SIGNAL BOOST

Alyssa Cole

Also by Alyssa Cole

Radio Silence (Off the Grid book 1)

Mixed Signals (Off the Grid book 2)

Eagle's Heart

Agnes Moor's Wild Knight

Be Not Afraid

Let It Shine

RADIO SILENCE

Edited by Rhonda Stapleton

ISBN-13: 978-1539694663

ISBN-10: 1539694666

And now, each night I count the stars.
And each night I get the same number.
And when they will not come to be counted,
I count the holes they leave.

– Amiri Baraka

1

The sun usually rises at about 6:20 a.m. on a late May morning in upstate New York. Daybreak wasn't even a pink tendril on the horizon when the baby started its nightly howling. I would have been annoyed if I hadn't already been awake.

If this was before electricity, and modern society, had stopped working, I would've dealt with my insomnia by scrolling through my smartphone, checking out dudes I would never have the nerve to contact on the latest gay hookup app. Or I would have turned on my gaming system, eager to explore vast worlds and be the hero of at least one story, even if it wasn't real. Now when I couldn't sleep I simply stared into darkness, waiting for something, anything, to break the monotony.

A crying baby would suffice.

The perpetrator of our nighttime wake-up calls, nicknamed Stump for his short little appendages and because his mother hadn't given him a name, quieted for a moment but then released a wail that rivaled the best of the Motown divas.

I couldn't blame him—honestly, I'd be screaming too if it wouldn't totally freak out everyone else in the house, which was packed tighter than a Gameland the day a new Jack Carjacker video game dropped. The guest list at Chez Seong now included my wonderful but meddling parents; my older brother, Gabriel, and my best friend, Arden, who spent most of their time projecting sexual tension at each other; and my teenage sister, Maggie, who was constantly redefining the meaning of *mood swing*. There were also Darlene and Stump, the woman and baby we'd taken in after she and her husband had held my parents captive. Yes, we were one big post-apocalyptically happy family, trapped in a house in the middle of nowhere as we tried not to think of our dwindling supplies and the fact that society had not returned to normal, as we'd hoped. That was enough to make anyone holler, but instead I had to keep my fear and anger bottled up inside, like a grown-up.

Maggie stirred in her bed across the room from me, but her mutant-teenager ability to sleep through anything meant Stump's cries wouldn't awaken her. Her mass of long, dark hair was pulled into a messy bun atop her head, revealing a face that was a strange mixture of child and woman. What kind of life would Maggie have if things didn't change soon? One of isolation, where she was married off to the neighbor boy for a dowry of expired candy bars?

I sighed and threw off my blankets, running a hand through my tangled hair. It was getting too long, resting on my shoulders now, and I'd have to ask Arden to give me another trim. I kind of wished she was still bunking with me, mostly so I could hear the string of expletives she was inevitably muttering as the baby cried out, but she'd moved into Gabriel's room down the hall, now referred to in hushed tones as the Shag Zone. The only thing keeping her from strangling Darlene for her poor parenting skills was the fact that she was blissfully besotted with my older brother—and that she'd already killed the woman's husband. I mean, that was awkward enough, as far as living arrangements went.

Still, I heard the door of the Shag Zone open and Arden's sleepy steps as she approached the room now inhabited by Darlene and the baby. She didn't bother knocking anymore, since retrieving the baby and comforting him had become a nightly routine. Darlene wasn't big on activities like eating, speaking or child-rearing these days anyway, so there was no point in waiting for a response.

I slid out of bed and emerged into the hallway just as Arden was walking by. "Boo!" I whispered near her ear as I jumped from my room into the darkened hallway.

Arden kept walking toward the stairs, not even breaking pace. "John, you need to come to terms with the fact that you will never make me flinch," she said as we walked down the stairs, searching for the least creaky spots.

"Don't take it personally. Besides, after changing this kid's diapers, nothing can scare me."

Having had my eyebrows singed off by the smell emanating from one of Stump's more memorable incidents, I understood what she meant.

"Dammit, baby, why do you have to wake us up?" she asked a burbling Stump as she settled them into the comfy love seat in the living room. "Don't you know how miserable it is for us to deal with you every night?"

Miserable? Our nightly hangout sessions were the one thing I looked forward to. It was the only time I really felt like I could be myself, whatever that meant. Not someone's son or brother, but just a friend. While everyone else slept, we made each other laugh, plotting who we would eat first when the food ran out or choreographing elaborate dances to songs sung a cappella. Sometimes, we'd make each other cry, like when she pulled out her tattered road map and we planned various routes to Northern California, where her parents lived—if they were still alive. Arden was the only one who really understood me, and even she considered the time we spent together miserable. Great.

I lit a tea candle, stuck one of Stump's premade bottles into the pan of water warming in the fireplace and snuggled next to Arden; this had become a nightly ritual too. She rested her head on my shoulder, moving slightly as she rocked the baby in her arms. Maybe she felt how stiff I was against her, or maybe she was just thinking the same thing I was, which wasn't rare, but her next words made me realize how ridiculous I was being.

"You know I hate being woken up and dealing with all this baby shit, but I really do enjoy this. Just you and me hanging out, like old times, except I'm holding a baby instead of a bag of corn chips," she said. "Thank you for always being here for me."

"I thought Gabriel was here to meet all your Seong-related needs these days," I quipped, still feeling tetchy even though I knew I was reading more into her words than she'd meant.

"Gabriel fulfills certain needs, but you're the Seong with first dibs on my heart and you know it," she said. I glanced at her, only to find her worried gaze fixed on me. I'd seen that look a lot lately. "Did you manage to get any sleep before this guy started screaming?"

"Nope," I said, grabbing Stump's warm, tiny foot when he pointed his leg toward me. I could have lied so she wouldn't worry, but she knew me well enough to catch me. "I think seeing you wiping someone else's ass of your own volition has traumatized me too much. I'll never sleep again. That and the whole downfall of society, of course."

Arden sighed with mock impatience. "John, it's only been a few months since all the electricity stopped working and we had to flee our home and join your family in the middle of bumblefuck. I mean, could you be any less patient? I think we should wait at least a year before expecting government intervention or an explanation of what the fuck happened."

I twisted one of her long plaits around my fingers and tugged, and she smiled deviously.

"You know, I only recently discovered how much I like that," she said. From the look in her eyes, I could tell she was thinking something about my brother that I didn't want to know about *ever.*

I released her braid and dramatically wiped my hand off on my pajama bottom. "Unlike some people, I haven't had an unending supply of peen to distract me from pondering my mortality. Thus, no sleep," I said. I meant it to be a joke, but as the words left my mouth I realized they were a bit too close to the mark. "And to think I used to complain about my lack of dating options back in Rochester. I'd even consider that creepy Asian studies major who kept wanting to show me his samurai sword collection at this point."

She shifted and looked up at me. I'd always thought her beautiful with her large eyes and luminous brown skin, but since she and Gabriel had gotten together, she'd been glowing. That said a lot, given the fact that we were in the middle of a full-blown dystopian drama. I'd never thought my brother could make a woman look like that, or that Arden would let anyone close enough to even try. I was ecstatic for them, and miserably jealous too.

"John..."

The pity in her eyes was what did it. If she had joked back or smacked me upside the head, I could have pretended things would be okay soon. But the look in her eyes so clearly screamed, *"You are alone and I feel sorry for you,"* that I couldn't stand it. I jumped out of my seat so fast she nearly toppled over sideways into the space I'd occupied. Stump, who'd been settling down, wailed again as he was jostled.

"I'm going to go check on the garden," I blurted out.

"Right now? Why don't you wait until morning?"

"It is light out. There's a full moon," I said. "Besides, something has been getting into the beets, and I need to assert my authority over the animal kingdom."

She stood and shushed Stump, patting his back as she began pacing. I handed her the warmed bottle to make up for my awkward departure. She smiled as she took it from me, waiting until Stump latched on and there was only the sound of his suckling to continue talking. "Okay, Farmer McGregor. Go show those cute little bunnies what for."

"Rabbits can be vicious, Arden," I said. "And what about raccoons? People think they're cute, but those wee opposable thumbs make them a formidable foe."

Not waiting for her to roll her eyes, I walked to the door and quietly removed the crossbar and turned several locks before creaking it open. Silvery moonlight illuminated the cornstalks swaying in the cool predawn breeze, the cucumber and tomato vines that had wrapped themselves securely around wooden stakes before bearing fruit, and the heads of cabbage that sprouted in even rows beneath them. Under my mother's careful tutelage, Arden had discovered yet another hidden talent: plant whisperer. Arden always told me I was good at everything, but my mint plants had withered and died, despite their supposed hardiness, and my potatoes had never taken. I wasn't much for omens, but it was hard not to take things personally when every patch of garden except mine grew in abundance.

I looked up at the brilliant night sky. Auroras had blazed for weeks in the aftermath of whatever caused the blackout, but they'd all but faded away now. The universe was unfurled above me like…like nothing. There was nothing to compare it to, no pithy metaphor that could describe that swath of blinking, twinkling, all-encompassing starlight. The Milky Way seared across the sky, unimaginable numbers of stars and planets reflecting their light toward me. Without light pollution dimming their brilliance, the stars dominated the night. They seemed to press closer, wrapping around the Earth like some delegation of curious observers who were also eager to know the fate of this forsaken planet.

I was so lost in my reverie I almost didn't hear the rustling. Something was approaching and it wasn't a bunny; the quiet deliberation in the movement assured me it was a human.

A bolt of fear straightened my back and made my hands clammy. I'd made a dumb move—leaving the house without a weapon. I couldn't open the door to slip back inside without the intruder seeing light seep through the front door. My family was in there, and Arden and Stump were much too close. What if Arden decided to come see if I was okay right now? My adrenaline surged at the thought.

Just then, I saw a shadow pass between me and the garden. A very large shadow. As it bent away from me, some primitive part of my brain realized that the shadow has its back to me and this would be a good time to make my move. I hesitated, but inside the house I heard Arden say, "John?" and the creak of her footsteps walking toward the door.

No.

I took off at a run, lunging at the shadow with a yell and catching it around the waist as I tackled him to the ground. Yes, this was definitely a *him* struggling beneath me. A him who was much taller, lanky even, but well muscled and strong. I tried to pin him down, but he flipped me onto my stomach, pulled my arm behind my back and threw his weight on top of me.

A voice rough with strain breathed into my ear. "Please stop struggling." There was the hint of an accent but I was too panicked to place it.

"Yeah, that sounds like a great plan, just lie here and let some crazy vegetable thief have his way with me," I said as I pushed back against him, trying to throw him off. He was immovable. I waited for him to stab me or punch me or do something to quiet me, but instead he chuckled. The sound reverberated against my back, and the sensation wasn't entirely unpleasant. How fucked up was that? I struggled some more but stopped when my ass pressed into his groin and something pressed back, something that made my dormant libido rise and do reconnaissance. He angled his hips away quickly, and I exhaled a shaky breath.

"I have a pretty good hold on you. You're not going

anywhere," he said, and then sighed. "I'm sorry I tried to steal from your garden. You caught me, so now I'll just get up and go. No need to battle to the death over a tomato."

"That depends on whether you ganked an heirloom." Arden's voice carried over to me just as fluorescent light flooded the garden. I glanced at the front door and saw her silhouette, armed with the shotgun. "Get off him."

He released me, and I scrambled from beneath him, turning to glare at him and completely unprepared for what I saw. I looked up into the face of the garden interloper in the bright light of Arden's lantern, and my heart stopped. Floppy dirty-blond hair hung down over eyes that were large, cornflower blue and strangely cool for a man who was staring at a woman with a gun. His cheeks were flushed from our grappling, matching the rosy pink of his wide mouth. His nose was large, and there was a certain jut to his brow and cheekbones that hinted at some Slavic background.

He was gorgeous. I mean, the sparse growth along his upper lip showed there was at least one person in the world who had more trouble growing facial hair than I did, but I wouldn't hold the patchy mustache against him.

Maybe it was the adrenaline rush or the fact that he was no longer a threat—or that I hadn't been around a man who didn't share genetic material with me in months—but I suddenly regretted I wasn't still beneath him.

"What are you doing here? Are you alone?" Arden asked, scanning the darkness. I pulled myself up into a crouch; there might be others closing in on us.

The intruder ignored Arden and squinted in my direction as I went to step forward, and then those impossibly blue eyes widened with fear. "Wait, don't move!" he cried, lunging at my feet.

Why, you idiot? I felt an odd twinge of sadness when he jumped my way. Arden was going to shoot him, and even if he was a thief he was the most beautiful man I'd ever laid eyes on. It was entirely selfish, but I didn't want him to die. I also didn't want Arden to have to shoot anyone else.

My foot came down on something hard, and whatever it was broke under my insole with a loud snap. At the same time, the man's warm hand landed on my ankle, encircling it as he gazed up at me in despair.

"My glasses!"

Arden came to a running stop behind him; she held the rifle by its muzzle but stopped midswing. I lifted my foot, and he released his hold on me, gathering the remains of his glasses as if it was a fledgling bird that had fallen from its nest.

He's gentle too. The long-dormant romantic sector of my brain really was stupidly choosing now to kick back into gear.

He rocked back onto his heels and blew out a sigh of relief that ruffled his unruly locks.

Adorable. Dammit.

"They broke evenly in half," he said with a grin, as if we

were all buds. Dumbly, I fought the urge to grin back at him.

"You didn't answer Arden's questions," I reminded him. "What are you doing creeping around here?"

"I was trying not to starve to death. I can't be the first post-Flare survivor to arrive looking for food. I would have asked, but it's the middle of the night and—" He raised one half of his broken glasses to his eyes and looked at Arden. He scrambled backward then and came to a stop against the cornstalks. "Holy shit, you have a gun? You have a gun. Why do you have a gun?"

"Exactly how blind are you without your glasses?" Arden asked.

My question was right on the heels of hers. "What do you mean by 'post-Flare'?"

We'd interacted with some of our neighbors over the past few months. We'd even bartered for some necessary items; my life was slowly becoming a role-playing video game. But no one had mentioned anything about flares.

"Are you going to shoot me?" he asked, holding half of his broken glasses by the arm to gaze up at us. He looked completely vulnerable, with one eye magnified so it appeared even larger, and I wanted to reassure him he had nothing to fear. But then I remembered the crazy assholes we'd encountered over the past few months. Some of them had tried to kill us, and they'd come very close to succeeding. My head throbbed at the memory of our arrival at the cabin, although I actually couldn't remember a thing since

I'd been knocked unconscious by scavengers. Hot or not, we couldn't take any chances. The bumbling European tomato thief act could just be a clever ruse—if he wanted our trust, he'd have to earn it.

"Not yet," I said, answering for Arden. "Answer our questions and when we've determined you're not a threat, you can go."

"The Flare was a solar event that initiated a large-scale geomagnetic storm," he said. "That storm hit Earth at maximum power and fried our electrical grids, at least in the northeastern section of the Americas. I'm assuming this was an Earthwide event, given that we haven't received reinforcements from other countries and I haven't seen military reinforcements or nongovernmental organizations. It's a bit more complicated than that, but there you go. Pre-Flare life was normal. Post-Flare, I have to scrounge around in random gardens risking my life for subpar tomatoes."

"Hey," Arden said, sounding wounded.

"Can I go now? I've answered your question."

I shook my head as he moved to stand. He stopped, and I realized that for the moment at least, this stranger was in my power. Nausea streaked through my belly; I didn't want this kind of power. I'd sometimes resented my older brother for always wanting to be in charge, but now I was in awe. I couldn't understand how Gabriel handled this kind of responsibility on a day-to-day basis.

"Why should we believe anything you've said?"

I asked. Whether I wanted the responsibility or not, I was the one who'd intercepted the floppy-haired thief and I was the one who should make sure he wasn't a threat. This was what I got for dramatically fleeing from Arden.

"Because I'm an astrophysicist," he said with that grin of his. "Kind of. An almost-astrophysicist."

I channeled my inner Gabriel and met his cuteness with a stony look.

"Okay, okay, I haven't gotten my PhD yet, so I'm technically just an astronomer, but—"

"Get up," I said. "We can't let you go until we're certain you're alone and not dangerous."

He seemed harmless enough, but we had to be sure. There was no way we could just release him into the night to go to tell his theoretical cronies that there was house that had a bangin' garden and people who looked well fed and had weapons. I grabbed a coil of rope that had been left over from sectioning off the garden.

"You can't be serious," he said. His grin was gone now; I'd killed it.

"Arden, keep the gun on him while I tie him up."

"John, are you sure?" Her voice was laden with shock—she was supposed to be the badass, after all—but I didn't know what else to do. My stomach was churning with anxiety and I could feel a headache building, which happened much too often since my head injury. I needed to do *something.*

"Dammit, no I'm not, but I can't let him go if there's a chance he'll hurt us!" I exploded.

"Okay," Arden said. "I understand."

"What? I *don't* understand," the stranger said, panic rising in his voice and thickening his accent. "I'm not going to hurt you. I swear on my *didus*'s grave. But I'm not going inside with you either."

I inhaled deeply, steeling myself against his reaction. I didn't know what a *didus* was, although it sounded like an uncomfortable bowel movement, and I didn't care.

"Hand over your glasses," I said. The side of my nose itched, but I didn't think scratching it would make me look scary or commanding, so I ignored it.

The look of fear that crossed over his face at that moment was something that would haunt me forever. It was as if I'd asked him to hand over one of his vital organs. "Are you crazy?" His voice was even higher, reaching falsetto levels. "I can't see without them. No way."

"Look, I don't want to do this either," I said. "If you give me the glasses, you can't go anywhere, so I won't have to tie you up or anything drastic. You'll get them back."

"Why should I believe you?" he asked, throwing my own question back at me.

"I don't know what you've seen out there, but in our experience people show their hands pretty early on in the game," I said. I realized I was rubbing the spot where I'd been hit by the rock and pulled my hand away from my temple. "If I wanted to hurt you, you'd be hurting right now. Let's go."

"Well, then do it." His gaze was intense as it bored into mine. There was fear, but more than that, there was honest challenge and a hint of something wild and desperate that told me he wasn't bluffing. "Just shoot me, because I'm not going in there with you."

"You'd rather die than come inside and answer a few questions?" I asked.

His reply was a stare that chilled me to my core.

Fuck. Sweat broke out along my hairline, even though the night was cool. I reached out to grab the gun from Arden, but when I pulled, she stubbornly held on. I turned to see what the problem was and found her staring at me, her eyes wide and glossy. Her voice was small when she spoke, how she sounded when she cried out in the nightmares that now plagued her. "Please don't."

The world really was upside down if I was playing bad cop and Arden was playing good, but then I remembered that she was the one who had to deal with the memory of being held hostage by strangers. She was the one who knew what it meant to end a life.

"Geez. Just take them, okay?" He handed me the two pieces of his glasses and put his hands behind his head. I didn't know why he caved, but Arden's posture slackened with relief, and I certainly wouldn't complain about not having to kill the first guy I'd met in months.

"I know this is scary, but as long as you don't have any plans to hurt us, we won't hurt you," Arden added as we headed for the house. I glanced at his expressionless profile. I didn't think he was the kind of guy who cared about such warnings.

I nudged the stranger forward through the door into our sanctuary and hoped I was making the right decision.

2

Stump was sprawled on a quilt that had been placed on the floor near the couch. Arden handed me the gun before rushing over to lift him up and out of the stranger's reach.

"I'm going to go get Gabriel," she said, giving me a worried look as she jogged out of the room.

I gestured for Chez Seong's first ever hostage to sit on the sofa, but he stood in place, squinting around the room like Mr. Magoo's hot grandson. He hadn't even been able to see my very obvious hand motion. I'd always had twenty-twenty vision, and just thinking of being stuck in a world like this, one without law and order, and possibly being unable to see was enough to make my skin crawl.

He raised a hand to his face and made a circle with his thumb and index finger as if making the sign for "okay." For a millisecond I thought he was giving some kind of signal, but then realized two things: one, no one could see into the living room, since the windows were boarded up, and two, he was peering through the little *O* formed by his two fingers.

"Doesn't look like the headquarters of a cannibal cult," he mused. "Kind of reminds me of my grandparents' living room."

"I thought you couldn't see without your glasses," I said, tensing.

He turned toward me, hand still hovering in front of his eye.

"Right now I'm using my fingers to create a pinhole lens. It's simple physics, really. The small opening filters out the light entering my retina, focusing it in a way that makes everything less blurry," he said. His tone had taken on the same nerdy affect as when he'd described the so-called Flare, and Lord help me but it was the sexiest thing ever to hear a man talk knowledgeably about physics.

"Like a camera aperture?" I asked.

His eyebrow rose from behind his fingers, and he nodded. He continued to stare at me, and it occurred to me how ridiculous this scene was, or should have been, but ridiculous was the last thing I felt as he looked at me. I knew he was just keeping an eye on the strange Korean dude who'd taken him prisoner, but the tingle of awareness that slowly passed through me was something different. It was the same sensation of eyes meeting in the cereal aisle at the supermarket, or in a bar full of straights, or in the quiet corner of a library. It was that subconscious level of gaydar that was always sending out subtle waves and that only registered when it received a ping.

PING.

Arden hadn't been gone long enough to make it to the Shag Zone. Nonetheless, she and Gabriel entered the living room, putting an abrupt end to our little moment.

Arden always said she thought Gabriel and I were more alike than I realized, even that we looked alike, but I think she was just confused by her love for me. Seeing how he handled his entrance alone made it abundantly clear that the Seong badass gene had missed me on the Punnett square. He walked ahead of her, his gait slow as if he was taking an evening stroll. His face was placid, but his eyes were intense as he kept his gaze on the stranger. I was the one who'd jumped the man, held him at gunpoint and taken him prisoner, but I could see him submit to Gabriel's control just as everyone else did. He dropped his hands to his sides and sat down on the couch. I don't think anyone saw me rolling my eyes because they were too busy staring at the older, hotter Seong.

"Gabriel was coming to see why I'd been gone so long," she said. "If the electricity weren't dead, I'd swear he has some kind of surveillance system set up." I'd thought she would be more relaxed now that he was with her, but she nervously jiggled a disgruntled Stump, who'd had enough adventure for the night and was ready for bed. "I gave him the short version of the story."

"That you found me in an indiscreet position with a stranger in our cabbage patch?" I asked. "Wouldn't be the first time he'd heard that."

The interloper's head turned sharply in my direction, but Gabriel smirked and Arden's baby-jiggling slowed down, which was wonderful because she'd essentially been priming a projectile vomiting machine. I took a few steps away so I was out of the line of fire.

"No, she mentioned that you claim to know what happened to cause the electricity to stop," he said to the guy. He grabbed an ottoman and took a seat, placing himself between the stranger and Arden. "Can you tell me more about that?"

If the tomato thief had shown up a few months ago, he likely would have been beaten to a pulp by now. However, Arden's magic hoo-ha had apparently given my brother at least some basic lessons in diplomacy. I could see from his stance that he was ready to strike if necessary, but he was listening first.

"My name is Mykhail, by the way," he said, his tongue darting out to swipe over his lips. His lips really were exquisite. He had a wide mouth with a pillowy bottom lip that pretty much guaranteed he'd make a good kisser, or at least provide good fun for someone who enjoyed nibbling like I did.

Mykhail.

"Okay…that's not what I asked," Gabriel replied. The little tendon along his jaw flexed, showing he was irritated, but he didn't say anything else. In the first few weeks after he and Arden had become official, I'd teased Gabriel about going soft. I quickly learned that just because he now joked and shared his emotions with us didn't mean he was no longer a hard-ass—it simply meant that he cared enough about Arden to try harder to control his reactions. If only Pavlov had known that love could engender the same change in behavior over a couple of weeks that took years of work with an annoying bell and smelly dog food.

"I know, but it seemed impolite not to introduce myself. Besides, it's harder to torture or maim someone whose name you know," he said with a shrug. Again, I noticed that hint of an accent, the way his tongue seemed to shape rounded vowel sounds just a bit strangely.

"Names don't mean squat. The last guy I killed was named Dale, and this is his baby," Arden said, offering Stump as exhibit A.

"Was he your ex?" Mykhail interrupted. "Because I can see a bit of resemblance between you and the little one. You guys have the same…nose."

"No!" Arden said, but I could tell she was biting back an exasperated laugh. "Look, I actually don't enjoy killing people, so if you do something stupid that forces my hand, I'll be sure to end you in the most painful way possible, just out of spite."

Mykhail nodded, and I saw his Adam's apple bob

in that long neck of his. Little did he know that a threat from Arden was a term of endearment; I wasn't the only one being charmed. He gave Gabriel the recap of what he'd told us about the Flare, minus his dig at Arden's tomatoes.

"How do you know this? And how could something like that happen without the government being prepared for it? It doesn't make sense," Gabriel said.

"Well, I know because I saw it. I was looking at the sun through my telescope—"

"As one does," I interrupted. I winced and shook my head at him. "Wouldn't that burn out your retinas?"

"Maybe that's why he needs glasses," Arden contributed.

"Will you both shut up and let the man talk? It would be nice to have this settled before everyone else wakes up," Gabriel said, and then sighed deeply and muttered, "Too late."

There was a high-pitched sound from the entrance to the living room and we all turned to find my mother there, resplendent in her muumuu and hair curlers, head thrown back in a loud, boisterous yawn that segued into an elaborate stretch. When she was done, she blinked owlishly at all of us and said, "Oh, I didn't realize you all were awake. You should be getting your beauty sleep! Especially you, Arden."

Typical Mama Seong.

She walked in and took Stump from Arden and sat

down on the couch next to Mykhail, giving him a bleary glance that quickly sharpened.

"Oh. Who are you?" she asked and then gave me a pointed look. "Jang-wan, who is this?"

"I found him trying to steal vegetables in the garden, Amma," I said. "He says he knows why the electricity stopped working."

Her mouth drew up into a tight circle and she gave Mykhail the look that had always rendered me a sniveling mess as a child, and sometimes even now. "You stole from my garden? Why would you do that, huh? We work very hard on that garden! The soil is no good around here and we had to spend so much time to get things right, and you just come and take from us?"

Mykhail hung his head with what appeared to be actual shame. "I'm sorry, ma'am. I was so hungry and this was the first good food I'd seen in weeks."

His stomach growled long and loud then, as if to back up his story. He tried to smother the sound with his hands, and my mother laughed and nudged his knee with hers.

"Ah, it's okay. Everyone has done something they aren't proud of before," she said kindly and then announced to the rest of us, "He looks like a nice boy. And a smart one, if he knows what happened. And cute, eh, Jang-wan?"

She winked at me, and my face flushed with heat. Of course, my mother would manage to embarrass me in front of my first hostage. Such was my life.

"Anyway, he was explaining this Flare? Why did you interrupt him?" she said, giving us all a disapproving glance before turning her saintly smile onto Mykhail and pretending she hadn't let slip that she'd totally been eavesdropping before making her presence known. "Go on."

Mykhail looked just as overwhelmed by my mother as we all were, but he was handling it admirably for a first-timer. He ran a hand through shaggy hair that would be gorgeous once he took a shower—right now it looked as if he'd tried to mop up an oil slick with his head.

"Well, I call it a flare but it was actually a coronal mass ejection," he said, ignoring Arden when she snickered and elbowed Gabriel. "Let's call it a CME for the twelve-year-olds in the room. Have you ever heard of a sunspot? It's like a bubble of energy on the surface of the sun. Sometimes a CME results from that flare."

"How does something happening on the sun affect anything here?" Gabriel asked. He wasn't being snarky—there was real curiosity in his voice. "I've seen a sunspot in a picture...it looked like a ball of molten lava. Wouldn't Earth be burned to a crisp if one of those hit us?"

"You mean like the venison Arden made last night?" my mom asked through pursed lips.

When I glanced at Mykhail, he no longer looked confused; he was smiling. A full-on, stop-you-in-your-tracks, be-still-my-heart kind of smile. His full, rosy lips pulled up at the corners and his dark blue eyes flashed with mirth. And then he turned that smile on me, and I was done. This was beyond *PING*; it was a full-body awareness of how beautiful Mykhail was and an approximate 99.99 percent certainty that he was of the same tribe. This realization didn't help matters. There was no clause in the gay code that mandated that any two of us under the same roof must immediately start having frenzied sex; I wasn't even promised a hand-job. The fact was, it would have been better if the hot dude smiling up at me was straight, because then I wouldn't be having inappropriate thoughts in front of half of my family. Then I wouldn't be wondering what his kiss tasted like, when the truth was I'd likely never know. I doubted I was his type; I mean, it seemed I wasn't anyone's type, and the months in isolation probably hadn't helped sharpen my social skills.

"You know, if I had to be kidnapped by cannibals eating any survivor who stumbles into their garden, I'm glad it was you guys," he said. "You're nice cannibals."

I couldn't fight it any longer. I smiled back.

"We'll be sure to put that on your grave marker. Mykhail GardenGnome—Lean, Tender, Eaten by Nice Cannibals," I said. I was tired of standing with the gun, so I sat on the edge of the ottoman with Gabriel, who moved over to give me more space.

Arden crossed her arms, rested them on both of our backs and said, "Please tell us more about the mass ejections."

"Okay, so these CMEs that result from solar flares are bursts of solar wind and magnetic energy. Usually they just shoot out harmlessly into the galaxy. Well, harmless to *us*. But if the Earth happens to be in the path of one of these things, it collides with our atmosphere and a geomagnetic storm occurs. This isn't like an earthquake, or something that's over in a few minutes. The energy from a huge CME can last for weeks. And that energy is drawn to certain things, like the high-voltage wires that make up our electrical grid."

"This has happened before?" Mom asked. Even Stump was looking on curiously, as if he wanted to know more.

Mykhail nodded. "A few times, yes, but on a much smaller scale. The only time there was ever a relatively large-scale event was in the 1800s, before most of the world was totally wired for and dependent on electricity. The Carrington Event. It took out telegraph signals and created an aurora that could be seen down to Florida for a few weeks."

"So that's what caused the aurora!" Arden exclaimed, and even though I wasn't thrilled about her elbow digging into my back as she jumped up and down, I shared her excitement. What Mykhail was telling us sounded absolutely insane, but just crazy enough to be possible. After months of conjecture, we were finally learning what had happened and why life as we knew it had been snatched away from us.

"Yes, it was kind of like a beautiful bruise on the Earth's geomagnetic field," Mykhail said. "The larger problem was that the CME that hit us was huge. There's a scale that measures these things, and it scares me how high up this event rated. Earth has spent millennia lucking out with small-scale events and glancing blows, but the CME that caused this was a monster and was on a direct path for Earth."

"It's hard to believe some random burst of energy from outer space is behind this," Gabriel said, shaking his head. "Why weren't we prepared for this?"

I was wondering the same thing. If a student was this well informed, the government should have had a plan in place to deal with this.

"People have been warning the electrical companies for years. It'll take years to rebuild the grid. The large transformers that have all been fried? They don't even make them in the U.S. anymore. There was a hurricane in Florida in 1992, a pretty bad one. It took every available small transformer in the U.S. to restore power there, and there was a worldwide shortage for the year after that. And that's one small swath of one state." There was a silence as his words sank in, as much as it was possible for them to anyway. It was beyond comprehension. "When I realized what was going on, I tried to call one of my professors, a guy who'd actually been ostracized for his obsession with CMEs and how we weren't doing anything to protect ourselves from them. But it was too late."

He had been swept up in our excitement as he told us about the Flare, but now his lips were drawn in a grimace and he was clearly flagging. The dark blue circles under his eyes were more prominent, and I realized just how ragged his clothes were. It was amazing what a nice smile could distract you from, but the spark had gone from his eyes and he stared past us into the dark corner of the room.

The Flare had happened months ago. Where had he been all this time? What had he done to survive? Not everyone was lucky enough to have parents with the stock of an entire store and an obsession with canning. I couldn't imagine what it was like depending on chance for survival, on stumbling into a garden or a cache of edible items just to make it to the next day. I'd felt compelled to stop him when I caught him skulking around, but now I regretted begrudging him a few vegetables when we had so much.

"You're tired, huh?" my mom asked.

"Yes," he admitted, and it seemed he was admitting it to himself too. He blinked rapidly, like Stump did when trying to fight a nap.

"Okay, then I only have one more thing to ask you. Do you mean to harm my family?"

"Of course not," Mykhail said. He was either a damned good liar or he was telling the truth.

Relief rushed through me at his words, at the fact that we wouldn't have to harm anyone. Both Gabriel and Arden had killed in our defense, and I knew it was a heavy burden to carry. When screams emanated from the Shag Zone in the middle of the night, none of us got annoyed. We knew they were the result of horrific nightmares and not from more pleasurable activities.

My mom nodded. "That's enough for right now, then. We can talk more in the morning."

"Thanks," he said, his voice low and ragged. His hands were squeezed together in his lap so tightly that his knuckles were white beneath the grime.

My mom stood and began issuing orders, and both Gabriel and Arden deferred to our resident Alpha. "I'll go make tea. Arden, you bring the baby upstairs, see if his mother is okay to take him. Gabriel, bring a pillow and fresh clothes for our guest—he can sleep in here. John, take him to the bathroom so he can freshen up, and then bring him back down. You'll have to sleep in the living room with him, okay?"

I didn't even have to look at her to know that she had the determined matchmaker's glint in her eye.

"Slow your roll, Mother dear," I whispered as I passed her.

"Listen to your mother like a good boy, Jang-wan," she chided in Korean, but there was a triumphant smile on her face as she turned to head for the kitchen. "Mothers know these things."

As I climbed the stairs with a silent Mykhail behind me, I realized that for the first time in my life I hoped my mother's matchmaking instincts were correct.

3

I was bent over the coffee table in the living room when Mykhail walked in, toweling his hair.

"You guys are pretty lax with your prisoners," he said to announce his arrival. "Allowing them to bathe, giving them clothes and free run of the house. I could have done anything while you were in here...doing whatever you're doing."

His words grew louder as he approached me, and my hands trembled a bit from nerves, almost messing up my careful work. I couldn't remember when a guy had ever made me so nervous that I'd physically lost my cool. It didn't make sense. He didn't have the kind of deep, sexy voice that generally revved my engine; it was weirdly accented and a smidge nasal. Despite that, the sound of it unleashed a tumult in my belly and nearly derailed my project. It wasn't just his words and the way they sounded. Everything he said was imbued with the effortless confidence provided by knowledge. He was smart, but he also seemed to give zero fucks about whether anyone else thought so. He just *was*, and for someone as lost as me, that was a huge aphrodisiac.

He leaned over my shoulder, and I could smell the freshly scrubbed scent of him. It was the same soap we all used, a cheap body wash, but there had to be some chemical interaction between the powder-fresh scent and his skin because he smelled delicious. The heat and smell and nearness of him gave way to a powerful image of what I could do with a guy still damp from the shower…

Something dripped on me, and I looked up into a face that really was much too beautiful up close. There should have been giant pores or blackheads or some imperfection visible to the naked eye, but his skin was milky smooth with a hint of pink at the cheeks. The blue smudges under his eyes were the only flaw, and they merely added an extra layer of vulnerability to him. Damp ringlets of hair curled around his face, the color a brown that would lighten to blond as it dried. Another drop of water dripped from the ends of his hair and splashed in my eye, saving me from embarrassing myself because it forced me to look away.

"This is an old house. The floorboards in this place are just as good as GPS when it comes to tracking your movements, so there was no need for me to stand sentry. Here." I handed over what I'd been working on.

"Jang-wan, this is… Thank you." He cleaned the lenses

of his newly repaired glasses and then slipped them on. Somehow, *somehow*, he still managed to look like the sexiest nerd in nerdtown. He gave me another one of those beautiful smiles.

I shrugged, despite the fact that I was more pleased by his reaction than I'd been by anything in a long time. I hadn't been feeling much over the past few weeks, but I'd only realized that after tussling with a beautiful boy in the light of the full moon. Now that I remembered what it was like to have my heart race and my stomach flip, the past few weeks of near zombietude were put in perspective. Maybe he was like one of those hitchhiking ghosts that kept a lunar schedule and helped lonely gay boys find themselves. Tomorrow morning he'd be gone, and years from now I'd hear of the beautiful boy named Mykhail who'd died from choking on a stolen tomato and haunted veggie patches all along the Canadian border. I inwardly scoffed at my tale, but it would at least explain his beauty.

"There's tea and cookies on the side table next to the couch," I said. He nearly tripped over himself running for the cookies, and I sighed when he was out of my radius. The guy was seriously messing with my head. "And the name is John, by the way."

"But I heard your mother—"

"Are you my mother?" I asked with an arched brow. I knew I was being needlessly rude, but what else were you supposed to do when a hot, totally unattainable man perfectly pronounced the name people had butchered for years?

I went by John instead of my Korean name for a reason.

He shoved a cookie into his mouth, and then another, before shrugging. "Sorry," he said around a mouthful of chocolate chips. "People always called me Michael at school and I hated it. I didn't understand why one combination of letters was so much harder for them to pronounce than another. But if you prefer John, I'll call you John."

I sighed. This guy seemed to have stepped right out of my dreams, or one of the fairy tales Arden told me when I couldn't sleep. "Look, sorry. I'm just tired and cranky. And I'm not supposed to be fraternizing with the prisoner." My words were facetious. It was clear to all of us that he was no threat, and he knew we meant him no harm either. Although we hadn't decided when he would leave, he was now more guest than hostage.

He graced me with a disarming smile. "Is that what we're doing? Fraternizing? I've led a pretty sheltered life, but I always imagined that entailed slightly more illicit stuff than chatting over cookies and tea," he said, taking a small bite of the last cookie and licking the crumbs from his lips. He shook his head. "If that's the case, I fraternized with my grandparents all the time. That just seems wrong."

I was surprised at Mykhail's sharp sense of humor; clearly the "boring scientist" stereotype was wrong. I couldn't remember the last time I'd met a guy whose conversation actually kept me on my toes, who understood the fine line between funny and trying to elicit a reaction. I wasn't religious at all, despite my parents' best attempts at pushing me into the Christian Korean social scene, but at that moment I definitely believed in a higher power. Namely, Satan. He had obviously sent Mykhail here to torment me with his perfect hotness.

I'd really only ever had one serious boyfriend, "Peter with the wandering peter," as Arden had dubbed him. I'd had my fair share of hookups, but I'd generally been too shy or too turned off by dudes with Asian twink fetishes to really date very much. I certainly never made the first move. Yet here I was talking myself down from stalking over to Mykhail, sliding my fingers into his dripping hair and crushing my mouth to his. He was tall and lean, and I imagined how the notch of his hip would feel under my hand, how the substantial length that had pressed against me as we tussled would thicken as I stroked him through the borrowed sweat pants he wore.

The thoughts were like a shock to my system. In the outside world, power lines, water mains and the various underpinnings of society lay dormant, gathering rust and dust. If the power ever came back on, I'm sure they would experience something similar to what Mykhail was causing in me. Long barren places within me were suddenly submerged in a deluge of sensation, and something bright and hot was coursing through my veins. I'm fairly certain I would have been capable of powering at least a toaster oven if the cord was plugged into the right orifice.

"John?" Mykhail was staring at me, his head tilted to the side like some kind of cute-ass puppy. Here I was about to start shooting sparks out of embarrassing places, and he was looking at me as if there was something wrong with me.

I really needed to work on my game if my seductive face made people concerned for my health.

"Go to sleep," I said, stretching out in front of the door. "Tomorrow is going to be a long day."

"Do you have some nefarious plans for me or something?" he asked over a yawn.

"You'll find out in a few hours, little rabbit."

I had plans for him, all right, but I was keeping them safely in the realm of dreams, where they belonged.

I didn't know what time it was when a gentle hand on my shoulder shook me awake. A form hovered over me in the dim living room and for a brief, hopeful moment, I thought it was Mykhail. I was disappointed when I realized it was someone about eight years too young and who lacked a certain important appendage and possessed entirely too much similar genetic material to be waking me for a morning booty call.

"What do you want, Maggie?" I rolled onto my side so she wouldn't see the embarrassing boner that had sprung to life at just the thought of Mykhail joining me on the floor.

"Breakfast is ready. More importantly, who is that cute dude on the couch?" she whispered. Even in the dim morning light, I could see her eyes shining. If she was a character in one if the old cartoons they played when I was a kid, big red hearts would have been shooting out of her eyes. In retrospect, those cartoons were kind of morbid.

Mykhail shifted and turned his back to us in his sleep. His T-shirt rode up as he turned, exposing ridges of abs and then the pale expanse of his back. Maggie sighed appreciatively, and I considered punching myself in the groin to avoid traumatizing my sister.

"Just some vagrant I caught stealing vegetables from the garden last night," I said, but she was too busy staring. "He'll probably be leaving soon. Please put your hormones back wherever you usually store them and go to the kitchen, will you?"

She huffed and stood from her crouch, giving one last appreciative glance at the couch before she shuffled out of the room.

I didn't get up immediately because I was grappling with the strange dread that rose within me at the thought of Mykhail leaving. Given that our relationship had started with a tackle and I'd known him for only a few hours, I was overreacting, but there was something compelling about him that had me hoping he would stay longer than breakfast.

"Get it together, John," I muttered. "You've gone through longer droughts than this."

"What?" Mykhail asked. I turned to him and my mouth went dry. He was stretching awake on the couch, a full-body contortion complete with arched back that exposed even more of his deliciously lickable torso. The motion was clearly indecent and was probably banned in at least thirty states. Did he wake up like that every morning?

"Nothing," I said, tearing my eyes away from the tempting scene. "I was just talking to myself, like a weirdo."

He finished his stretch and collapsed contentedly back onto the couch. "It's not so weird. I've spent a lot of the last month talking to myself," he said. He turned his head toward me. "You've been with your family since the Flare?"

"For most of it," I said. "Arden and I made our way here from Rochester." I didn't tell him about being attacked, or my parents being kidnapped. It didn't seem like the kind of thing he needed to hear just then, and I didn't exactly love rehashing those memories.

"You're lucky," he said. It was barely more than a whisper, but the pain in those two words may as well have been spoken into a bullhorn. Before either he or I could say anything else, Arden stuck her head into the room.

"Good morning! Mom Dukes said we could have a special treat today since we have a guest," she said, her eyes wide with excitement.

"What, she's going to let us heat up our rice instead of breaking our teeth on cold clumps of it?" I asked, and then instantly felt like an unmitigated ass when Mykhail jumped up excitedly and cried, "You guys have rice?"

Arden laughed. "Please don't say that in front of John's mom, or we'll never hear the end of it. She already calls us ingrates all the time."

"Give me half your portion of rice, and I won't say anything," Mykhail said, tugging the string of his sweat pants to keep them from falling down as he approached. "Give me the whole portion, and I'll insult her cooking and her hospitality. What do you say?"

A peal of laughter escaped from Arden's lips, and from my own. She gave me a look that we hadn't shared in a very long time. The "this guy is cool, right?" look that shimmered with excitement. The "we should hang out with this person" glance that hinted at possible adventures to come. I wasn't the only one enchanted with our so-called prisoner.

"If you insulted my mother's cooking, you'd wish we were a cannibal commune," I said. "Someone gnawing on your bones would be gentle in comparison."

In the kitchen, everyone was seated on the benches at the long wooden table: Mom, Dad, Gabriel, who had Stump strapped to him with a length of cloth that doubled as a Baby Björn, Maggie and even Darlene. The woman's hair was knotty and she looked as if she hadn't changed her clothing in a very long time, but even she had been compelled to check out the new arrival.

Her presence shocked me for a moment, pulled me out of my laughter. She had been here for months, but Mykhail already felt like one of us, like he had been before he arrived. I was often annoyed by Darlene's presence, but as we settled into the empty spaces at the table, I felt bad for her. I sometimes felt like a stranger in my own home. She *was* one. I was a jerk for not thinking about that before, but it had been easier for me to relegate Darlene to the role of postpartum widow and ignore her than to deal with the emotional impact of what she was experiencing. When forced to read *Jane Eyre* in high school, I'd thought Mr. Rochester was a huge asshole, but maybe I should've cut him some slack.

I made a brief round of introductions. Mykhail glanced in Darlene's direction and then leaned my way as we took our seats across the table. "So I asked if you were cannibals last night, but I neglected to follow up with the 'white slavery ring' question," he whispered. "Who is she?"

Oh, just the wife of the man who kidnapped my parents and tried to kill me and my brother. She sank into a catatonic state after Arden killed her husband, forcing us to take in her and her baby and to raise him in her stead. Want some oatmeal?

"Ummmm...it's complicated," I said, making ixnay motions with my hands. "Like, please-don't-bring-it-up-at-the-table complicated."

His brows knit in wary confusion, but he nodded in agreement. I was reaching for the instant coffee when a scent hit my nose that inspired more lust than even the Mykhail Burlesque Stretch Morning Show.

"Is that...?" Arden began to ask in a reverent tone just as my mother walked in with a platter piled high with bacon.

"Bacon!" my dad shouted, slamming his hands on the table although he was usually the most reserved in our group. He narrowed his gaze at my mother, his salt-and-pepper mustache bristling as he gripped the table. "Kitty, you said that there wasn't any bacon left. I asked for it on my *birthday* last week, and you said we were all out."

"Yeah! Why would you lie to us, Amma?" Maggie's eyes were wide with betrayal, even as her gaze drifted to the steaming pile of breakfast meat. It had been weeks of oatmeal or rice with the occasional breakfast of bartered eggs.

"I didn't lie. I said 'I can't find any more bacon in the freezer.' That was because I moved it to the deep freezer," my mom said with a dainty shrug. Her curlers had been removed and her choppy black bob swung around her ears. "But aren't you glad for that misunderstanding? Because now you get to have a surprise. I thought our guest was looking too thin."

She set the platter down and shoveled a pile of crisp, fragrant meat onto Mykhail's plate, and then added a spoonful of freshly made rice. Everyone chattered now, with Gabriel pretending to hide the remainder of the bacon in the baby sling and my dad threatening him with a butter knife. Maggie and Arden tugged at either end of the plate, and my mom brusquely passed out scoops of rice. There were only two still spots at the table. Darlene was silent as usual, but even she knew a good thing when she saw it. She picked up some of the bacon that had been doled out to her and nibbled at it. The barest of smiles graced her lips, which wouldn't have been remarkable but for the fact that I'd never seen her show signs of happiness before.

Something else was happening with Mykhail. He was silent and unmoving beside me, but his tension was palpable. I felt him trembling through the bench seat we shared, and when I turned to look at him, his face was a splotchy red from the effort it took to hold back his tears. His shaggy hair hid his eyes, but when he quickly passed his palms over his cheeks I knew that he was wiping away moisture.

"Thank you," he said in a voice that was clogged with emotion. Something in his voice—the gratitude, or the way it wavered as he struggled to sound like he *wasn't* crying—undid the reserve I should have had with a near-stranger. My hand moved to his back of its own volition, but I made the decision to move it in small, comforting circles instead of snatching it away. He leaned into my touch just the slightest bit, lean muscle and sharp vertebrae warm under my palm, and then cleared his throat before continuing. "I'm sorry, I just didn't think that I would ever have the chance to taste bacon again, or to enjoy a family meal. Thank you."

Quiet had descended on the table. Everyone was looking at him—or at us, rather, as I continued to comfort him. It felt good to be touching him this way, much too good to be doing it in front of my parents.

I gave him a final awkward pat on the back and then pulled my hand away. I studied my plate and selected a nearly charred strip, my favorite, before speaking. "I almost cried when I saw we had bacon too. Don't feel bad."

I glanced at Arden, who was chomping on a crisp piece of bacon and sending pointed looks to Gabriel while not so subtly tilting her head toward Mykhail and me. When she noticed me staring at her, she pretended to be stretching her neck.

I pointed my fork in her direction and held it in warning.

"We're happy to share with you," Dad finally said, breaking the silence. "Do you mind if I ask where you were coming from? Where you're headed? It's none of our business, of course. You don't have to give the bacon back if you don't feel like answering."

Although he was the quieter of my parents, he had his own way of getting what he wanted from people. He was the definition of kindly father figure, complete with deep crow's-feet and a graying mustache, but he was also the man who'd taught me how to navigate by the stars, survive in the wild and break a person's wrist with minimum energy expenditure. Not all people wore their badassery on their sleeve.

"I don't think you'd want the bacon back at this point," Mykhail said, sounding a bit less doleful. A weak grin spread across his face. "Unless you need fertilizer for the garden."

"Oh, gross," Maggie and Arden exclaimed at the same time, although Maggie said it with disgust and Arden with glee.

"Sorry," Mykhail said. He chewed for a while. "I was heading to Burnell University, to see if my astrophysics professor was there."

Of course he was a Burnell guy. Their undergrad was great, but they were mostly known for their grad school that recruited the cream of the crop. Their alumni often went on to do things like invent world-changing devices and win Nobel

Prizes for curing diseases. I'd been hurt when I'd received their form rejection, but had come to terms with it after having such a wonderful time at Rochester. I hadn't regretted not getting in until this moment, knowing there were guys like Mykhail walking around.

Mykhail continued. "Dr. Simmons knows a lot about solar flares and has done extensive research into how a CME could affect the electrical infrastructure. He's actually the founder of the North American Electrical Grid Initiative, which has been lobbying for years to get power companies to pay attention to the possibility of solar flares. If anyone is working on fixing this, it's him. I was thinking that if I found him, I could help him."

The table again broke out into noisy chatter as everyone began to lob questions at Mykhail. I gave a fleeting thought to the fact that he hadn't answered the "where were you coming from" portion of the question, but I was too intrigued by his words to focus on that. What mattered was the fact that he was doing something—traveling by himself with no safety net of family, friends or even a food source to keep him safe. I'd been holed up for months bitching about how unhappy I was, but here was a guy who was actually trying to change things.

I work with computers. I'm good at repairing electronics. Maybe…

I realized in that moment what it was I'd been feeling these past few months: useless. My family appreciated me—it was nothing so banal as feeling unloved. Just a sensation of being trapped, unable to do anything that would have real consequence in the grand scheme of things. Where Mykhail was going, I could probably help more than just a few people. I could contribute more than a handful of wilted mint leaves or comic relief. My thoughts began multiplying now that a new probability had been introduced, one that was scary as hell but might be worth the risk.

"Burnell isn't so far from here," I announced, my voice cutting through the ruckus. "It's only a few days' hike. Arden and I steered clear of the campus on our way here, but we passed it."

Arden glanced at me, eyebrows raised as if she was the only one who could sense the undercurrent of excitement in my voice. Mykhail flashed me his full smile, and my heart bumped in my chest as the seedling of an audacious idea began to sprout roots.

"Is that true?" he asked. There was relief lacing his question. "To be honest, I've kind of been wandering around hoping it was in the general vicinity. I'm used to driving, thus my idea to walk didn't work out and I got turned around. That's why I ran out of food. I thought I'd be there already or..." He lifted one shoulder casually, even though the rest of his sentence couldn't have been anything good.

"Aren't you an astronomer?" Gabriel asked. "Shouldn't you be able to follow the North Star or something?"

Mykhail flushed red again, from embarrassment this time. "I thought I could, but turns out that without GPS I have a terrible sense of direction," he admitted. "Just because you can pick out Corona Borealis doesn't mean you know where it's pointing you. Trying to travel alone wasn't the best idea, but I didn't have much choice."

I can read maps. I can navigate without GPS.

My natural sense of direction was great, and navigation was one of the many skills I'd learned from my dad that'd helped Arden and me make it to the cabin alive. My family was particularly proud of this ability, and because of it I'd become the human compass on every hike or situation where someone was too lazy to pull out their digital map.

No one said anything though, which was strange, since my family was usually eager to reveal information about me to strange men. Instead, everyone stared intently at their plates. I wasn't the only one who'd done the math and come up the answer that it would make sense for me to go with Mykhail, but I was apparently the only one who thought it was a good idea. The muscles in my neck tightened as the silence drew on. I didn't say anything. It seemed like if I did I would be crossing some line that had suddenly appeared in the sand, a line that separated me from Mykhail. The idea was still there though, germinating.

"Well, you can stay here for a day or two, get your strength back. My husband will help you figure out how to get to the university before you go." My mom smiled as she spoke, but it didn't quite reach her eyes. "John, come help me with the dishes."

I'd fully expected her to try to throw me into some compromising situation with Mykhail, so I stared at her in confusion for a moment longer than she appreciated.

"Come work that bacon off!" More feigned cheerfulness.

I stood reluctantly, and only as I brushed against him did I realize that Mykhail and I had been so close that our shoulders had nearly been rubbing. I looked down at the beautiful garden thief and felt my idea experience another growth spurt. The roots of it wrapped stubbornly around some part of me that had been looking for an excuse to escape for weeks. Then I thought of my family and how my leaving would affect them and I realized I'd have to weed it out. It couldn't come to fruition without hurting all of them.

"Coming, Amma," I said, and walked away from Mykhail without looking back.

4

"What did I do to deserve this punishment?"

Hours had gone by since breakfast. After washing the dishes, my mother had roped me into trying to repair a radio that had she'd dropped, even though we had several working radios and none of them were picking up transmissions. The soldering iron jumped in my hand as I rushed through the job, growing increasingly irritated as peals of laughter drifted down from the living room. Each explosion of gaiety sent pinpricks of irritation down my spine. My feet tapped impatiently and my thoughts wouldn't stay focused on the busywork my mother had forced onto me. Mykhail would only be staying for a short while before he went off in search of his professor. It wasn't fair that instead of basking in his adorableness I had to sit and listen to my mom complain that she might never know what happened to the couple in the K-drama she'd been obsessed with before the blackout.

She stood a few feet away, labeling mason jars of preserves. "In the last episode to air, a group of henchmen kidnapped Su-Hwa, but Dong-Yul thought she had run away from him. Instead of remembering all the love they shared, he let himself be swayed by doubt! When the electricity stopped, he was standing at the altar with the horrible woman his parents were forcing him to marry..."

I tried to pay attention, but an ungainly bark of laughter from upstairs pulled my attention to Mykhail again. I hadn't felt this anxious since I'd sat hunched over my computer monitoring eBay sales, ready to dive in at the last moment and swipe couture clothing and vintage video games from slow suckers who thought they'd won an auction. Mykhail was a million times more enticing than a Hermès scarf or Mario Kart cartridge though, and I didn't have to pay delivery charges to see him.

Another burst of laughter from upstairs broke my last shred of restraint. I put down the soldering iron, enjoying the dramatic clank of it against the metal surface of the work table. "If I hold on to that for one more moment, I'm going to use it to seal my ears shut, Ma. I'm taking a break."

My mother narrowed her eyes in my direction, but I raised my eyebrow and glared right back at her. For a minute I thought her parental force would overtake me, but eyebrow apparently beats mom glower in the staring contest hierarchy because she sighed and looked away. I couldn't feel entirely victorious when my usually proud mom suddenly seemed so pensive. The little boy in me wanted to tug at her sleeve and ask what was wrong, or to make her one of those fugly drawings of rainbows and mermaids that she had always hung in place of honor behind the counter at Seong's Grocery.

"Mom—"

"Go have fun, Jang-wan," she said. "I know you've been so unhappy here, just...don't do anything crazy, okay? This boy is cute, but he is a stranger still."

Her words should have had a dampening effect, but instead the seedling of possibility stirred in my chest again, like the insensitively named Mexican jumping beans my parents had sold in their store when I was a child. I'd loved the unpredictable movements of the little brown spheres and had been horrified when I'd learned a living creature was trapped inside the seed pod, struggling for survival. That was how I felt now, bouncing off the walls of the house. But Mykhail's arrival had bought with it the possibility of something more.

"Stop getting ahead of yourself." I took a deep breath, trying to heed my own advice, stood and gave her a quick peck on the top of her head. The familiar scent of her hair cream, the one she'd used for as long as I could remember, wafted up at me. Emotion tickled the back of my throat, but I tried to tell myself it was an allergic reaction to cheap product. "I'm just going upstairs."

"A mother knows things," she said. Her words weren't as lighthearted as they'd been the night before. "Now go make sure Arden isn't teaching Maggie some new curse word or how to twerk or something."

I tilted my head to the side as I tried to process what she'd just said. "What do you know about twerking, Ma?"

No sooner had I said the words than she slapped the table, jumped to her feet and began jerking her hip region around in a spastic motion that made me turn and run from the cellar in horror.

Her voice chased me up the stairs. "Mrs. Park showed me when we volunteered at the soup kitchen over Thanksgiving!"

And she called Arden a bad influence.

When I walked into the living room, I found Arden, Gabriel and Maggie crowded around the coffee table. They were playing a board game, Risk, and although four mugs of tea ringed the table, Mykhail was nowhere to be found. A jagged shard of sadness pressed against something soft and easily punctured within me. *Had he left without saying goodbye?*

Just then, a shaggy golden head popped up from the other side of the coffee table. "I found the dice!" he said with real excitement, as if he'd discovered an errant gold nugget instead of a chunk of plastic. His gaze flashed to me. "Jang-wan! Where've you been, man? Come help me out over here."

I opened my mouth to warn him off saying my name again, but the words died on my lips as I watched him shake the dice in his cupped hands. His eyes were squinched shut and the tip of his tongue peeked out of the corner of his mouth, as if he was really concentrating. It should have been strange to see a lanky hottie playing a game with the enthusiasm of a child, but it was totally endearing instead.

"No, I'll just watch," I said. I moved to perch on the edge of the couch and hoped my stride was more fluid than it felt. I'd wanted so badly to be in his presence, but now I felt awkward and too self-aware. *Do I always walk this weirdly? Should I swing my arm now, or put my hands in my pocket? Why is everyone looking at me?*

But it wasn't my family's attentions that made me feel like a rusty tinman who needed his joints oiled. It was Mykhail's. I told myself that he always had this mischievous light in his eyes, but I'd seen his gaze lose its shine more than once since his arrival. He looked genuinely happy to see me now though. He'd called me over to join him as if it was normal—more than that, as if it was expected. I again felt that surge of connection I'd experienced at the breakfast table, the one that had drawn my hand toward him in an irresistible act of comfort.

"John, what are you talking about? You love playing Risk," Arden said from beneath Gabriel's arm. They were cuddled together with the fireplace in the background, a Norman Rockwell painting for the post-Benetton era. "You get to indulge your Machiavellian impulses and use skill and logic to annihilate everyone. Actually, yeah, you should just watch. I've conquered half of Eurasia and I don't need you fucking up my flow."

"I definitely need your help then," Mykhail said. He reached one of his long arms over, fingers stretched just enough to wrap around my forearm, and tugged, dragging me to the ground beside him. I landed with a thump and looked up into his eyes, the deep cerulean blotting out the drab wooden paneling and shabby mauve furniture behind him. I was momentarily stunned, overcome by a strange spinning sensation that came from someplace deep and ancient and unknowable within me. It was the same feeling I got when I stared up at a night sky studded with stars.

He looked away and continued speaking as if nothing had happened, a good reminder that I shouldn't read too much into his behavior. I sat up straight and tried to muster my dignity, which I'd apparently left behind on the arm of the sofa.

"I'm Ukrainian," Mykhail said with a shrug. That explained the hint of an accent I kept hearing. "While my people are practiced in repulsing those who try to conquer us, we're not so great at the large-scale takeover. That's where you come in."

"Is that why you've just been massing your troops in Alberta and slowly ceding the rest of your Canadian territory?" Maggie asked from behind a hank of hair that had fallen in front of her face. "I thought it was some kind of clever ruse and that no one could really play that badly."

"My whole life has basically been the anti-Risk." Mykhail nudged one of his artillery figurines with the tip of a delicately tapered index finger. "Doing what my parents wanted, and my grandparents wanted, and my teachers wanted. I'm not very skilled at aggressive attacks."

He glanced at me, and I wondered if there was any underlying meaning to his earnest confession, but he scrubbed a hand through his hair sheepishly and looked away. I didn't get Mykhail; in a way, he was so completely open with us, this group of strangers he barely knew and who'd initially taken him under physical duress. I was used to walls that needed to be scaled and knocked down to get at a person's true feelings, and here he was just laying it all out there. Like Maggie, I was suspicious—it had to be a trap.

"While Arden can give you lessons on being an antiauthoritarian rebel later this evening, I'll certainly help you with game strategy...for a price," I said. The words were barely out of my mouth before I realized what I was saying. Arden called me the logical one in our duo, but I was taking a play out of her book. This was pure impulse.

His head whipped in my direction and his gaze met mine. He studied me, the angle of his glasses hiding everything but the fact that his eyes were wide with curiosity.

"Nothing salacious," I said quickly—I knew without looking at her that Arden was opening her mouth to say something pervy. "I've been reading a lot about the cosmos while we've been cooped up here, charting constellations with a star wheel and tracking the constellations. I doubt we'll have many more astrophysicists raiding the garden, so I should take advantage of this opportunity. Maybe some Astronomy 101 in exchange for my world domination lessons?"

I pasted what I hoped was a normal, noncreepy smile on my face and hoped he couldn't tell that my hands were clammy and my heart was racing.

"Ooo, that sounds fun!" Arden exclaimed. She began bouncing up and down excitedly, but Gabriel, God among brothers, hugged her in place and said, "We have plans tonight, honey."

She glared up at him. "Like, what, stare at the ceiling some more? No, we do—ohhhhh, yeah. That thing we have to do. Maggie has to do it too."

"Star talk is boring," Maggie said with a curl of her lip. "You don't have to worry about me trying to crash their date."

"Hold up, hold up, hold up," Mykhail said, and I braced myself for the inevitable put-down. Why did she have to call it a date? I stared at the floorboards, carefully searching the whorls in the hardwood for some prophecy that involved Maggie's lips being glued shut.

"Boring? Are you kidding me?" I looked up at Mykhail to see both of his eyebrows raised in disbelief. "I know you're young and you're probably more concerned with…I don't know what teenagers care about, actually. But come on. The big bang? The fact that out of so much chaos and insanity, out of huge aimless chunks of matter bashing into each other, everything exists? That we exist? It doesn't get much more exciting than that."

"Maggie doesn't much care for anything not guitar related," Gabriel said. It could have been an insult, but it was said with admiration. He had grown to love Maggie's playing, and the close bond that had formed between Arden and our sister because of it.

"Oh, perfect!" Mykhail said. Risk was forgotten, and he held his hands out like a composer about to launch into a symphony. "Do you know about string theory?"

I had some basic understanding, but I took in the puzzled expressions around the table and spoke for the majority. "Um, I'm going to go with no."

He nodded excitedly. His hands moved as he talked, sketching illustrations of images that none of us could see but him. "Okay, so everything in the universe is made up of waves. Think about it—sound waves, light waves, radiation waves. Subatomic particles, which ride these waves, are basically the same thing as notes on a staff. A tiny vibrating staff, or tiny vibrating strings." He wiggled his fingers. "When you study physics, you're studying the harmonies that can be played on these strings. Chemistry is the study of the melodies. The universe is the greatest symphony ever, the most advanced philharmonic you can imagine, and we're nothing but cosmic music in a tiny section of the overture."

There was silence after he finished. Everyone stared at him as if he had two heads—well, after being pressed against him in the garden, I was well aware he had two heads, but right now I was vastly more interested in the one sitting on his neck. It was fascinating to see how his passion illuminated him, how his love for his field was practically bursting from him. I was suddenly filled with yearning for those times when I'd been so consumed with interest in a topic that I could go down an internet research hole and not resurface until Arden kicked my door in and shook the potato chip crumbs from my clothing. I missed learning new things and sharing that knowledge.

"You know, if my science teachers had explained it like that, maybe I would have cared more," Maggie said. "That makes it sound freaking awesome!"

"Maybe you can help with the chemistry lesson I'm going to give Maggie later?" Gabriel suggested in the guise of a question. Since he'd aced med school, I didn't think he was asking for help with the homeschooling curriculum he'd devised because he needed it. He seemed so comfortable with our new life, never complaining, that it was easy to forget that he was probably hungry for mental stimulation too.

While my brother bonded with my crush, I was still in the thrall of his passionate words. Vibrating staff, indeed. There was nothing more attractive than a man who knew what he was talking about, and *cared* about what he did. Mykhail wasn't lecturing us. He was once again laying himself bare, sharing this thing that was such a huge part of him. It was wonderful. And it was a major turn-on. If my astronomy lesson was going to be anything like this, I'd have to strap down my crotch beforehand.

He clapped and rubbed his hands together. "Alright, Coach, you ready to take over the world with me?"

That was the very least of the things I was ready to do with him, but it was a start.

I cracked my knuckles. "Let's do it."

5

I sat on the front porch later that night, wondering what the hell had possessed me. At my prime, I walked the fine line between droll and demonstrative that evoked either insta-love or insta-hate in people. Since the blackout, however, I'd felt like a dull, unvarnished version of myself, as if someone had cut away all the fun bits but the snark, which is just the poor man's self-defense mechanism. Unfortunately, man cannot live by snark alone.

I occasionally glimpsed my old self during my nights with Arden and Stump, but after leading Mykhail to a ruthless decimation of my friends and family at Risk, I'd felt fully John, fully Jang-wan, for the first time in weeks. I'd joined him in a joyous, ungainly victory dance. Without any preamble, we'd both swung imaginary lassos over our heads and performed a syncopated little horse ride. After booing and hissing, the others had given in to the bacchanalian frivolity and joined us.

After that, the lot of us had been recruited into a canning assembly line by my parents, and my dad had nearly choked on a pickled string bean when Mykhail told a story about how one of his relatives had managed to smuggle family gold out of the USSR using only her feminine wiles and a very large wig. Instead of searching for witty bons mots to fool everyone into thinking I was okay, I had laughed and *actually* enjoyed myself.

Maybe it was the freedom of knowing what had caused the blackout, but since Mykhail's arrival, the darkness that had hovered over me had lifted. The house that had become a prison felt like a home again. And I wanted to leave more than ever. Isn't that always the way?

When I'd read about black holes in my antiquated astronomy book, I'd teared up at the description of an event horizon, the region around a black hole from which no escape is possible. It hit on the strange dread and apprehension I'd been feeling each day we were trapped in the house, as if I was struggling against some inexorable force that threatened to pull me in. I cared so deeply about my family, but if I stayed it was only a matter of time before I was sucked into the void.

It was ridiculous, from any angle I looked at it, especially because I was pretty much the least traumatized person in the house. Both my parents and Maggie had been abducted. Arden and Gabriel had been forced to kill, and Darlene had lost her husband first to madness then to a shotgun blast. It felt wrong to be so desperately unhappy when I had the least reason to complain. I told myself wanting to leave was selfish and I should just deal with my weird emotions like everyone else, but the denial technique wasn't working.

There was a pall over everything for me, a desperate fear and uselessness that gnawed at the edges of my thoughts. Everyone else seemed to acclimate to the new normal, but my mind was in a constant state of rebellion. There had to be *something* happening in the outside world, some rebuilding or restructuring that lacked the assistance of a stylish Korean tech geek.

I didn't want to go away forever though. Burnell University wasn't so far away. I could make a round trip journey in a week. Maybe less…

"You're here early. I didn't take you for a teacher's pet."

I swung my flashlight in the direction of Mykhail's voice and found him coming around the side of the house. His hands were shoved into the pockets of his jeans and the light bounced off his glasses, hiding his expressive eyes in an unsettling way. I pointed the beam of light away from his face. When he reached me, he bent down and flipped off the power switch, hand gliding over mine casually, as if it was normal for near-strangers to touch each other this way. A riot of sparks lit my nerve endings from fingertip to elbow, but he was already looking over his shoulder, his gaze scanning the night sky.

"Well, I'm not usually the first to arrive but I guess I'm excited to learn about Uranus," I blurted out, muddling the witty comment I'd carefully crafted over the course of the day. I cringed, but he just smirked and tugged the sleeve of my shirt, indicating that I should follow him as he stood to his full height and walked away.

I sat in a self-recriminating silence, face burning as I imagined Arden shaking her head sadly at my attempt. *Oh, honey, no.*

"We need a few minutes for our eyes to get adjusted to the darkness," he said when I caught up to him. We walked past the garden. Mykhail's gaze was still scanning the sky but his feet managed to sidestep a stray cucumber. "That's Polaris. It's the most visible star, so we're going to use it to track the movement of the sky. These rocks…no, this deer poop will mark our place."

I craned my head back, but Polaris was lost in the jumble of bright dots. Without the pesky, light-dampening effects of human technological progress, the sky looked entirely different than I was used to. There was too much to see, and the markers I'd once considered bright now blended into the background. I used to be annoyed at the light pollution that prevented me from seeing the night sky in all its glory, but I hadn't thought then about the cost of such a desire being fulfilled.

Mykhail touched a hand to my shoulder and leaned in close, shifting my body to align my gaze with the blazing star. His long pointer finger came into my field of vision. "See? It's right above us."

I could see the star now and had gained my celestial bearings, but my other senses were relaying much more important information to my brain. The warm solidity of Mykhail's chest pressing against my shoulder as he repositioned me for better viewing. The clean soap smell that clung to him and was more enticing than any aftershave. The endearing lilt of his accent that clipped certain words and rounded random syllables. The only thing missing was taste. Something hot and urgent danced in my stomach at the thought of how close his lips were to mine. Just the turn of a head, the pressing of my toes into the ground as I leaned forward…

I fought a tremble, and the urges that were pressing me ever closer to Mykhail's body.

"You see the blinking ones?" His mouth was next to my ear, the warmth of his breath much too similar to a lover's caress.

I nodded and made a sound that was halfway between "uh-huh" and "mmm."

"Those are the variable stars. I've always felt a kind of kinship with those guys." He pulled away from me and started walking back to the porch. I followed his gangly stride and sat down beside him. "Each time one of them flickers off, it's like it's fighting against some crushing force that wants to extinguish it. Maybe that's it for our valiant friend. After millions of years, it's given up the ghost and blinked out for the last time. You start to mourn its loss, and then—bam! It lights up again."

I reached under the ledge of the porch and handed him one of the juice boxes I'd stashed there. Wine would have made it seem too much like a date. Besides, my inhibitions were already dangerously low.

"You just made me want to weep for a hypothetical star," I said. I struggled to pierce my straw through the aluminum-covered opening in the juice box, trying not to look too undignified. After several failed attempts, Mykhail reached over and shoved his straw into the hole of my box with amazing accuracy, then plucked my straw from my fingers and speared his own. He spoke again before I could even begin to process the metaphorical implications of his actions.

"You should cry. One day it will blink out for good. But it will have shone brightly for millions and millions of years. It would have existed, and that's enough. There's no point in trying to shine when you can't anymore." He took a sip of his apple juice.

There was something reverent in his voice as he spoke of the theoretical extinguished star, something melancholy and tender that was both alarming and all too familiar.

I stared at him. "Was that supposed to make me feel better? If so, maybe you should stick to astrophysics."

"Listen to me." He shook his head. "This is star stuff. It should be fun! Look at all these constellations. I always miss Orion in the spring, but Ursa Major is great. You see the Big Dipper in there? Most people think it's a constellation, but it's just a star cluster within Ursa Major. But a glorified frying pan is easier to identify than an abstract bear, so that's what wins the popularity contest."

I was disoriented by the tonal shifts in the conversation, and by his closeness, and by the way his lips wrapped around that tiny straw as he drank his juice.

"Why did you start studying astronomy?" I asked. I wanted to exert some control over the convo, and I honestly wanted to know. "You said earlier that you did everything because other people wanted you to, but you're really passionate about this. Did the love for astronomy come before or after the decision to study astrophysics?"

He made a noise that was somewhere between a laugh and a grunt and aggressively slurped the dregs of his juice box. "Astrophysics is about the only thing that I ever wanted that I actually went after. It's the only part of myself that I couldn't hide away because it made my family unhappy. I remember watching *Cosmos* for the first time. My grandmother picked up the DVD from the library because she thought Carl Sagan was *krasyvyy*."

"Pardon?" I gathered from the way he smiled at the memory that his grandmother had thought Sagan was a babe, and really, who could resist a smooth operator in a turtleneck and a tweed jacket?

"Sorry, my Ukrainian slips into the mix sometime. I actually haven't spoken much English over the past few months." He crumpled the juice box in his fist and dropped it to his feet. "Anyway, she put on that DVD and as soon as he started talking about the big bang and the origins of the stars, I was hooked. What he was saying made much more sense than my Sunday school teacher, and Sagan didn't seem like someone who would hit you with a ruler for asking questions. I watched the first few episodes over and over again, and harassed my baba until she got the next DVD.

"She was upset that she'd exposed me to what she called 'an atheist garbage peddler,' but it was too late. Soon I wanted books, and a telescope, and to go to astronaut camp instead of *Plast*—that's the Ukrainian Boy Scouts. My parents were furious, but I didn't care.

"I used to look for hidden treasure in my grandparents' apartment and at the faculty housing when I visited my parents. But then I realized that the sky was full of secrets more valuable than gold doubloons or a pirate's map."

He jumped to his feet, and I followed. I could feel the nervous energy emanating from him when he spoke, could sense his agitation.

"What's wrong? Did I upset you?" I asked.

"It's just so hard to explain," he said. He stopped and turned to me, grabbing my hand and flattening it against his chest. I could feel the rapid hammering of his heart beneath my palm. Its staccato pace beat a mysterious rhythm into my skin, one that spoke of beauty and desire, a once-familiar melody that I'd forgotten after countless disappoints. His chest expanded under my hand and then the words rushed out of him. "I can't explain what it felt like to suddenly understand that the universe was so vast, that there was more to life than church, and honoring your country, and staying out of your parents' way. It was a revelation. Do you know how Sagan described the feeling he got when he had some new insight about all of this?"

He waved his hands above his head in the direction of the stars. His cheeks were stippled in rose and his eyes were wide behind his glasses. His heart still pounded beneath my hand. I would've thought him angry if I didn't know he was talking about astronomy. This was passion. I remembered spending hours figuring out how my computer games worked as a kid; when I got older, that time had been spent learning code. But I hadn't been fervent about anything in a very long time.

I shook my head, eager to hear what else he had to say.

"He said it was like falling in love." His voice was low and rough now, and his eyes had gone dark. "That soaring sensation, that moment when everything clicks into place and you just *know*. Isn't that beautiful?"

You're beautiful was what I wanted to say, but even caught up in the thrall of Mykhail's impassioned rant, I couldn't allow myself to be that cliché. Instead, I slid my hand from his chest, up around the back of his neck, and I pulled him into a kiss.

I don't know if he was opening his mouth to protest or to continue his rant on the beauty of the universe, but my mouth pressed against his parted lips and my tongue slid in without preamble. There was no soft brushing, no tentative nips. My lips sealed to his and our tongues tangled confidently, as if this wasn't our first time and they were greeting each other after a long absence. It was warm outside, but every one of my hairs stood on end as a shiver of pleasure zipped down my spine and straight to my groin.

I grabbed at his hip with my other hand and pulled him against me, adjusting the angle of my head so our lips wouldn't part. He tasted of apples, sweet and crisp, and I wondered if he'd tasted like that even before the juice box because it fit what I knew of him so well. Sweet. Fresh. Delicious. His lips matched my every move, while his tongue explored my mouth, palate and teeth, as if the mysteries of the universe could be found therein. I could feel the beat of his heart in the notch of his hip where I held him to me, in his neck, in our kiss. He pulsed, everywhere. For me.

My cock stirred to life in my pants, pressing against my zipper. I rocked my hips forward, just a little, and he mimicked my motion, his heavy length nudging my stomach just above the waistband of my jeans. Every nerve in my body lit up like a circuit board in response, wild desire urging me deeper into our kiss, pulling my hips forward to meet the friction of Mykhail's tentative thrusts.

I didn't know how much time we spent like that before I pulled away, but my lizard brain executed an executive override before one or both of us passed out from oxygen deprivation. It was then that I noticed his hands were still raised above his head, fingers stretching toward the cosmos as they had been when my kiss had ended his ode to the stars.

I stepped away from him, and he turned and marched in the opposite direction, hands still awkwardly above his head.

"We have to find that deer poop," he said in a shaky voice.

I was too shocked to speak. I'd had some strange responses to my overtures, but a sudden need for animal feces wasn't one of them. Then I realized that he was looking for our Polaris marker, as if the kiss hadn't happened. The brief press of our bodies had left me with shaky legs and an erratic pulse, but he was sticking to his Astronomy 101 syllabus. Suddenly, Mykhail being a scat enthusiast wouldn't have been the worst thing that could've happened to me.

Humiliation put the kibosh on any residual lust sparking in my system and I forced myself to follow behind him. I'd misread his signals and overstepped my bounds, and that was *after* making a bad Uranus joke. He'd returned my kiss with a fervor that seemed all too real—I hadn't been mistaken about that mouth of his—but the dust cloud he'd left in his wake undercut any hopes for another.

"I swore this was the spot, but... Oh, here it is." He raised one of his feet to look at the sole of his Converse and then scraped the shoe back and forth over the grass to clean it. "Look up."

I followed his order because it gave me something to do besides marinate in awkwardness. Polaris was gone. Perhaps it had looked down on my sad attempt at seduction and fled when overwhelmed by *fremdschämen*.

"The stars swing from east to west usually, so..." Mykhail was still giving his lesson, his gaze searching the night sky. Conveniently, that meant he didn't have to look at me.

"Over there," I said, pointing at the brightest star in

the sky as I homed in on it. I may have misread Mykhail, but my sense of direction was always impeccable.

"Yeah. See how far it's traveled in the time we spent talking? The Earth is always moving even when we think we're stuck." When I looked at him his gaze was fixed on the ground and his color was high. He poked at the tape binding his glasses, pushing them up the bridge of his nose before muttering a stream of Slavic on a sharp exhale.

"My Ukrainian is rusty, so can you say that in English?" He was probably cursing me for being a creep, but I kept my tone cordial. It wasn't his fault I'd tried to maul him without getting his explicit consent. Of course, in the leopard shifter romances Arden and Gabriel had talked me into reading, the hero never asked first. It was supposed to be more romantic that way.

Mykhail sighed. "I've never done that before, okay? I've never kissed or been kissed by anyone— Wait, that's not true. Oksana Leskiv tried after prom, but that doesn't count because she ended up licking my nostril instead. But that's beside the point. This was my first time, and I didn't know how to react. Sorry."

Oh my God. I felt like a slug who'd just accidentally showered in kosher salt as all the lush sensations of our kiss evaporated. I'd creeped on an uninitiated gayling, kissing him without style or finesse. I'd taken something he'd probably been saving for someone special, and worse, part of me basked in the fact that I'd been his first. I guess all my late-night "fuck the patriarchy" talks with Arden had been built on a foundation of denial. Throw one sweet virgin my way, and I was ready to mount him on the spot. Damned shifter romances.

"No, I'm sorry," I said, trying to pretend I wasn't completely shocked. If he was in the closet, he must have been hiding in the deepest recesses, in the crevice where you keep your nude pictures, high school journal and other top secret materials that could be used to blackmail you. Because honestly, if someone as generally harmless as me couldn't keep my hands off him, how had he gone so long without so much as a kiss? I was curious, but first I owed him an apology. "If I had known, I wouldn't have—"

"Don't apologize!" He still couldn't look at me, but his cheeks blazed red. "I enjoyed it. Like, *really* enjoyed it. I'm glad I got to do it before..."

"Before what?" I stepped closer, taking the liberty of holding his hand. He seemed so confused and distressed that I was compelled to comfort him. His fingers were stiff in mine, but he didn't pull away.

"Before I leave," he said firmly. His gaze met mine again, but it was as blank as the lenses of his glasses reflecting light. "Your dad helped me chart a course to the university while you were up in your room after dinner. I'm leaving in the morning."

Something in me froze when he uttered those words. My blood slowed and thickened, and the beginnings of a headache pounded in my sinuses as I swallowed against a surge of emotion. What the hell? He was cute and a good kisser, but I'd met plenty of those before and didn't mind when they passed through my revolving door and kept it moving. But Mykhail was different.

"You can stay if you want," I said. "I won't bother you again."

"Bother," he muttered and shook his head. He pulled his hand from mine, gently so it didn't seem like a rebuff even though it was. "It's better this way, Jang-wan. I'm not the kind of guy you need."

I disagreed strongly with that sentiment, but tried to laugh it off. "Handsome, intelligent, great kisser. Sweet to boot. You're right, who wants that?"

He grinned, but it didn't reach his eyes. "My baba had a favorite proverb for when she thought I was getting ahead of myself. '*Dyyavol zavzhdy zabyraye svoyi podarunky.*' 'The devil always takes back his gifts.'"

"I'm starting to think maybe your grandma should have gone a little easier on you," I said.

"She said the same thing before she died." His voice was low and forlorn, not at all like the man who'd marveled over bacon and made everyone in the room feel lighter in his presence. This was Mykhail the variable star, and he had just gone dark. "I'm not who you think I am. Trust me when I say no good can come of getting attached to me."

He left me standing there bewildered, turning his words over in my head to see if they made sense from any angle. Was I the gift, or the devil? Either he was fond of elaborate put-downs or something was very wrong.

It was the end of the world, and I had time to kill. I intended to find out which was the case.

Sleep didn't come that night, joining me in my dry streak. The heat of Mykhail's lips and the coldness in his eyes took turns tormenting me. I was already up and pacing the hallway, baby bottles locked and loaded, when Stump let out his first hiccuping cry. The door to the Shag Zone swung open, and Arden slipped out. She looked tired, but not like someone who'd been recently awoken.

"I thought you'd be downstairs already. Are you this eager to handle *Diapersplosion: The Reckoning,* or are you hiding from your boy toy?" she asked, giving my arm a playful squeeze. I was supposed to be the friend who made witty but incisive remarks. I was clearly off my game.

Arden froze in the doorway to Darlene's room, and when I peeked over her shoulder I saw why. Darlene was out of bed, again, and she was holding Stump. She still looked worse for the wear, but she appeared to have finally bathed and washed her hair. Her lips were pulled into a line that teetered between a smile and the frown that preceded a sob.

"I…I'd like to come down with you tonight," she said. The words sounded practiced, as if she'd stood in front of a mirror psyching herself up. "After I change his diaper."

"Of course, that would be great!" Arden graced her with a toothy smile, and then elbowed me.

I earned an exasperated look on top of the blow when I only managed to sputter, "That would be… interesting!"

After the diaper change, we marched down the stairs in an awkward line. I didn't know what to make of this sudden change in Darlene's behavior. It seemed I wasn't the only one jarred out of a stupor by Mykhail's arrival. Maybe all it took to see what a mess your life had become was the presence of someone who didn't know what lows you could sink to.

I was leading us to the kitchen to avoid waking, or seeing, Mykhail, but the sound of strumming from the living room drew Arden inside, and I reluctantly followed. Mykhail sat cross-legged in front of the hearth, Maggie's guitar nestled in his lap as his fingers flew over the strings in a strange, upbeat melody. He played with his head bent forward and eyes closed, the light of the gambling fire highlighting streaks of bronze in his hair and tipping his eyelashes in gold. His hands were positioned strangely, giving the usual notes a different sound from Arden's powerful strumming and Maggie's own developing style. His playing was serviceable, but it was his beauty that made me want to charter the Seong Household outpost of the Mykhail GardenGnome fan club.

"So that string theory stuff wasn't just conjecture for you," Arden noted as she sat on the sofa. She would usually be rocking Stump, but Darlene held on to him as she settled next to her. I pushed the warming pan close to the flames with my toe and dropped the bottles in, and then sat next to Mykhail. He opened his eyes and blinked at me a few times before reaching for his glasses. If he felt anger, or anything, about our earlier encounter, it didn't show. Part of me was relieved, the other part offended.

"Bandura lessons were required at the Ukrainian camp where I spent most of my summers. It's kind of like a lute meets a banjo, and definitely not as cool as a guitar. My roommate freshman year of college let me play his acoustic, and I taught myself a little."

I was noticing that most of his stories involved either his grandparents or places people sent their kids to get them out of their hair. Were his parents dead? If he wasn't an orphan, his parents had probably not been the most attentive.

"My dad taught me to play," Arden said. Her voice had that soft, wistful edge that it always got when she talked about her parents. "It was one of those things I looked forward to every day after school."

"Dale used to play keyboard in a band, when we first met. When things were good," Darlene offered.

Her words were rushed, like a double Dutch player who feared being slapped by the ropes as she jumped in. It was the first she'd spoken of her husband in a long time. It was the longest sentence she'd uttered about anything in a long time, for that matter. I waited for her to begin weeping or withdraw again, but she bounced Stump on her thigh and ran a hand over his smooth scalp. "On our first date, he brought me to his room and played 'Brown-Eyed Girl' and that was it for me. He had such a beautiful voice."

The only recollection I had of her husband's voice was him snarling through the back door that I'd better let him in or he'd blow me back to where I came from. If I hadn't feared for my life I would have asked him if he meant Albany, where I was born, but I figured he meant Korea. I decided against tarnishing her memories with my anecdote.

"What do you think of the name Morrison for this little guy?" she asked. Her eyes were wide as she looked at us. "We could call him Morris for short."

I thought it sounded like a name for a stray cat you fed at your back door, which wasn't entirely inappropriate in this situation, but Arden answered more diplomatically. "I think that's great! Do you want us to call him Morris from now on?"

Darlene looked Arden in the eye—I don't think she'd really even acknowledged her since the vitriolic attacks of her first days with us—and smiled. "I don't mind him having a nickname, but his real name is Morrison Dale Leverton."

"That's a great name." Mykhail strummed a fast-paced, whimsical ditty, and then began to sing in an off-key but palatable voice. "Morris D. Leverton, and his mother named Darlene. They survived the Flare and met the Seongs, now they can do anything." That wasn't entirely accurate, but I was willing to let it slide for the sake of a good story. He nodded in my direction, and I scrambled to think of an appropriate song. For some reason, only words that rhymed with shot and killed and dead came to mind, perhaps because they were the elephant in the room.

"Uh… Morris D. Leverton, also known as Stump. Born in the light of a solar flare, he takes astronomical dumps!"

That garnered a laugh from everyone, and then Darlene's thin voice cut through the laughter. "Morrison Leverton, I—" she began to sing, then stopped and shook her head. "I'm no good at this stuff. I wish Dale was here. He could always come up with something funny. But he's gone now."

Morris squealed with excitement and waved his arms in the air, wanting more entertainment. He raised his arms toward Arden, but her smile was gone now, her expression blank. She silently retrieved the bottle, handed it to Darlene and left the room. One of the benefits of Darlene's silence was not having to be reminded about Dale; now that she was coming out of her shell, we'd have to learn to deal with his attack and its aftershocks all over again.

"Oh, I didn't mean to drive her off," Darlene said. "I can't do anything right." Her face started to sag into its familiar scowl.

"Has anyone explained to you how to live with the woman who killed your husband?" Mykhail asked. He waited for Darlene to shake her head. "That's because there are no guidebooks for that. No right and wrong. No one explained to Arden how to deal with killing him either. You're both doing the best you can in a situation neither of you asked for, so don't beat yourself up."

I left them to their therapeutic chat and followed the sound of clanking ceramic. Arden was in the kitchen, using the end of the broomstick to nudge a box of tea down from a high shelf. The box fell, and she caught it in one hand, which would have been impressive if a spice jar hadn't come tumbling down after and crashed at her feet.

"Dammit!" She hopped away from the skittering shards and the garlic-scented powder that hung in the air. "Motherfucker!"

The scene was so endearingly her that I smiled, despite her annoyance. I grabbed a dustpan and kneeled before her while she used a broom to sweep up the mess. "Everything is changing." Her voice was irritable, but resolute. "Darlene's coming back from la-la land, and you're going to leave me here with her."

I choked on a sudden cough and wished I could blame it on the cloud of garlic powder she'd just pushed in my direction. "What are you talking about? Who says I'm leaving? You're the one who's planning on going to California to find your parents as soon as it's safe."

Although she hadn't heard from her parents since

before the Flare, she held on to the hope that they'd survived. Her mom was sick, but Gabriel had assured her that her illness didn't have to be deadly without treatment. Still, she was determined to get to California as soon as it was possible.

"You're damn right, I am," she said. She opened the tea box, then closed it and chucked the thing at me. It bounced harmlessly off my shoulder, but her expression was painful enough. "The look in your eye every time Mykhail opens his mouth broadcasts your intentions loud and clear, John. Why wouldn't you go? You like him, he likes you. You've been miserable here for weeks now, and if you go you can be useful to him while finding out how this electricity situation is going to be resolved. So don't bullshit me about this."

I stood and looked at her carefully. I wasn't angry; I was relieved. I'd been on the fence about going, and Arden's outburst made everything so clear. "He doesn't like me, but I still want to go. I don't know why—I've never been the most adventurous Seong—but I feel this urge that I can't get past. The trip should only take a few days, round trip."

The tears began pouring down her face before I finished talking. She stepped toward me, heedless of the broken glass, and pulled me into a tight hug. Typical Arden. "I don't want to guilt-trip you, but I'm going to be so worried about you. You're my only family that I can account for now, and I know it's selfish but I want you here."

My nose burned and my throat was tight, but I managed

a weak joke. "You only want me here because you hate mixing formula." I squeezed her tightly. "I want to be here, but…I don't want to be here too. If I stay, and nothing changes, I'll go crazy."

I struggled to find the words to explain what I was feeling, but then she squeezed me even tighter, making speech impossible.

"He'd better be packing some heat if you're willing to follow him." She sniffled and wiped her tears on my shoulder. "It's dangerous out there, and you shouldn't settle for less than premium, grade-A cock."

My laughter bubbled up, cutting through the thickness in my throat. "I wouldn't know, but I also wouldn't be opposed to finding out." I thought of our kiss, awkward as it had turned out after. If it was any indicator of how good sex could possibly be… "I just need something, and I know what I need isn't here. I love you and my family so much, but I have to at least try this. If he says no, I won't force it."

"Well, you're the one who talks people out of doing stupid shit, so don't expect me to stop you. I just want you to be happy, and if risking your life in pursuit of Ukrainian peen is what it takes, so be it." Her cool lips pressed to my forehead as if she was the Pope absolving my sins.

"I'm supposed to be the dramatic one, darling." I grabbed her by the arm and spun her, dipping her back like we'd just tangoed. "I know you really want that last packet of Twinkies, but you don't get it unless I come back alive, so don't count me out just yet."

"Never," she whispered, looking up at me. "I *know* you can do anything. You're the one who needs to prove it."

I stared down at my best friend. Beneath her brashness was so much love that it threatened the very plans she was urging me to follow.

"Or you're just really fiendin' for some D," she added. I dropped her on her butt, then collapsed laughing beside her on the cool tile of the kitchen floor.

The door creaked open and a shaggy blond poked his head in, eyes wide behind his glasses. "Darlene went upstairs with the baby."

"Aw, were you lonely?" Arden asked, rolling onto her back. She was clearly joking, but he nodded and walked into the kitchen, taking a seat at the table. She raised herself with her elbows to stare at him. Only when he started fidgeting, his long fingers twining with each other, did she speak again. "John is going with you to Burnell. We want to make sure you get there in one piece."

I was reminded of one of the primary reasons for having best friends: they would do your dirty work for you without batting an eyelash. I was glad for it, but I still inwardly cringed and hoped that the moment would be over with quickly. I was certain he would say no and that my dreams of adventure would be over before they'd even begun.

"Wait. You want to go to Burnell?" Mykhail asked.

His hands rested on his knees and his back was straight. He looked positively rigid compared to Arden and me sprawled on the floor.

"I want to see what's happening beyond this one-mile radius. Since you said you didn't know how to navigate, or do much of anything, I thought I could tag along and make sure you get there in one piece. But I don't have to go with you if you'd rather be alone." I scratched my nose. I realized it was true; I could venture out by myself. But he was my passport to something more than just a walkabout. "The thing is, you're going to find someone who would definitively know what was up with the electricity and with getting things back online. I'd really rather have a goal than wandering aimlessly and hoping to find a way to be useful."

"So you want to be my guide. That works out well for me," he said, an odd tone in his voice. He scrubbed a hand over the back of his neck and then shook his head, as if amused by something only he could see. Then he smiled at me, wiping away any disquiet I was feeling. "I won't promise you anything, but if you want to make a trip I won't turn down a companion who knows how to navigate."

I grinned in return, but I'd be lying if I didn't admit to the slightest bit of disappointment. Maybe I'd expected him to give me a smoldering look instead of taking me along for practicality's sake. I felt like the useful tool one picked up on a quest in an RPG game instead of the item that made a player fist pump in triumph when obtained. Well, if I was more med kit than flamethrower, so be it.

"It's settled then," Arden said. Her sprightliness covered the break in her voice. "Now you just have to tell your mother."

"Tell me what?" Amma stood in the doorway, and she did not look amused.

7

We slept late the next morning, exhausted by extended negotiations with my mother. First she flat-out refused to let me leave, as if I was fourteen instead of twenty-four. Next, she castigated me for wanting to desert my family at a time like this. Then, she demanded that we tell her exactly how long the trip would take, what route I would follow and what we'd do in case of emergency. When she finally demanded that I prove my ability to defend myself if I was attacked again, I snapped and challenged her to an arm-wrestling match.

She won, but since I didn't fold immediately, she gave me her reluctant blessing.

Hours later, I was moving down a hug assembly line comprised of my family as they lined up on the porch. Seeing them all there, together, suddenly made it clear what I was doing.

I was purposefully leaving them, the most important people in my life. I could feel the bonds that tied me to them stretched taut and I hoped that none of them would be severed in my absence. A crushing despair settled onto my shoulders and gripped me by the throat, making it hard to speak as I bid farewell to each family member. Gabriel's gruff "Be careful." My dad's crushing embrace, capped off by a clumsy kiss on the cheek. The way Maggie bit her lip and hid behind the long curtain of her hair.

When I got to Arden, she smiled and pressed something warm into my hand. "This is for you. I figured you would miss it, so..." She shrugged benevolently. I looked down to find she had gifted me one of Stump's diapers. Her smile, and the way both of our hands were wrapped around the tightly balled bundle of poo, triggered a torrent of tears that slipped down my cheeks even as I laughed.

"This better be from Stu—Morris, and not some weird roleplaying you and Gabriel got into this morning," I said. "Dammit, Arden! I can't even wipe these stupid tears away now. If I get pinkeye on this trip..."

"If you get pinkeye from baby poop and not from debauched sex acts, I'll disown you," she whispered as she pulled me in for a hug. She took the diaper back and averted her glossy eyes.

Gabriel came up behind her, and she leaned into him. I was sometimes envious of the ease of their love, of how simple they made it look even when they were arguing, but now I was grateful because I knew they had each other. Together, they could take on just about anything. I still thought the fact that Gabriel was still among the living wasn't a result of dumb luck and a well-placed walkie-talkie but because Arden had willed it to be so. Would I ever care for someone deeply enough to make people consider telekinetic bullet redirection as a reality?

A cloud of rubbing alcohol in my face shifted my attention to my mother. "I was aiming for your hands," she said, not bothering to hide the lie. It seemed she hadn't entirely forgiven me for making this trip. She pumped the antibacterial spray onto my hands and rubbed it in as she gave me the same advice she had when I'd headed off to camp as a kid. "Take the multivitamins I packed in your bag, because you need more vitamin D. Remember not to eat those red berries that grow around here. I only packed a couple of pairs of underwear for you, and those berries run right through you. And—" All at once I was assaulted with a memory of her cleaning my hands after one of my messier meals as a child, joking and laughing with me in Korean to keep me from squirming away.

More tears slid down my cheeks. "It's from the spray, Amma," I said, and although my chest hitched and I sniffled, she nodded.

"Be careful, okay? I know you're a grown-up, but you're still my son. Make sure you come back." She kissed my forehead and then handed me a pack of tissues. "Your face is all red and your eyes are puffy. Go splash water before Mykhail sees you like this..."

She was back in matchmaking mode, which meant she forgave me. Relief, just a bit of it, released into my system.

"Kitty, let the boy go," my dad said, squeezing my shoulder. "John knows what he's doing. I have complete faith in his ability to get there and back in one piece. Now, if he can find a cache of Applewood bacon on his way back, that would be something impressive."

I blew my nose and shrugged the heavy pack onto my back. Mykhail, who had already given his thanks and said his goodbyes, was waiting for me at the edge of the woods. Earlier in the morning, he'd pulled his nearly empty backpack from the bushes where he'd hidden it. Now we were both oversupplied for our journey, our bags stuffed near to bursting. My mother had even snapped a bulging pink fanny pack around my waist at the last minute. The hideous item did nothing for my outfit, but sartorial issues weren't a priority anymore. After my first trip to this cabin, when Arden and I had survived on the sad remainders of our pantry, I didn't mind the extra weight or the fashion faux pas.

The spring day was warm, the sky was blue and I looked back only once. My family and Arden stood on the porch. I raised a hand in their direction, and each one of them lifted a hand in reply immediately, as if we were bound with an invisible tether. Instead of making me sad, I got a little bump of joy seeing them all waving in unison like the cheesy intro to one of the 90s sitcoms I'd grown up watching in syndication.

Mykhail and I began our journey in silence. We walked under the boughs of spruce pines and maples, and I breathed in the scent of wild flowers and grass that carried on the breeze. It was the same air I'd inhaled every day for months, but it stirred a sense of freedom within me now, the same feeling I got when dipping my toes into the ocean. There was a whole world out there, waiting for me. Waiting for us.

I glanced at Mykhail, who stared sullenly at the ground as we marched forward. Perhaps now that we were actually on our way, he was realizing that he didn't want a travel buddy. My stomach lurched at the thought of having forced myself into his plans, and a desperate embarrassment momentarily held me in its stinging thrall. I shook it off. I hoped he wasn't having regrets, but if he was, too bad for him. I was here, and I didn't plan on spending my trip with Debbie Downer.

"Last time I made a journey, some guys knocked me out," I finally said to break the silence that was anything but comfortable. "I think by the rules of probability that makes us pretty safe."

"Yeah, Arden told me about that. Right after she threatened to cut my balls off if I let anything happen to you." He didn't look at me, but I saw his lips curve up a bit. "It must be nice to have people who are so protective of you. I was tempted to sneak away and leave you while the tearful goodbye-fest was going on."

The smirk was still firmly in place, but there was an

edge to his voice that I hadn't heard before. I told myself I was overthinking, but his next question didn't help things.

"Why are you coming with me? I already told you that nothing can happen between us, so I hope it's not that."

I cringed as embarrassment clenched the back of my neck and spread through me in a wave of self-doubt. My pride demanded I turn around and head home without saying another word, but then I imagined the pitying looks on my family's faces when I slunk back in. Fuck no. I was out for an adventure and I was going to have one.

"You've made it perfectly clear that you're not interested in me, and while you're cute, I do have a little more self-respect than to put my life in danger for a piece of ass." I was just a smidge over the self-respect line, really, but he didn't need to know that. "I came because I want to find out exactly what's being done to fix the electrical grid, and to help if I can. I don't want my family's survival to be at the whim of some imaginary force that's going to make everything better."

"You're willing to give up all that? All those people who care about you?" He stopped and turned to face me. His cheeks were rosy again, the cherubic characteristic undermining the surprising anger that burned in his eyes.

"Who says I have to give up anything?" I countered, my own anger growing. "I intend on being back home within a week. Why do you care? If you're not interested in me or my companionship, don't hide behind some misplaced sense of concern for my family."

He gave an annoyed sigh that was very close to a growl.

"Jang-wan, you know that anything could happen to us out here. You haven't left this area for months. Do you think everyone is living a happy little cloistered life with bacon and board games and love?" His Adam's apple bobbed in his swanlike throat and his wide mouth was stretched into a scowl. "I never said I wasn't interested in you. I'm interested enough that if something were to happen to you because you thought I might change my mind, I'd feel even worse than I already do."

Conversation with him was like being recruited into a game of tug-of-war, only my end of the rope had been slicked. One moment it seemed as if he didn't want to be alone, the next he was angry at me for joining him. He ran away from my kiss, then worried about my well-being.

"Mykhail, I'm a grown-ass man. I can take care of myself. You're the one who said you'd be hopelessly lost without my help. If you're going to keep second-guessing me, I'll gladly flounce and leave you to find your own way."

His nostrils flared, a delicate expression of his supreme frustration. Not with me, I realized, but with himself. When he spoke, his voice was rough. "I've hurt enough people. I don't want to hurt you too."

I didn't know what he meant, but any fool could see that he was struggling under the weight of something terrible. I'd thought of Mykhail as an open book, but I realized now that wasn't entirely true. He hadn't divulged where he'd been since the Flare had plunged us all into darkness, or who he'd been with. Curiosity tugged at my pigtails, but I shooed it away. There would be a good time to question him about that. The despair in his eyes warned me that it wasn't now.

I reached out and tentatively placed a hand on his shoulder. "I'm the cannibal serial killer, remember? You should be more worried about *me* hurting *you*."

The furrows in his brow smoothed out, and with a blink, the haunted look in his eyes was replaced by relief. He brought his hand up and briefly rested it on mine, fingertips stroking over the back of it with an absentminded tenderness. Sweet sensation curlicued through me, flooding my body with a bright need for more followed by a dingy chaser of disappointment. He didn't want me in that way, I reminded myself.

He sighed and turned away, staring through the trees at some abstract point in the distance.

So this was what they meant by unrequited. I pushed the thought away, as well as the bit of hope that flared at his touch. I'd played the role of doormat before and, crush or not, it wasn't a role I was willing to reprise.

"Just think of me as the Samwise to your Frodo," I said, and then realized I couldn't have chosen a more apt pairing, if all the slash fic I'd read before the internet died was to be believed. Being a loyal, lovestruck hobbit wasn't one of my personal relationship goals, but here we were. Why couldn't I be the Frodo in all of this? Or the Aragorn, for that matter?

He raised his eyebrows and spoke in a scratchy, high-pitched voice that I supposed was his attempt at a hobbit imitation but sounded more like Yoda. That should have been enough to kill my infatuation. "Where do we go from here, Jang-wan Gamgee?"

I pulled the compass from the pocket of my pants, the dull metal disk warm in my palm as its needle spun and finally settled. It pointed straight at Mykhail.

"Very funny," I muttered as I stuffed it back into my pocket.

Mykhail gave me a quizzical look, but I shook my head and started walking, and he fell into step beside me.

We eventually decided to walk along the roadside, where there was less underbrush to trip us up but ample opportunity to dart into the trees if need be. After my initial jubilation at setting off had faded, I was able to discern the low-level fear that thrummed in my veins. *The woods are lovely, dark and deep.* The line of the poem I'd once thought magical now seemed menacing, warning of the dangers that lurked ahead of us. It felt silly, given the way the spring sunlight sluiced through the greenery, carpeting the asphalt with intricate undulating patterns. The shush of the wind through the leaves was comforting, like the white noise app I used to play before bed every night to calm my internet-addled mind. There were other sounds though: rustling bushes, breaking twigs, squeaks and chirps that came from no discernible location.

It was midafternoon when a sound slightly ahead of

me made me gasp and jump toward Mykhail. My humiliation was immediately compounded by the small brown-and-white animal that darted into the road then back into the safety of the trees.

"I always forget how loud chipmunks are for their size," I said. I pulled my back straight and tried to emit some measure of comportment.

Mykhail maintained the same gangly stride he'd displayed all day, one that emitted an ease that I wasn't quite feeling yet. "They can be deadly, you know." He shot me a faux-serious glance and my nerves trilled in response. "I once saw a group of them carry a man off into the woods."

"Very funny. You didn't even jump though. Have you had your reflexes tested lately?" Heat rushed to my face as I thought of how I'd pounced on him under a blanket of stars. My hair brushed against my overly warm neck and I pulled it up into what Maggie called my manbun.

He shrugged. "I only run from things when I'm frightened."

My thoughts again flashed to the night before, of him speeding away from me into the darkness. To the moment just before that, when our kiss had aligned perfectly and it had briefly seemed that the possibilities before us were endless.

"Well, what does it take to frighten you?" I prodded.

"Honestly, at this point, not very much." His voice was colder now. He pushed his glasses up into his mussed hair, once again making his striking cornflower-hued eyes the center of attention. I usually didn't pay attention to stuff like that—I mean, nearly everyone had eyes and, judging from his prescription, he didn't even possess a pair that worked very well—but their strange beauty was so vibrant that each time I saw them I was struck speechless. I wondered if I'd ever stop being startled by them and realized I would...when we went our separate ways and the shade eventually faded into a dull memory.

He continued and the way the joy left his face made me wish I hadn't asked. "I've tried to look at this whole catastrophe as an experiment. My hypothesis was that a major cosmic disaster would result in humanity joining together to overcome and rebuild. That hypothesis had been disproven multiple times, until I met your family."

It was strange, watching him transform as he spoke. Easygoing and charming Mykhail receded with a stiffening of the neck and a hardening of vocal cadence. It was like the part of a sci-fi film when a character you knew and loved was revealed to be an android in disguise. Except with him, I couldn't tell which persona was the act. Maybe neither of them was.

"Where were you before you showed up in my garden?" I spoke softly, not wanting to demand information that should have been offered willingly, but hadn't. I was more than curious about what had happened that could freeze him from the inside out like this. What had he encountered that had left him so cynical? Who had he met, and what had they done to him?

"Walking." His stride stretched even longer, and I trotted to keep pace with him. He was trying to evade something, and I didn't think it was me. I thought he wasn't going to elaborate, but then he took a deep breath. "I walked for a long time after I left. The home is pretty far from here." He squinted into the distance, and even though I knew there was nothing ahead but trees and roads, I followed his gaze.

"What home?" I asked. It didn't sound like he was describing the place where he'd grown up. I shuddered involuntarily, what my mom called "passing through a ghost," but the foreboding in my stomach didn't get in the way of my concern for him. Mykhail was still a stranger to me in many ways, but I could tell by the way his jaw clenched and his hands clutched the straps of his backpack that he was struggling against something. The urge to take his hand was strong now, but I walked closer to him instead. He could reach out if he needed me.

"My baba, she lived alone while I was at college. She was independent—you don't tell a woman who's fought against tyranny for her entire life what she's going to do. But even a strong will can't mend a broken hip, and when she fell getting out of the shower last year, my parents decided to send her to a nursing home." His voice was flat, but I knew it wasn't because he had no feelings on the matter. It seemed to be the opposite, in fact, as if he was walling something away to protect himself from too much emotion. I thought back to when my parents had gone missing; I knew the technique well. "Well, it was kind of a hybrid nursing home, assisted living facility. There were a couple of nurses, but mostly hourly staff. My parents are on sabbatical in Kiev and they didn't even bother to come visit her. Simply had her carted off like refuse."

I'd already gleaned that there was no love lost between Mykhail and his parents, but the glint in his eyes bordered on more than simple family strife. I didn't know what the correct response was. Maybe he wanted me to go off on his parents and call them dirtbags, but family was usually more complicated than that. "I'm sorry," I said, keeping it simple. When he glanced at me, I simply met his gaze, signaling as best I could that I was listening.

"She liked the place," he continued. "It was full of other Ukrainians, and when she recovered she got her own little studio apartment. So it wasn't very different from the life she was used to. She gossiped and reminisced about the old days with the women, and flirted with the men. But she got really sick right before my fall semester started. Pneumonia. I took the semester off, and that's where I was when the Flare happened. There's a town up ahead."

He did reach out then, just the lightest laying of his hand against my chest to get me to slow down. I'd been listening to his story so intently, parsing it for details, that it took me a moment to catch his last few words.

"Oh yes. That's Belleville," I said. "Only about forty people live there. It's less a town than a few houses along a road with a general store."

"When was the last time you had contact with anyone here?" His hand was still on my chest, and when he came to a stop I was forced to follow suit or push past him. "Has your family bartered with them, or has anyone passed by your property?"

"No, but I think my sixth-grade English teacher moved here. Mrs. Jacobs was nice."

"Unless you have a personal invitation that was extended after you were twelve, we should probably go around." He said the words casually, but it wasn't actually a suggestion since he didn't wait for me before starting toward the woods.

"Sure," I said. I wasn't spoiling to talk to strangers just yet. The thought actually terrified me, after being cloistered for so long. But there was something in the way his eyes scanned our surroundings that bothered me. "Is there anything you'd like to share with me right now, Mykhail? You said you only run if you're frightened, and right now you look like you're about to jet."

He stared past me, and when I turned to follow his line of sight I was ready to jet with him. Something glinted in the distance, and then a dusty red pickup truck on wheels too big for its body pulled into the road. It stopped and idled, the sound of its engine thrumming menacingly. I was anthropomorphizing, but I couldn't help the way my stomach flipped as the vehicle sat "staring" at us. I was grasping for the title of the movie about the possessed car when Mykhail grabbed the front of my shirt and pulled me toward the trees. My pulse kicked up and my body tensed, teetering on the edge of fight or flight.

"Remember how we first met?" he asked over his

shoulder. He swung his other arm in front of him, pushing branches out of our way.

"I jumped you, and Arden almost shot you. Your classic boy-meets-boy tale." I tried to make the words light, but I was beginning to understand where this conversation was going.

"That was one of the more welcoming receptions I've received." I bumped into his pack as he hesitated over which direction to go. "I've been run out of a couple of small towns like that. The last one I went through had a body hanging from a lamppost in the town center."

The baseline fear that had settled under my skin spiked, raising the hairs on my neck and arms. I wanted to pull away from him and run. I'd amped myself up for an adventure, but at that moment every particle in me wanted to beam back home, where Arden and my family had protected me throughout this ordeal. But we were already half a day away, too far to expect help from anyone but each other. "What the hell? Now you tell me? This would've been nice to know beforehand." Fear made my words sharp and I pushed at his backpack. He was moving too slow for my panic's liking as the low growl of the truck's engine began to move in our direction.

"Is it really surprising to you?" he asked in a harsh whisper. "You got knocked unconscious by a stranger months ago. Did you think community relations had magically gotten better since then?"

"Well, no, but why didn't you just stay with us if things were so dangerous?" I scouted the possible hiding spots, drawing on my instincts as the reigning hide-and-seek champion of the Seong household. Nothing. There was nowhere to go, except maybe… I yoked him by the backpack and pulled him behind an oak tree just wide enough to provide coverage for both of us if we squeezed close together.

I was suddenly hyper aware of everything: the wheeze of my rapid breathing as my adrenaline kicked in, the sound of tires on asphalt, the twigs that littered the ground around us that would make quietly escaping virtually impossible.

"Because there's something I have to do," he finally answered, settling against my backpack so that he covered me from behind.

"Get to the university?" I whispered, ignoring the warmth of him all up the back of me. I was thankful for the pack that served as a barrier between us; apparently even a situation as dangerous as this couldn't suppress my body's reaction to him.

I felt his shrug as it lifted and lowered my backpack. "No. Honestly, I didn't care if I made it there until you said you wanted to go. I'd rather not see you hurt because of my whim."

Confusion and unease twisted inside me. I was starting to notice a pattern in the way he talked about what exactly he was doing, or not doing, and why. A realization hovered just outside my peripheral vision, but the silencing of the engine on the stretch of road we'd just evacuated cleared every thought from my mind, save one: *oh shit, we're about to die.*

The *fwump* sound of car doors being slammed shut was followed by the crunch of boots on the ground. Two sets. I didn't hear the click of a safety or the pump of a rifle, but I knew they were armed. There could be no other reason for the confidence in their approach. My hands slid to the garish fanny pack my mother had snapped on. I'd been trying to recover from my diaper-induced crying jag when she'd told me its contents, but I'd caught the last few words—*gum, those strawberry fruit snacks you like and the handgun, okay?*

Suddenly Mikhail's hands were moving over my chest, pulling at my shirt. I was completely terrified, and it was a damned miracle that I didn't yelp in surprise or make some other unseemly noise that would attract attention.

I turned my head to glare at him. *You choose now to reciprocate?* Then I realized what he was doing—pulling the hem of my dark shirt over the glaring pink fanny pack. I would've attributed it to his sense of self-preservation, but he didn't seem to have much of one. That meant one thing: he was making sure they didn't see *me*. I didn't know why it affected me so much. It was an automatic movement committed blindly in a moment of panic. But that was why it hit me so hard; in a moment of absentmindedness, my safety was at the forefront of his thoughts. A ragged hope within me that had been crushed into the ground the night before now raised its antennae and tested its crumpled wings.

"I think he went in these trees, here," a voice rang out in the silence of the woods. A woman's voice, older and kindly, like the grandma in a TV commercial. "Should we hunt him down, or wait for him to make a move and then kill him?"

I shuddered at their casual discussion of ending one of our lives. They hadn't seen that there were two of us from that distance, but they surely wouldn't be bothered by having to take someone else down, judging from the woman's cold-blooded conversation.

"Do we have to kill him?" A man, middle-aged from the sound of it. "Maybe we can lock him up in the cellar like the last guy that passed through—"

"The thief who wouldn't stop screaming his head off and trying to escape every time we turned our backs? No. You know what we have to do. We can't chance losing anyone else to these scavengers."

The faint sound of footsteps approached, growing louder. They walked slowly, making it seem as if time had turned to molasses.

Fear scrambled in my veins, urging me to move, to turn, to run, but Mykhail's arms clamped around me, holding me in place. He leaned in close to me, the tips of his shaggy hair tickling my ear before his quiet voice did. "Jang-wan."

I turned my head to look at him. His eyes were closed as he held me in my panic, and his mouth moved as if he whispered something to himself. When his lids fluttered open, his gaze was already locked on mine. The burning determination in his eyes startled me, but not so much as what happened next. Even as the footsteps of people hunting us approached, he lowered his head down to mine and kissed me.

His lips were soft, but there was an urgency to this kiss, a longing in the firmness of his mouth and an unfathomable tenderness in the slide of his tongue over mine. I already thought Mykhail was very much an open book, and his kiss was no different—he didn't hold anything back, transmitting his emotions in the tremble of his lower lip and the bump of our noses as he lined his mouth up with mine. My pack still separated us, but his hands brushed shyly over my stomach and chest.

Our positioning was awkward and my neck ached from angling back and up, but I couldn't move away from the short-circuiting pleasure that zinged through me from my feet to my head. It wasn't fair being kissed like this though, because something lurked behind the perfection of our tangling tongues and the excitement of Mykhail's growing confidence, something that made it feel like a goodbye instead of a beginning. It should have been romantic, being held by this beautiful man and kissed as if I was someone he cherished, but I was already shaking my head before his lips parted from mine and he adjusted his glasses.

"Stay here. I mean it." Five short words, and then a serene expression settled onto that sweet face of his before he moved away from me. My reflexes were good, but it happened so quickly that I didn't have time to stop him. My fingertips just caught the hem of his shirt, but he tugged away easily as he stepped out from our hiding spot.

"Looking for me?" he said with a wave. He was all boyish charm, even as the first bullet whizzed past him and into the trees behind us.

9

Dead. I had to be dead, because all of my vital organs seemed to cease functioning as Mykhail stepped into the line of fire with a smile. I wasn't a lip reader, but now I realized the words his lips had been forming before they'd pressed against mine: a prayer.

I hadn't been to church for years, since Maggie's confirmation, and one of the realizations I'd come to since the blackout was that I didn't quite believe in anything, but the words that roared in my head in response were *Jesus, no*!

"That was a warning shot," the woman gritted out. She sounded so angry, although Mykhail had done nothing to her and never would, even if given the chance. "Put your hands up and walk toward us."

Mykhail raised his hands and moved, widening the distance between us until he was out of my line of sight.

I got a last glimpse of his wide mouth, pulled up into a seriously inappropriate grin, and his golden hair burning brilliant in a shaft of sunlight that had hopscotched through the leaves above.

An inarticulate sound of distress lodged in my throat, but I swallowed it down. I leaned my forehead against the tree and tried to steady my breathing. *Imagine this is just another game of hide-and-seek.* I commanded myself and tried to take slow, deep breaths and pull my frazzled thoughts together enough to form a plan. *Panic is for amateurs, and you're a pro.*

"What are you doing in our woods?"

The woman's voice was hard, but Mykhail's was bright and unconcerned when he replied. "I didn't know these trees were spoken for, ma'am. I'm just passing through. I'm not looking to hurt anyone."

"You think that's the first time we've heard that?" The woman's voice was even harder now. "Last time I fell for that, I let some hungry men in my house. They cornered my daughter first chance they got, then ran off with our food. Why should I think you're any different?"

I heard Mykhail sigh and remembered his disproven hypothesis on human nature. My hands rested on the fanny pack, and I wondered if I should risk the noise unzipping it to get the gun would create. One small sound could result in a jumpy trigger finger, and the guns were trained on someone who had quickly become far too valuable to me. Imagining a world without Mykhail's goofy smile and easy touch made me feel ill. I didn't want to push his assailants over the edge, but I couldn't leave him unprotected either. I pulled at the zipper slowly, moving it millimeter by millimeter.

Mykhail spoke, his voice as casual as if he was giving directions. "Well, I'm not attracted to women, for starters. Also, I've been pretty much asexual until two days ago, and I haven't turned into some kind of ravening sex beast since then, so there's no threat of assault from me." He chuckled, as if he was talking to friends. I hoped the gun-toting duo found it as endearing as I did. "Maybe that was too much information. Basically, I'm a decent human being who doesn't enjoy hurting others. If I did, my life would be much easier right now."

I heard a grunt from the man, then the clearing of his throat and hocking of a loogie large enough to make an audible impact with the ground. "This is turning into a goddamned therapy session."

"She started it," Mykhail pointed out. "I'm just trying to assure you that I want nothing from you. I have everything I need to make my journey, and, I don't mean to be rude, but my sights are set a little bit higher than Belleville."

There was a silence and my hand stilled on the zipper.

"Why should we believe you?" the woman asked. "The men who came before you said they were soldiers, said they were just passing through and—"

"If you don't believe me, just kill me." Mykhail's voice was completely calm, amused even, like a child who has just double-dog dared someone. What was he playing at? After years of gaming, I was pretty good at planning attacks and counter-attacks, and asking a deranged enemy to kill you wasn't in any of my playbooks.

Fear welled up in me, and anger at the people who wanted to hurt him. Annoyance at him for goading them, and at myself because I'd enacted this same scenario with him only a couple of days ago. I remembered how he'd refused to go into the house, despite the weapon we had trained on him. He'd only relented once Arden had gotten upset and intervened on his behalf, as if he—

"You alone?" the man asked, interrupting my whizzing thoughts.

"You gonna shoot?" Mykhail asked in return, tone bemused.

I slid my hand into the fanny pack and closed it around the barrel of the handgun. I hoped I wasn't making a noise that would tip them off, but I couldn't tell. My heart beat loudly in my ears, drowning out sound, drowning out logic. It didn't matter if I'd just met him, or if he felt the same way about me. I remembered the moment I thought Gabriel had been shot, the sick dread that had slammed into me. I wouldn't experience that again. Besides, there was something about Mykhail that made me feel as fiercely protective of him as I would about any member of my family. I couldn't sit here while his life was arbitrarily ended in front of me.

I'd never be able to live with myself.

Someone huffed a sigh, and then the man's voice rang out, annoyed. "Cripes, Mabel, this boy isn't a threat. While we're out here dicking around with him, someone looking to do some real damage could be sizing us up."

"But Harold—"

"But nothing! I'm tired and I want a drink. I'm not killing anybody else unless I damn well have to. You can kill him if you want, but you have to handle the body yourself."

There was a long silence and then her angry "hmf" of assent. Relief wrapped around me, warmed me through like the electric blanket Arden and I had snuggled under as we watched TV on cold autumn nights.

"You're letting me go?" Mykhail asked. "Why?"

"Are you crazy?" the woman asked, giving voice to my thoughts. "Lay facedown on the ground and don't move until five minutes have passed. Stay away from our town, and we won't be forced to hurt you."

Their footsteps receded, and the growl of their engine did the same shortly thereafter. I counted off the seconds in my head, unsure if I should trust that both of them had driven away and that we were indeed safe. I was good with numbers, but my scrambled thoughts kept throwing me off track, so I finally just waited. It seemed like forever, but eventually I heard Mykhail stand. I peeked around the tree, ready to berate him for his unfathomable behavior, but his expression stopped me. He'd spoken candidly with the two people hoping to protect their town, but pain was etched into his every feature now. His eyes met mine, just briefly, and the distance between us in that instant seemed much farther than a few feet of overgrown woodland. There were light-years between me and the broken man who met my gaze, and I briefly felt the impotence of the astronomer who stared longingly at Saturn's rings but knew they were lifetimes beyond lifetimes out of reach.

"Why did you do that?" I asked. My voice was quiet. Not because I feared being overheard, but because he seemed so very close to cracking and I knew I didn't have the right tools to put him back together. Not yet, at least.

"Why not? You have a family to go back to. I don't." His voice broke and his mouth closed into a grim line as he brushed leaves off his jeans and shirt. He picked at minute particles that were perhaps only visible under the magnification of his glasses before looking at me. When he spoke again, his voice was calmer, although still a bit wobbly. "Besides, I've never gotten to be anyone's knight in shining armor. I wouldn't say it was fun, but I don't regret it. I don't regret any of what just happened."

A hint of a smile tugged at those lips that had so recently touched mine; the kiss he'd laid on me before embarking on his chivalric quest had fallen to the wayside in the face of the two seriously pissed townies. But that smile reminded me how soft his lips had been, and the bittersweet pleasure of being on the receiving end of someone's last kiss. Except he was still alive, thank goodness, and now I wasn't sure how to proceed. I could sit him down and ask what in the entire fuck he thought was okay about asking someone to shoot him as a diversionary tactic, but his raw emotion in the aftermath made me fairly certain that I'd best save that question for when Mabel and Harold weren't on our heels. I opted for a diversionary tactic of my own.

"Does this mean I'm your damsel in distress?" I asked, raising an eyebrow at him as I zipped my fanny pack shut. "I'm not sure I'm entirely okay with that label, but if it gets me another kiss like that, I guess I can tolerate it."

A blush stained his cheeks at my words. "We should go before they come back."

I didn't mind his evasion. Besides that sadness that kept threatening to overwhelm him, he'd just had a near-death experience, and it wasn't his first. Plus, the whole kissing dudes thing was new for him. I wasn't going to be the guy who pushed him too hard, too fast. I knew how that could screw someone up, and he didn't need to be any more emotionally mixed-up than he was. I wasn't some kind of sexual martyr though. We had only a few days together, but if he was willing to risk his life for me, it wasn't entirely out of bounds to think that maybe he'd kiss me again before that time was up. A boy could hope, at least.

Patience, grasshopper.

"After me, Sir Knight," I said, pulling out my compass. "We'll circumvent Belleville and find a place to hunker down for the night."

"There's still time, you know. For you to go back. I don't think that's the last trouble we'll have." He kicked at a rock in his path, followed it with his eyes as it ricocheted off a gnarled tree root. He looked anywhere but at me.

"Do you think I'd just abandon you after that?" I asked. He'd just volunteered to play decoy for me, and he thought I'd leave him so easily?

"I think you *should*. It's the logical choice, and the safe one," he said. A thin trickle of humiliation and sadness slid down my spine at the dismissal. He looked in my direction, but his gaze was turned inward, as if he puzzled over some erroneous data. "But I don't want you to go. I never imagined this happening when I left the home. This is a dumb question, but does it always feel this weird?"

"Does what always feel weird? Acting a fool and almost getting yourself killed?" I snapped. I was still testy with him for thinking so little of my loyalty, even if his reasoning made sense. All of his rationalizing boiled down to him trying to get rid of me, and after that kiss it was even more embarrassing.

"No, I know what that feels like pretty well. That's an adrenaline rush, like jumping out of a plane. It's kind of peaceful, in a way. I'm talking about liking someone, and wanting to be around them a lot."

Oh.

He pushed his glasses up his nose and looked at me earnestly, the same way he had when asking if he should attack Maggie's stronghold when we played Risk. The thrill of acknowledgment filled me to overflowing, followed by the sobering chaser of reality.

"Have you really never liked anyone before?" I asked. How could he be so inexperienced? It didn't make sense. I led us away from where he'd stood at gunpoint for me, trying to get us back on track to our destination.

He fell into step beside me. "I've had crushes on guys before, obviously. I just didn't expect reciprocation. Or want it. I never really considered pursuing a relationship because there was always a better reason not to."

I knew men and women alike who'd made it into their twenties and thirties without having relationships and without having sex. None of them were scary bridge trolls with borderline personality disorder; they were kind, funny, attractive people. Some of them just had no interest in it, while others were waiting to meet someone they clicked with. But even knowing that this situation was common wasn't enough for me to reconcile the idea with the man before me.

"I understand, but still...do you have some dark secret? Like, a prehensile penis that you're scared to freak out your partner with?" I glanced at his crotch and pressed my lips together before I continued down that path any farther.

Mykhail laughed. "I wish. It would have come in handy these past few months, when I was doing the job of ten people." He looked away from me. "My parents warned me against 'getting myself into situations.' They didn't care that I'm gay, per se, but they worried about how it would be perceived by others. It was a distraction from my studies and lowered my chances of gaining tenure, they told me."

I'd heard a lot of weird reasons for staying in the closet, but that was a doozy. Plus, I'd had loads of gay professors, so it wasn't factual either.

"And my grandmother was so religious, and reacted so negatively to news about gay rights, that I couldn't deal with disappointing her. Mostly, I just never felt like dating anyone."

"So you parents told to keep it on the down low and you just...listened? Did they have a camera on you 24/7? Unless it was a requirement that you share your sexual exploits at Sunday dinner, you could still have led a full life without them knowing." I kept my words gentle. I wasn't chastising him; I'd known guys who simply hadn't thought of that option.

"I'm a virgin, not naive," he said a bit tartly. "I wasn't hiding. I was never that interested in sex or relationships, ergo I never sought out sex or tried to have a relationship. If I'd met someone I really clicked with, I wouldn't have denied myself."

I thought of the way he touched me easily, constantly. Not interested in sex, my ass. He made even the most benign motions sensual, as if all that repressed sexual energy was yearning to get out and I was the lucky recipient. But I had obviously hit on a sore spot for him.

"Sorry," I said. "I'm being an asshole, but not on purpose. Your level of sexual experience isn't relevant to anything, and if not boning strange men is what you were comfortable with, then it was the right choice for you. Lord knows I could have used a bit more discretion in some of my past relationships."

Mykhail gave a little laugh, which I hoped meant he didn't mind me getting all up in his business. "To be honest, letting other people make decisions for me was what I did, even if it made me unhappy. My parents didn't know the real reason I hadn't had a relationship. I was lucky, they told me. I had opportunities they'd never imagined and I shouldn't be selfish."

He didn't look angry about this, even though the hypocrisy of telling your son that being himself was a selfish act made me want to break something.

"Why now?" I asked, really meaning, *Why me?*

He shrugged again; I was starting to understand that the nonchalant action was actually a sign of discomfort. "Baba had another saying: '*Nai bude zle, aby nove.*' It basically means, 'I don't care if something bad happens, as long as it's a new experience.' She was usually being sarcastic when she said it, but I'm not. For the first time in my life, I'm free from restrictions, bar one. I'm trying to live a life without fear of repercussions. I'm trying to experience what I can before...before we get to the university."

So that was it. Despite how his mere touch overwhelmed me, how I couldn't look at his mouth or his fingers or him in general without wanting a taste, this was analytical for him. He wasn't speaking about me specifically, but his words explained a lot. His liking me was a social experiment, testing another, more sensual hypothesis. For a moment, I wanted to just crumple to the floor and join the trampled leaves moldering on the ground. It wasn't the end of the world—I already knew what that felt like—but it was still a punch in the gut to think that what was a revelation for me was research for him.

I didn't know why I was disappointed. He'd told me flat-out and more than once that I shouldn't expect anything from him. But after that kiss...I thought I'd felt something deeper, something more than being the gay sensei to a man who'd lived like a monk rather than stand up to his family. I tried to push down the tumult of emotions rushing through me, to close myself off and think of him as nothing more than a traveling companion. That was the only way to avoid getting hurt. But part of me already knew that it was too late.

I liked him, *really* liked him, and despite it being illogical, I'd kiss him again if given the opportunity. I hung my head and focused on putting one foot in front of the other. I'd done walks of shame before, but they had nothing on this one.

Drama queen John needs a time-out. I could just imagine Arden giving me that judgmental but empathetic look that eviscerated me every time.

"You didn't answer," Mykhail reminded me. "Do you think it's normal, how I'm feeling?"

"Yeah, it's probably nothing special."

He gave me a serious nod, and we walked on in silence. He was deep in thought, while I was trying to convince myself of the lie I'd just told. I was far from inexperienced, and "nothing special" was the absolute last way I'd describe the chemistry between Mykhail and me. But like a good teacher, I'd let him figure out his opinion on the matter for himself.

10

We carefully skirted our way around the town—my skin crawled as we did, as if I could feel the townies fixing me in the sights of their rifle scopes—and forged our way toward the university. We eventually stepped out into an open area of greenery, the edge of national park land, which I hoped meant we'd have less unwanted company.

"You said you went University of Rochester? What was that like?" he asked suddenly, as if he was picking up a conversation where it had left off. I'd been thinking about my family's well-being and on the verge of a panic spiral when he asked, so I welcomed the distraction.

"It was great," I said. "I applied to Burnell, you know, but I probably wouldn't have fit in there. I made a lot of great friends at Rochester." Friends who may or may not all be dead now, with the exception of Arden. I pushed that morbid thought away. "Since the courses were kind of easy for me, my GPA was awesome, which was another bonus. Of course, that GPA has probably been lost to the ages now, since all our school records were stored electronically. If society ever does get back on its feet, we can all say we had 4.0s."

"I definitely didn't have a 4.0," Mykhail said. "I was about to flunk out and thinking of quitting to save the administration the trouble when I met Dr. Simmons."

I gave him an incredulous look. "What? How is that possible? You obviously know your shit when it comes to astrophysics." The idea of flunking out didn't match at all with the passionate, intelligent guy I knew Mykhail to be.

"There's a difference between knowing your shit and caring about it," he said. "I loved learning, but after a certain point the entire idea of academia just left a bad taste in my mouth. Were you really excited about your major?"

"Eh," I said, twisting one of my hands from side to side. "Kind of hard to get excited about computer science. I enjoyed learning new stuff, and being able to code and fix issues, but I wouldn't say I loved it. But I still spend—rather, I spent—a lot of my time learning even after I graduated, so I guess it made me happy. I considered majoring in fashion design but I can't draw for shit."

I regretted that even more now. There were no camera phones, or even an old Polaroid or daguerreotype, to capture Mykhail's features for me. It was romantic to think that I'd never forget his face, but the truth was once we went our separate ways, he'd eventually fade from my memory bit by bit until he was just a vague concept of something that might have been.

"Well, if it makes you feel better, computer science will probably be more useful to rebuilding society than fashion design," he said.

I cracked a smile. "I'll have you know that I've been thinking up some fetching hazmat suits for when the nuclear reactors start failing. Leopard print with fur around the visor."

"Hmm. I like the idea of animal print, but the fur would be too distracting," he said, scrunching his nose adorably.

"Oh-ho, it seems our astrophysicist has an opinion on fashion," I teased. I raised a brow at him. "Too distracting from what? The devastated nuclear landscape?"

"From your eyes." He looked embarrassed as soon as the words left his mouth, but he kept talking. "They're nice. Like this porter ale I used to drink, dark and rich."

I didn't mean to stop walking and stare at him, but aside from the fact that he was using malt alcohol as a simile, he had just given me the nicest compliment I'd ever received from a guy. I'd been called cute before, and handsome, but if anyone ever said anything about my eyes it usually involved words like *slanted* or *chinky*. Hope took this opportunity to slip past my resolve not to expect anything more from Mykhail. Because a dude didn't compliment another dude's eyes unless he was flirting. Right?

"I'm going to scout ahead," he said. His ears glowed pink as he pulled in front of me.

He'd obviously been slowing down his pace for me, because he shot ahead like a bloodhound on the trail. Our hike hadn't been very trying overall, aside from the interruption by the Belleville protection force, but now we were confronted with rocky inclines that left both my lungs and my thighs burning. Even though I was the one wearing fancy hiking boots, Mikhail was a mountain goat in his Converse, nimbly hopping up the steep terrain.

He was a few feet in front of me, clearing the rise of a particularly steep hill, when he stopped in his tracks. I noticed immediately because my eyes were glued to his ass, using the bunched muscles as motivation to keep moving forward. I'd been replaying his musing about my eyes, but that thought was dispersed by my burgeoning fight-or-flight reaction.

"Holy shit." I couldn't tell if his voice was low with fear or something else, but I reached for my gun to back him up just in case. My hand dropped when he remained still without warning me off or running. I didn't entirely understand his motivations, but at this point I knew he wouldn't let me just walk into trouble, so there wasn't a horde of zombies or angry people with pitchforks waiting over the rise.

I saw it as I walked up beside him—the metallic wreckage of something huge and obviously not of this Earth.

"Oh my God, Mulder was right," I gasped, sidling closer to him and plucking at his sleeve. Maybe Mykhail had been wrong about his solar flare theory and Arden had been on point when she came up with conspiracies during our late-night talks: aliens, dude.

"It's a satellite," he said with the excitement of a kid who'd just discovered where his parents had hidden his gifts a week before Christmas. "Let's go!"

And then he was off, stumbling down the hill, all floppy hair and long limbs. I picked my way down, not quite as eager to reach the dubious metal debris. I didn't know very much about satellites—my geek knowledge didn't extend that far. Was there a gas tank in that thing? Could it explode if someone started prodding it? I picked up my pace. "Be careful, Mykhail!"

"How cool is this? This was in space!" He ran his hands over the twisted metal, sticking his fingers into indentations and poking at panels. A few Cyrillic letters had survived the impact, but other telltale signs of the satellite's origins had been obliterated.

I pulled out the hand sanitizer and shoved it at him. "Isn't this how people get weird space viruses or possessed by aliens?"

"You know that bacteria can't live in space, Jangwan," he said, shaking his head at me. Still, he squeezed some of the solution in his hands and rubbed them together, for my benefit. Was that because he was so used to doing what he was told? "Don't tell me this doesn't excite you at all. This was shot into space at just the right angle, the perfect trajectory to get it into orbit. Asteroids have sped past it, and it's circled the Earth countless numbers of times!"

His cheeks were flushed again, and he seemed close to hugging the crumpled thing.

"Well, what's it doing here, on the ground?" I asked. "I've never heard of a satellite just dropping out of the sky."

His eyes narrowed as he fidgeted with a hinged metal flap. The twisted shard of metal came loose in his hand, and he stared at it for a long time before carefully placing it in the side pocket of his bag. A sharp piece of space junk seemed like a weird memento, but to each his own.

"Remember I told you how the Flare messed with the Earth's magnetic field?" he asked as he adjusted his backpack. "Even smaller solar flares mess with our atmosphere. They emit ultraviolet and X-rays that are absorbed by the outer layers of the atmosphere, heating it and making it expand, and that causes drag on the satellites. The solar flare that hit us was enormous, meaning it created a huge disturbance." The smile on his face faded and his pale brows furrowed. "I hope this satellite was really high, and that's why it fell. Depending on exactly how the solar flare hit, it could have affected things closer to the ground, like airplanes."

I hated flying, hated the loss of control and the fact that I had to depend on something invisible and not emotionally invested in my well-being to keep me aloft. The thought of planes, hundreds of them, just dropping out of the sky, plummeting toward land and sea as thousands of people instantaneously realized their lives were over... My lungs tightened so that each breath I took was labored. A disturbing tickling sensation that was anything but funny began at the crown of my head and crawled down my neck, and the muscles in my back and shoulders tensed.

"Hey, are you okay? Crap. Calm down, Jang-wan." Mykhail was next to me now, pulling me away from the wreckage and to a spot of grass shaded by a maple tree. I sat down, more like my knees buckled beneath me, and he dropped onto the grass next to me. I focused on my breathing, trying to stave off the panic attack with deep, diaphragm-expanding inhalations. He placed an arm over my shoulders, the motion tentative, after we'd slid off our packs. "I didn't mean to upset you. That's just speculation. I haven't seen any planes on the ground, have you?"

I didn't know why the horror of a hundred imaginary planes hit me more forcefully than people with guns and rocks who'd attacked me head-on, but it seemed too large to comprehend.

"I just—" I took a shaky breath. "I just don't know how we recover from this. How can a world where thousands of people fell from the sky go on? How many people have died of hunger or are dying of it now? How many people have been killed? And what about the people who killed them? How does a society bounce back from that?"

His grip on my arm tightened as the questions spilled out of my mouth, but I couldn't seem to stop them. I was in some sort of panic spiral as the magnitude of what was going on slammed into me full force. I'd thought a couple of near-death experiences were something that I could overcome, but I hadn't *really* thought of the big picture. Now I realized how much work implementing a societal recovery would be. In the movies, when weird shit fell out of the sky, the feds were on it; I hadn't seen any government officials,

American or Canadian, in months. Was it because of our remote location, or had everything really gone to shit? Suddenly, my heroic quest to take part in some kind of reconstruction seemed ridiculous.

"It's impossible. It can't be done." My chest felt banded by this knowledge: we were royally fucked, and there was nothing I could do to change that.

"You're freaking out right now, which is okay, but that's not really true," Mykhail said. "There's no reason to think that life won't eventually return to normal for a lot of people."

"Tell that to the dinosaurs!" I snapped. "Sometimes a species just can't survive a world-altering event."

"Jang-wan." His voice was gentle, the tone used to lure someone away from the edge of hysteria, but I wasn't having any of his logic or reason. I was light-headed and overly warm, panic making me want to jump out of my skin. I started to pull away from him, the need to run or scream driving my movements, but he solved my need for action by pulling me toward him and kissing me. Again.

He couldn't have surprised me more if he had slapped me.

My mind shorted out to a beautiful blank when his mouth connected with mine, probably a result of the immediate loss of blood in my brain. Because Mykhail wasn't just kissing me as he had last time, and he wasn't just shyly touching me, either. One of his hands rushed up my back, palm gripping my neck as his fingers slid into my hair and caressed my scalp. His other hand rested on my knee but slowly moved to my thigh, igniting a sharp spike of lust that nailed me in place, waiting for more of his touch. My cock had been patently uninterested in my meditation on mortality, but it thickened so fast in response to his kiss that the slide of its head against the fabric of my underwear made me gasp. Mykhail trembled at the sound I made, and at my erection bumping against his elbow. His tongue delved farther into my mouth as his hand crept down my thigh and closed around my shaft.

Just from that first contact, I was ready to burst. It had been some time since a hand other than my own had been in that region, but the tingling that shook my spine and nearly cramped my toes in my shoes was something I'd never thought possible just from a guy copping a feel. Especially someone as inexperienced as Mykhail.

"Fuck, Mykhail." Both of my arms were stretched behind me, supporting my weight, but now I shot a hand out and placed it over his. "You don't have to do this." I really wanted him to, of course, but that didn't mean I'd take advantage of his naivety.

He pulled his hand away from my hard-on, and I willed the Earth to just open up and take me then. Perhaps a statue would one day be placed on the spot memorializing St. John, patron of all men who'd died of stupidity after telling a beautiful guy to stop jacking them off.

But his hand didn't stray far. He took off his glasses and placed them an arm's length away from us in the grass. I didn't know if he feared them being broken, or if seeing out of focus made him feel less self-conscious, and I didn't care. His eyes were completely visible now, dark azure, and focused intensely on me. His expression was just as arousing as his touch had been. Maybe more so. As he ran his tongue over that wide mouth and stared at me, I knew that innocent Mykhail was thinking very naughty things. Desire was a solid ache in my bones, a tangible itch that was impossible to rid myself of. I needed Mykhail, and it appeared he was more than willing to help.

"I want to touch you," he said. He fumbled with the clasp on my fanny pack for what seemed like forever, and then its weight dropped to the grass at my side. His hand snaked back down to my crotch and unbuttoned my pants. "I don't know if I've ever wanted anything more than this really, and I'm a guy who's wanted for a lot. I don't understand everything happening between us—I shouldn't be doing this, but I've broken a lot of my own rules since I met you."

"You have a rule against giving handjobs in the woods?" I asked. My voice was husky, and I was pressing my ass into the ground so as not to seek out his hand with my dick. "That's highly specific."

He leaned forward and ran the tip of his tongue down the length of my neck, then retraced the path with his warm mouth, stopping to nip and suck at my sensitive skin. "I shouldn't feel this way about you. This should be nothing more than a kiss or a touch. But I feel more than that, which means you might feel more than that too. It's not fair to you, but that's not enough to stop me. You'll have to tell me if you don't want me to do this."

Again, his words thrilled and confused me, his resistance to the obvious chemistry between us heightening the attraction instead of diminishing it. He thought he was protecting me somehow—that was what we wanted from the people we cared about when it came down to it, wasn't it? I didn't quite know what to make of it though, his insistence that we couldn't be. He was inexperienced, and probably scared of a sexuality he'd suppressed for so long. Maybe he just thought that hooking up during a crisis wasn't the best idea. Whatever the problem was, I was confident it could be surmounted; it was hard not to be optimistic when his hand was caressing my length and his eyes were broadcasting desire. I ignored the alarm going off in my head, the one that told me matters of the heart were never that simple, and gave in to my impulses.

He rubbed his mouth against mine while his fingers fumbled at my zipper, carefully navigating it over the bulge in my pants. His hands were shaking as he pulled my cock free of jeans and underwear and, Lord help me, that turned me on even more. His fingertips traced the outline of my dick, from the base of one side up over the flanged tip and down the other side. Sweat broke out along my temple and I bit my lip to keep from making some embarrassing noise at his simple exploration. His touch was curious but not entirely clumsy, and the need for more, faster, warmer roiled in my veins, like a kettle just before the steam hits the spout.

"Should I stop?" he asked. I heard the thread of anxiety in his voice. Did he really think I could reject him as my cock jutted toward him, eager for his touch?

"Please don't even think about stopping."

He took me in his warm palm then, his grip light as it moved up and down my length. I closed my eyes and dropped my head back; the bright spring sunshine warmed my body and created rouged patterns behind my eyelids. The breeze slipped between his fingers and caressed my shaft, swept through the soft patch of hair at its base. I'd never been one for exhibitionism, but the sensation of exposure during such an intimate act added to my pleasure.

"Does it feel good?" he asked. I thought that was obvious, but then I remembered that he'd never touched any dick but his own prior to this. I rocked up into his hand in answer.

He took his hand away and quickly replaced it, now slick with saliva. His grip was tighter, squeezing up and down as he pumped my cock in quick bursts, occasionally brushing his thumb over the sensitive head. I opened my eyes and met his gaze, which was still locked on mine. He was studying my face, cataloging my reactions. When he found a rhythm that left me panting and thrusting into his palm, he stuck with it, adding a twist of his hand that provided an extra level of friction.

My pleasure escaped from my mouth in yelps and cries that broke the silence of the forest that surrounded us. Each stroke of his fist built upon the other, the push and pull answered by something in my blood and skin and bones that went incandescent at his touch. And the way he looked at me, so intense and eager to get me off, to give pleasure...

I was used to guys who wanted to take, even if they disguised it as a gift. But Mykhail couldn't hide how my reaction to him spurred him on. I lifted a hand to his face, then ran it down his neck and rested it on his shoulder, gripping him. I could feel the flex and release of his muscles as he stroked me at a faster pace, the way his body shook from the exertion and the excitement.

"I'm gonna come." I was a bit ashamed that he could get me this close to the edge so quickly, but I couldn't ignore the tingling that claimed my entire body, or the way my balls were tight and my cock jumped in his slick hand.

"Good," he replied in a husky voice, and then his mouth claimed mine again. This kiss wasn't tinged with sadness or sweetness. It was possessive, his tongue driving into my mouth to tangle with mine, even as his grip tightened and he increased the speed of his pumping. I didn't have time to register all of those things until afterward though; in that moment, pleasure arched through me like an electrical charge. I surged up against him and groaned my release against his lips. My hips thrust spasmodically as I spurted into his hand.

In the aftermath, there was only the sound of both of us breathing and a bird taking to wing overhead. He held my softening member tenderly, and I imagined what we looked like lying in the grass, sated. Well, one of us was sated at least. I reached for the fanny pack and dumped out its contents, searching for the pack of tissues. I handed him one and wiped myself off too.

"I hope that isn't a spy satellite," I said when I'd finally caught my breath, inclining my head toward the wreck that had triggered my meltdown.

He smiled and reached for his glasses, cleaning them with the edge of his shirt before putting them back on. "They would have gotten quite a show. That was probably the hottest thing I've ever seen, and before you ask, I did have an internet connection so I've seen porn before. The way you were so free..." His cheeks went crimson again.

I didn't quite know how to take a compliment about my O face, so I busied myself with zipping my pants. "Do you want me to, um—" *Debauch you?*

"No, I don't think I'm ready for that quite yet." The huge hard-on he sported begged to differ. I was tempted to call him on it, but I realized that he wasn't talking about the physical. If everything he'd told me was true, he'd just had his first sexual experience with another person. It was heady to think that his first act had been giving me pleasure, but it was probably even more emotionally charged for the guy who'd denied himself for so long. If he wasn't comfortable being on the receiving end yet, I wouldn't push it.

"Well, maybe we should rest up a bit and walk some more this evening before finding someplace to hunker down." I pulled a granola bar out of my bag and ate it in two bites before settling back into the grass. I lazily stuffed the contents of the fanny pack inside, pausing when my hand closed around a smooth, egglike object. It was a cell phone, one of the disposable prepaid track phones they sold at my parents' store. They'd meant it when they told us they were giving us everything we could possibly need on the trip.

"Weird." I flipped it open and turned it on, just in case, but of course there was no signal. Cell towers had fizzled out with the rest of the electrical grid. I waited a moment, compelled by hope and not logic, but when the Searching status where signal bars should be changed to No Service, I closed the phone and slipped it into my pocket.

"You rest. I'll keep watch," Mykhail said. A faint smile hovered on his lips as he glanced down at me.

"Your eyes are really beautiful." I don't know what compelled me to voice the cheesy thought that popped into my head whenever I looked at him, but he gave a wry grin in response.

"Do you know why blue eyes are blue?" he asked. He was speaking in what I'd dubbed his Professor GardenGnome tone, so I assumed it was a rhetorical question and let him continue. "It's because there's no melanin in the iris. The color you see is just the light around us being scattered and reflected back into space. Unlike brown eyes, which have melanin and absorb light, blue eyes are just a reflection of the world around them. I wonder if that's why people are so captivated by them?" He tilted his head in my direction and shook his head. "I guess a simple 'thanks' would have sufficed, huh? Thanks."

"I guess I'm not the only one who can't take a compliment. You know, maybe you should have been a philosophy major," I said, and then laughed at his expression of dismay.

He lifted one shoulder. "Now you know how I spent the brain power I could have been using to craft amazing online dating profiles and make first-date banter with strange men."

"Grindr's loss is science's gain," I said through my grin. "Aren't you tired too? You don't have to stand guard." I sank into the grass as that special kind of post-orgasmic drowsiness descended on me. I wanted nothing more than to pull him into my arms and sink into a deep nap, together, even though in the past I had been resolutely anti-cuddling during sleep. Dealing with someone else's bothersome tossing and turning wasn't fun for me, since sleep had been hard to come by even before the Flare and the insomnia, but I'd make an exception for Mykhail. Besides, cuddling could lead to fun rewards upon waking. I'd just had one of the most intense orgasms of my life, but I was already craving more from him.

"I'm not done with my knight-in-shining-armor role-playing," he said. He reached out a hand and tentatively patted my hair, as if his fingers hadn't just been deep in the strands and intimately wrapped around something else. "Get some sleep, Jang-wan."

"Okay, Sir Rabbit," I said. I rolled onto my side and stared at his hand, fingers splayed in the grass and pointed in my direction. It clenched into a fist just before my eyes fluttered shut and I slid into a nap.

11

I awoke to the scent of smoke, my dream having morphed into a nightmare that involved my family's cabin and all of our stored food burning to ashes because I'd knocked a candle over. I jumped up with a start, and my gaze immediately locked on Mykhail's. He wore the sheepish expression of someone who'd been caught in some depraved act. I shifted my gaze downward, expecting to find his hand in his pants. He was gripping something much more bizarre than his cock, though—a magnifying glass.

I blinked several times, wondering if I hadn't really woken up and this was part of some surreal dream, but it appeared to be real life.

"You carry a magnifying glass with you?" I asked as I stood and stretched.

A curl of smoke rose from the ground, and he gave it

a victorious smile before looking up at me. "Well, yes. What if I need to magnify something?" He pushed his glasses up the bridge of his nose by the mass of tape in the center, and the whole thing was so entirely *him* that all I could do was laugh and shake my head.

"If I'd known you'd be so bored that you'd be driven to roast ants, I could have skipped the nap," I said. I unzipped a side pocket on my fanny pack and searched for a mint. When I tugged out the metal tin, a seemingly spring-loaded ribbon of condoms jumped out in its wake and landed on the grass in front of me. I briefly imagined it as some kind of horrifyingly awkward jack-in-the-box with my mother's head on the end, cackling and saying, "The best sex is safe sex!", something I'd heard all too often when she passed me clippings of articles on gay men's health along with boxes of Trojans.

I grabbed the offending prophylactics and stuffed them back inside, foregoing the mint and hoping Mykhail didn't think I'd started the trip already assuming he was going to put out. I was tempted to see if she'd stuck some lube in the bag, but then remembered that the she in question was my mom and nearly died of mortification.

Mykhail missed my one-act play on the perils of a nosy mother because he was hunched over the magnifying glass again, focusing the sun's rays into a white-hot beam. "I'm trying to see if this is really an efficient technique for starting a fire," he said.

"I can show you a much easier method," I said. "You just take two thick sticks and rub them together."

A rosy blush colored the skin where his glasses rested, and it seemed that we simultaneously remembered what had bought on my nap. A stirring of desire whispered down my spine, but I ignored it.

I cleared my throat. "Are you ready to get going?"

He grabbed his pack and nodded, and we set off on our way.

The evening following the nap passed both too quickly and too slowly. We covered a huge swatch of terrain, avoiding ditches and potholes in the uneven ground as evening descended. I referenced the map with a penlight, checked our coordinates using a compass and then took a moment to consult with the stars.

"See Cassiopeia right there? Her foot points northeast right now. If we keep going in that direction for about a mile and then make camp for the night, we should have a pretty easy hike tomorrow and arrive there at some point late in the night or the next morning. It depends on how much hiking time we get in and whether we have any obstacles, like inclement weather or having to hide from crazy people."

My ego ticked up one or two notches just from the impressed raise of his brows. I was a little sad thinking about our journey coming to an end, although the sooner we got there, the more likely it was that we'd find out more about the Flare and what was being done to recover from it.

"How did you learn star navigation?" he asked. "It doesn't seem like something most people know."

"Well, my dad isn't a survivalist or anything, but he grew up in a pretty rural area of Korea. He was always really interested in learning the best way to do things and how to be self-sufficient, and he loved tinkering with things." His tinkering didn't always have the greatest results, as various scorch marks around the house could attest to, but Mykhail didn't need to know that. "I was the only one in the family actually interested in those things, so we spent a lot of time doing stuff like camping and navigation challenges, where you competed against other teams to find a specific location. He taught me how to read the stars so I'd never be lost."

And I'd left him behind. I suddenly missed him terribly; his awkward smile when I made penis jokes, the way he loved me so fiercely and had never let me doubt it for a moment.

"I have no idea what that feels like. To share fun hobbies with your parents." He didn't seem to expect pity, but his next words made me want to drag him back to my family and pull him into a group hug. "I don't know if my parents are dead or not, but if they are, it wouldn't change our relationship very much."

"Mykhail…I wish your parents had appreciated you more. They missed out on knowing someone really wonderful."

He glanced at me, face impassive as if I was talking about someone else. "I had Baba. Can you tell me more? Like, how did your parents react when they came home and found Arden and Gabriel together? Were they always okay with it?"

I didn't know if his Baba was any great shakes,

given what he'd told me, but I honored his unspoken request to change the subject. "My mom tried to be weird about Arden and Gabriel sleeping in the same room, saying it was a bad example for Maggie, but I don't think she really cared. Honestly, I think she was just trying to exert some authority after being tied up in a van for days and realizing her family had changed while she was gone. Anyway, Arden countered that Maggie walking in on them banging in the cellar would set an even worse example. Then Maggie got mad and yelled that it wasn't as if she didn't know what sex was, and my dad nearly choked on a piece of beef jerky. And that was the first meal we all shared together after my parents returned."

Mykhail laughed with abandon, and something in me warmed at the way I could draw this unvarnished merriment out of him, especially in light of the darkness in him that surfaced at unexpected moments. I knew people thought I was funny, but that *he* thought so was important to me.

We stopped at a secluded copse of trees, where Mykhail finally gave in to the fatigue he'd been fighting. Although he'd said he had no real desire to get to the university, he'd pushed himself hard. The nervous glances he shot me when he thought I wasn't looking made me wonder if he wanted to get there more quickly so we'd be safe, or if there was something awaiting us there that I should be concerned about. I doubted he was luring me into a trap though, so I didn't press it. Besides, I was on edge, too, expecting trouble to jump out from behind a tree at any moment. Things were going smoothly, but I didn't want to be lulled into a false sense of security.

Mykhail seemed to enjoy hearing the stories about how we'd passed the time since the Flare, so after instructing him on how to build a fire, I told him about Maggie and Arden's music lessons, and gardening with my parents, and the homeschooling classes Gabriel had set up. He didn't talk about what had happened to him in the past few weeks, but told stories about his fellow grad students in his astrophysics program. My favorite was the guy who got a tattoo of Carl Sagan on his back without vetting his artist first; when he removed the bandages, he'd discovered that the artist had gifted him with something that resembled Kermit the Frog in a toupee and turtleneck.

After micromanaging his fire pit construction, I cooked two cans of franks and beans. We ate cowboy-style, straight from the flame-licked cans, as we laughed and learned about each other. It was nice; I even refrained from making any *Brokeback Mountain* jokes. It would have been like any old pre-Flare date if not for us constantly looking over our shoulders to check that we weren't being stalked by people ready to kill us for our supplies. But even the need for constant vigilance couldn't kill the happy buzz that thrummed through me; hell, it wasn't as if I'd never been to a dicey place where a gay Asian dude had to fear for his life. At least now I could rest assured that homophobia wouldn't be the driving reason behind any decision to attack me; it was more likely to be hunger or hysteria.

We placed our sleep rolls side by side after dinner, the exhausting day making even sitting up too much work. Our hunger for food had been sated, but we asked each other question after question, driven by a ravenous curiosity.

"Why did they have to dis Pluto like that?" I asked. The stars moved slowly overhead, giving a surreal, dreamy cast to the night. We were both staring up at the sky, our hands at our sides. If I stretched my pinky I could have touched him, but there was something more thrilling about keeping that little bit of distance between us. "Imagine, you're a planet all that time, and suddenly some know-it-all scientist comes along and snatches your wig without even an apology."

He snorted. "Look, Pluto is just fine where it is. It's not a planet. It's a dirty chunk of ice that got to live the highlife for a generation. If you feel bad for it, think of all the other dirty chunks of ice in the Kuiper Belt that wondered why they couldn't be planets too. It was bad for their self-esteem."

I giggled. Like, actually giggled. I should have been ashamed, but if you couldn't giggle with the boy you liked, what was the point of being alive?

"What fascinates you the most about the universe?" I asked around a yawn. I expected him to say something about alien life-forms or faraway planets, but I should have known better.

"The universe is spreading," he said after a long pause. He yawned, too, and then continued. "I think you know that theory. But, within that, the planets and stars are moving apart from each other at a faster rate than the universe is expanding. No one knows why. So, eventually, a person lying in this same spot will look up and see maybe one or two stars. At some point far in the future, they'll see nothing. They'll be entirely alone."

His words were soft, as if the thought pained him but he'd resigned himself to the inevitability. Something twisted in my heart in the silence that followed, because he spoke like someone who already knew what that loneliness felt like.

"Mykhail—" I was answered by a soft snore. When I glanced at him, his mouth was slack, lips slightly parted, and his long lashes were damp in the starlight. I hoped his sleep bought him someplace more peaceful than his mind allowed for during his waking hours.

My insomnia persisted, despite my change in location and our arduous hike. The hard ground and rocks poking into my back didn't help, either. In that weird pocket of space-time that held all those who should be sleeping but couldn't, I thought of my family and imagined what they were up to. I recalled the events of the day and how close we'd come to a quick and senseless death. I wondered about the future and how quickly our time together was passing, and if this strange warmth in my chest was anything more than a crush, or if it even could be.

Mykhail turned to me in his sleep, shivering from the chill in the air. I didn't know if I was crossing some line, but I inched closer to him. Just to keep him from freezing, of course. The planets might be moving away from each other, but he didn't have to be alone. Not when I was here and willing to share what comfort my presence could offer him.

He didn't awaken at my motion, but wrapped his arms around me and pulled me into the sweat-and-soap smell that clung to him. I went still as stone, my anxiety ramping up as

I decided whether to pull myself away and wake him, or to stay still and risk having him think I'd taken advantage of him in his sleep. I never made the choice.

Apparently, even a stone could get a good night's sleep if being cuddled by the right guy; I awoke to Mykhail hovering over me, propped up on one elbow with his other arm still around me. His drawn brows were contrasted by a fragile smile. I almost laughed at the confusion etched so plainly on his face. *My open book*, I wanted to say, but instead I settled for, "Morning, Bunny Fou Fou," which was only marginally less confusing for him. "It's a song about a rabbit," I explained.

He looked thoughtful as he got up and shook the dust from his clothes. The cool morning air slid in and replaced the warmth of his embrace. I wanted to pull him back down to me, to twine our legs and fingers together as we planned out the rest of our day, but one night of spooning did not a couple make.

"I've never had a nickname before," he said. "Baba called me Misha, but everyone named Mykhail gets called Misha."

"I can stop with the rabbit stuff," I said. Not everyone enjoyed being called out of their name, and he certainly went out of his way to address me correctly.

"Don't," he said quickly, then seemed embarrassed at his own eagerness. "I mean, it's fine. It doesn't matter either way."

He struggled with his sleep roll, managing to bundle it incorrectly three times. His neck was stiff, his lips were pursed and he looked as if he didn't know what to do with himself. I placed a hand on his back, lightly, and saw the muscles jump then relax one by one when I didn't pull away.

"I have some carrots in my bag if you want a snack before we head out, Bun."

He shook his head in amusement, and we prepared for the rest of our day in unison.

12

"Great. It's going to rain," I complained as we hiked later that day. The windy morning breeze had transformed into a late afternoon gust during the time since we'd awoken and continued the journey to Burnell. The birds that had been riding the invisible currents above us earlier were now gone, having sought shelter in the trees. When I looked over my shoulder, I could see dark clouds massed behind us and heading our way.

Mykhail shivered, swung his bag around to the front and pulled out two slim plastic packets. He handed me one, and I stared at the creepy hooded couple on the label. "Poncho. I still can't believe how giving your parents are. Even after being abducted while helping someone, they took me in without hesitation and stocked me with supplies. And they trusted me enough to let you come with me."

"First of all, I'm an adult. They didn't *let* me do anything," I sniffed. He didn't dispute that, but his lips puckered in an expression of disbelief. I was tempted to drop a kiss on them, but I realized that was something a couple would do, and we definitely weren't a couple. The moment passed and his mouth reverted to the scowl he'd been wearing all morning.

I made a noise of surrender before continuing. "Okay, fine. If they trusted you to get where you were going without falling off a cliff, they would have made me stay home." I grinned, but he didn't. Our day had started off well, but a dour mood had crept up on him over the course of the hike. He'd gone from good-humored and talkative to distant and withdrawn. He attributed his mood to bad dreams, but I wasn't sure he was being entirely truthful. After the connection we'd made as we camped, an emotional one that seemed nearly as strong as our physical attraction, it was disconcerting. I faltered, searching for something to pull him out of his funk. "I'm kidding. If you think my mom would send me off with the first cute boy who came along…okay, maybe she would. But they gave their blessing for the trip because they know you're a good person. My mom wouldn't risk a bacon-incited mutiny for just anyone."

"I think I saw a structure through the trees. Maybe we can wait out the storm there," he asked, ignoring my comment and squinting behind his lenses. "I really wish I'd gotten a new prescription before this happened."

I looked in the same direction, but the foliage formed a verdant barricade. I wondered if he'd really seen something or was simply trying to change the topic.

"I didn't see anything, but let's be careful in case there are people around. No more walking in front of guns like you can catch bullets in your teeth," I said. My heart squeezed with residual fear thinking of how close he'd come to death and how little it had fazed him. "You can get a new prescription once we see the man behind the curtain. Dr. Simmons, the great and powerful!" I linked my arm through his and began a "We're Off to See the Wizard" skip step. I channeled my best Judy Garland and blinked up at Mykhail. "Dr. Simmons, I just want to save the world and go home. My friend Mykhail would like some new eyes."

He didn't join in my skipping, and his morose expression didn't brighten. "I'm used to being nearly blind—I'd prefer a new heart. And the man behind the curtain was a fraud, in case you forgot." He gave his head a distressed shake, untangling his arm from mine.

Enough was enough. Maybe it was because I was tired of his moping, or maybe it was because his behavior was an unpleasant reminder of my behavior over the past few weeks, but I snapped at him. "Look, I know you had a bad dream or whatever, but I'm not gonna deal with Sad Clown Mykhail for the rest of the trip, okay? If you need to take a minute to meditate or do some tai chi, go for it. If I can do something to help, let me know. I understand that shit is difficult right now, but we have to keep our heads up."

Mykhail actually withdrew from my words, and I felt as if I'd just kicked a puppy. But he nodded. "You're right.

I'm just worried and I can get pessimistic when I'm worried. I keep thinking Dr. Simmons might not even be there. He could have been away from the university when the Flare struck. He could be dead. And we would have traveled there for nothing."

I hadn't really given much thought to the professor, actually. He was a means to an end, a convenient escape hatch from the malaise of a life lived entirely in a two-story home. I hadn't even remembered his name was Simmons. All that had mattered was he was likely to be doing something about the blackout, and that I might be able to help. I'd spent a good portion of my life being the one who pointed out the flaws in the plans of others, but it seemed I had a blind spot when it came to myself.

"I haven't seen him in over a year, and we left off on bad terms. He was upset when I took time off to help with Baba because I had to abandon the research I was doing for him. I'd like to set things right." There was the slightest hint of...something in Mykhail's voice that raised my suspicion. Reverence? Or was it longing? I wanted to categorize the feeling that flared up in me as concern, but it was something much more base—jealousy. It was ridiculous being envious of some random old fart who Mykhail looked up to as a mentor. And even if he wanted to bareback the guy across the Orion Nebula, it wasn't as if I had any right to stop him.

"What was the group he founded called again?" I asked, trying to be an adult instead of succumbing to jealousy. "The one that made people think he was crazy?"

"The North American Electrical Grid Initiative," Mykhail said. "The Initiative has been trying to get electric companies to flare-proof their transformers since the 90s, but the lobbyists screwed them over at every turn, and here we are."

I tilted my head. "Electric companies have lobbyists? I guess that explains why my electricity bills were so damn high."

Mykhail nodded. "Dr. Simmons was advocating that the U.S. go back to the microgrid system. A microgrid can be shut down more easily, and the transformers are smaller and easier to replace. Basically, they cost less and require less work. The system is safer because several small linked grids instead of one big one means that one part of the system going down doesn't take out the whole shebang."

"Can you explain to me why we weren't using that system?" I asked. "Maybe I'm missing something, but that sounds pretty much like the ideal."

"Microgrids are safer, but it means you can't shuttle electricity from sector to sector as needed, which is what made those companies their money," Mykhail said. "Huge companies balked at completely changing the setup of their system on the off-chance our planet was hit by a geomagnetic storm. Maybe if it had been a more tangible risk, like an asteroid, they would have gotten with the program."

Now that we were talking science stuff, the dark cloud that had hovered over his head all day seemed to dissipate. I, on the other hand, was getting more and more annoyed. All the suffering that people were experiencing could have been prevented, but it hadn't been deemed profitable enough.

"Let's stop talking about this," I said, waving my hands in the air. I slid on my poncho before continuing. "Maybe you give magic handies, but I've been feeling slightly more optimistic about humanity's projected survival since my satellite-induced freak-out. I'm not ready to slide back into nihilism just yet." The image of Mykhail working his hand up and down my cock blotted out thoughts of electrical lobbyists and a history that couldn't be changed. I nudged him with my elbow. "You've got a pretty good technique for someone who's led an asexual life until now. Did you watch instructional videos or something?"

Finally, *finally*, I got a smile out of him. "I said 'pretty much asexual.' It wasn't that I didn't have a sex drive. I just didn't feel like acting on it with others. I've done plenty of experimentation on which techniques felt best to me." He gave a short, embarrassed burst of laughter. "It's nice to have an outside opinion though. Like I have my own personal peer review board."

The weight his mood had placed on our walk began to lift. The teasing, fun Mykhail had reemerged from behind the clouds, even if the sun hadn't. I smiled up at him. "If you need me to check any data or give additional feedback, I'm at your disposal. Anything for science."

"Duly noted." Just for an instant, there was a flash of the Mykhail who'd gotten me off with his hand and a single, gritted-out word: *Good*. His tongue was a flash of pink over his lips and he took a step closer to me. The whole world seemed to go silent around us, and my body buzzed with the desire for just one touch from him. I didn't care if it was his hands or his tongue or any other body part he felt like prodding me with. My need for him blotted out thoughts of storms and shelter, and from the way he leaned his head down toward mine, I wasn't the only one feeling it. But then a peal of thunder shook the world around us. A few seconds passed and lightning flashed, blotting out his features in a burst of white.

"Shit, the rain will be here soon." I hadn't needed to count off between thunder and lightning to realize that. Although I'd discovered a newfound interest in exhibitionism, it didn't extend to placing myself at risk of electrocution.

I whirled in the direction Mykhail had been staring before, where a small structure rose up out of the greenery. It was a quaint, ramshackle little thing, comprised of wood and stone and draped in vines. It could pass for a carriage house or backyard studio on a large estate but was plonked in the middle of nowhere, as incongruous as the satellite had been the day before. The randomness of it all made me think of the board games we played back at home, and how our avatars were forced to overcome whatever obstacle we placed in their path. If I was religious, I'd say a higher power had provided this little shelter for us, but I couldn't get down with that. Some all-knowing, all-seeing being just hanging out and moving me around like a piece on a Risk board? Totally creepy.

Whether it had been placed there by Ceiling Cat or some other deity, one thing was certain: we had to make a mad dash for it.

"Come on." I grabbed his hand and started running. Sheets of cold rain charged over the hilly terrain after us, and we couldn't outrun it. The stinging shock of the rain as it slapped at us from all angles urged us on. We didn't let go of each other's hands, even as we slipped and slid and our ponchos blew up into our faces. When we made it to the front door, I let out an incredulous laugh.

Mykhail? He raised his right hand and made the sign of the cross, finishing the motion with a flourish—a kiss that he mimed passing up to heaven. "Some habits are hard to break," he said with a shrug before beginning to pry open the door of the boarded-up church.

13

The space we walked into was Spartan, not like the fancy basilica that I'd been shuttled to on special occasions when I was a kid. It was more chapel than cathedral. The place wasn't festooned with gilded edgework and weeping statuary that begged piteously for your tithe. It was simple, wooden, sparsely decorated. There was no stained glass, just thick, obviously old panes hidden behind peeling wooden shutters. Leaves and other small debris littered the floor, but the pews were empty and it looked as if the place had been cleaned sometime in the past year at the very least.

"All the crucifixes are gone. You can see the outlines of them on the wall," Mykhail noted after making a quick circuit around the place. "The room back there probably used to be the office, but it's empty. I guess the place was decommissioned."

"You can do that?" It seemed counterintuitive. How did something once holy suddenly become just an ordinary shack in the middle of nowhere?

"Well, *I* can't, but an archbishop or other higher-up church official can. Sometimes if a church isn't making enough money or they need to sell the land to a secular buyer, they just take all the holy stuff and go."

"That seems a bit mercenary. But maybe I'll reap the benefits of the Church's capitalism. Do you think there are any of those host wafers lying around?" I asked. My stomach growled hopefully in response.

"I don't think they'd just leave the body of Christ behind when they left," Mykhail said, his voice just a wee bit sharp.

"It's just bread before they bless it, right?" I asked. My stomach roiled again at a memory of the sweet bread that melted on your tongue, and how Gabriel had always given me his when we went to church because he knew how much I loved it. He really had always been willing to risk hellfire for me.

"Not if you're Orthodox." Again with the peevishness. I was so used to hanging out with heathens, who'd usually become so by circumstance or as a method of self-preservation, that I hadn't even considered he might be a believer. If he was, that would go a long way in explaining the whole "I just didn't want to have sex" thing.

"I'm sorry. I didn't mean to offend you, if you believe

in...all of this stuff," I said, steepling my fingertips. "I just assumed you wouldn't be religious, because science."

"I'm not, really. It's just conditioning," he said, but his voice was still curt. "Science doesn't preclude religion, by the way. Sometimes when I'm looking through the telescope, at a far-off planet or a dwarf star, I think there has to be a God. Or a devil. It would take one or the other to create that type of beauty."

I stared at him for a moment, letting his words sink in. It still shocked me every time he spoke this way, as if he was able to take the complex passion he felt in every particle of himself and spin it into something beautiful but simple to understand. He would make an amazing teacher one day, if the world ever got back to normal. I allowed myself a brief fantasy of Mykhail grading papers as I tapped away on my keyboard, us working quietly together like a normal couple.

That was a nice daydream, but in reality I was exhausted. I walked over to one of the pews and sprawled on it, heedless of my boots as they thudded on the faded wooden bench. My parents would have killed me, but I reminded myself it was no longer sacred ground. "I've found myself thinking similar stuff since the Flare," I admitted. "We didn't know what had caused the blackout for so long. Sometimes late at night, I would have these epic arguments with myself where I debated whether or not it was the End of Days or simply the end of life as we knew it. I kind of wished there was some deity up there, because otherwise, there was no greater plan behind what was happening to us."

Mykhail was silent for a while, then came over and squeezed himself into the other end of my pew. His long legs were bent at the knees, but his toes still touched mine. "My baba was religious. She always had been—it was what got her through war, and loss—but after my grandpa died, she became so focused on it. She had always been so logical, but by the end she'd started to talk about being one of the left behind. She had watched some religious movie that was in the home's DVD library just before the Flare..."

His voice trailed off, swallowed by the sound of the rain pounding on the gabled roof and slamming into the weathered siding. The structure was old but sturdy and built to withstand a good squall. As we sat in silence, listening to Mother Nature howl her grievances, I didn't fear that the chapel would fall apart at my feet.

I wasn't so sure about the man across the pew from me.

I still didn't know what'd happened to his grandmother, except it had been recent and he'd witnessed it. I knew it was tearing him apart, and that it was so painful that it could cause his vivacious spirit to snuff out like a lamp in a high wind. I was annoyed by some of the things he'd told me about her, but the woman obviously had some hand in creating the wonderful and caring person I felt such a connection with. She had to have some good qualities.

"Your baba sounds like a strong woman. Why don't you tell me something about her that makes you happy? Something good that you'll always remember?"

His head lolled back on the arm of the pew, as if

searching the chipped and peeling ceiling for a memory. Then, unexpectedly, he burst out laughing. "Oh, this is a good one! She took me to Manhattan once. She'd spent a good part of her life there, since it was where her family settled after fleeing the Communists. But for me, it was terrifying. I'd grown up in a suburban bubble, and my parents never bothered to take me into the city with them when they had to teach classes there. I was about five, I think, and everything about the city seemed huge and terrifying."

I imagined a tiny, bespectacled version of Mykhail, his too-big eyes made even larger by his too-big frames, looking up fearfully as big-city life bustled around him. My heart constricted and if I had ovaries, I'm sure they would have been exploding just then, a sensation that had recently entered Arden's lexicon.

"Well, we were walking around Herald Square, and suddenly a scary-looking homeless man lunged out at us, shaking a cup full of change." He glanced at me, abashed. "He wasn't really scary, when I think back on it, but I didn't know anything. I was a dumb kid. Anyway, he's shaking his cup in her face, and she says, 'Oh thanks, I needed some change.' And she reaches into the man's cup and fishes out a quarter! He was too speechless to even react." He burst out laughing, holding his belly, while I stared at him nonplussed.

"Your warm memory of your grandmother involves her stealing from a homeless man? That certainly is...special."

He wiped his eyes. "When we came out of the store, she went up to him and made me show him the fake vampire teeth I'd gotten from the bank of toy dispensers. And she said, 'Mykhail, this man doesn't have very much, but he gave me money to get you a toy. What do you say to him?' And I thanked him very politely, as I'd been taught to do with adults, and flashed him my vampire smile. The man seemed so pleased that he'd been able to do something for me. He and Baba spoke for a long time, and when we left she reached into his cup again, but to leave something there.

"After we walked away, she said 'Charity is well and good, but if you can let a person feel like they've done something, if you can make them feel human, that is an even greater gift.' I was just happy I got some cool vampire teeth out of the deal. I've been thinking about that story a lot lately though, and how right she was."

This was hugely unexpected from the hectoring woman I imagined, but then I thought of Mykhail's moods and how they could jump drastically from his baseline joie de vivre. Maybe it was genetic.

"She sounds like a pretty amazing woman." I slid to an upright position, opened my backpack and pulled out a sleeve of saltines and a can of cocktail sausages—Mykhail had to be starving, but he was too lost in his reveries to do anything about it. I remembered the jut of his ribs as he stretched on the couch in my living room, and I placed one of the little sausages on a cracker. "Eat," I said and passed it to him, but he leaned up and nipped it right out of my hand, his lips closing around my fingertips. Everything in my body tightened at the moist, warm pull. He returned to his casually sprawled position, but there was nothing relaxed about the bulge at the crotch of his pants. He ignored it, likely because the boner-plus-Baba-talk combo was uncomfortable for both of us, so I did too. Or tried to at least.

"She had some incredible stories," he said. He wiped a hand over his lips and licked at the corners. "Do you want to hear about the time she jumped out of a window into an idling car?"

"No, that doesn't sound interesting at all," I drawled, reaching over to feed him another cracker. "Boring. Tedious, even."

He grinned as he chewed, and just like that it was story time again. Instead of my best friend regaling me with fictional tales of derring-do before bed, there was a man who already felt as much a part of my life as anyone I'd ever let in.

One of my favorite childhood movies featured a boy who escaped into a secret room during a storm and discovered a fantasy world that was both beautiful and troubled. That was what I felt like as I sipped bottled water and listened to Mykhail's stories about his life with Baba, a woman who'd emotionally smothered her grandchild but also launched herself from a window rather than be caught by the secret police. What had she felt like as she cut through the air? Had she been gripped by the same fear that had pushed Arden and me out of our Rochester apartment? Or had she simply seen it as another necessity, like raising the grandson her daughter was too busy to pay attention to?

Mykhail's voice cracked often as he spoke of her, but he smiled in a way I hadn't seen before, his gaze off to the side as if he was watching the memories play out from the corner of his eye.

"Hey, hold on," I said after we'd laughed and spoken for what seemed like hours. Evening had long since turned to night, and the candles we'd lit gave the church a sanctified air. The storm still raged outside; it seemed as if it would never end, but it would, and we needed to make use of it. "I'm going to collect some rainwater in these. I have one of those filter caps, so it will be drinkable. Better to refill now than to be caught without water when we need it."

He nodded. "Oh, yeah. This is why you came with me, to make sure we do all that common-sense stuff."

"Yes, I do have my uses," I said with a toss of my hair as I strutted toward the exit.

I pushed open the door against the howling wind, slipping off my shirt and tossing it behind me. The thing had just fully dried, and I didn't want cold and clammy sleepwear. And I was no bodybuilder, but maybe I wanted to show Mykhail some skin too. Doing crunches was one of the things that had kept me sane during my insomnia and I had to show off my burgeoning six-pack to *someone*.

It was dark and foreboding outside, the vibrant green of the wooded area muted to a dull olive. The rain fell and fell, battering the leaves, but nothing else moved. Nothing I could see anyway. Still, I had a distinct sense of foreboding as I carefully propped up our bottles so they wouldn't tip over as they filled. Maybe it was because I'd been with Mykhail for so long, the man who activated that animal part of my brain that wanted to take and to feel, or maybe it was just straight paranoia, but I felt like I was being watched. Thankfully, the driving rain meant the bottles filled quickly. I trotted back into the chapel and pulled the door shut; I was probably overreacting. After all, I hadn't felt anything before two men had attacked Arden and me, and they'd had to track us for a while before making their move.

When I walked back inside, shaking off my unease, I found Mykhail kneeling at one of the pews, head bent in genuflection. His lips were moving in silent prayer again, and dust motes danced about his head in the lightning that flared through the shutters. He was beautiful, but it was a terrible beauty, like a pietà statue that captured the tragedy of mourning for posterity. His clasped hands went limp as he finished the prayer, but he didn't move from what had to be an uncomfortable position.

"Is story time over?" I ventured as I sat down next to him, laying a hand on his shoulder. "I like the Baba stories."

He looked up at me, eyes dark and intense. "I have another story," he said. "This one you might not want to hear."

My stomach churned at the desolation in his voice, and the anger. I wasn't so sure if my next words were true, but I wanted them to be. "If you trust me enough to share, then I want to listen." I ran my fingers through his thick hair, easing through the tangles caused by the storm's gusting winds. I continued the motion even after he spoke his next chilling words, mostly because I didn't know what I'd do if I stopped.

"Okay. Now I'll tell you the story of how I killed her."

14

I figured it had to be some kind of metaphor, the words of a devoted grandson who simply hadn't been able to help an old woman in need, until he continued.

"She wasn't the first one who asked for death, but she was the last one I agreed to help. Before her, I couldn't deny Mrs. Tereschenko, who was in so much pain from the cancer that she'd stopped receiving treatment for. Or Mr. Dzubenko, who was wasting away because I didn't know how to work his feeding tube."

Horror, undiluted horror, crept through my veins as pieces of Mykhail's story began to fall into place. His grandmother had been sick, and he'd gone to her assisted living facility to be with her. That was where he'd been when the Flare hit, before he'd wandered off and eventually made his way to my garden.

"Oh. Oh, no." I whispered the words as my hands stilled in his hair. He shuddered beneath my palm, and when he spoke, it was with that faraway voice, the one that came from a distant planet where the injustice of this world couldn't touch him.

"The night shift was smaller than the day shift at the home, and they were working with a skeleton crew because of the holidays. A lot of the aides stayed after the Flare first occurred. They cared about the residents, and they didn't want anything bad to happen to them!" His brows furrowed, and he gave me a despairing glance. "But they had families too. They decided to leave and return in shifts, so someone with experience would always be around to care for the more sickly residents. Help would come eventually, we thought.

"When the first wave of workers didn't return, the families of the others were still waiting…so they made off one by one, and eventually there was just me."

"What do you mean?" I asked, although I understood perfectly. I just didn't want to. "You're saying the staff at the facility where your grandmother lived left you in charge of the elderly residents? You, who had no idea of how to care for them?"

"I had some idea," he said in a low voice. "And it wasn't just me. A few of the more mobile residents helped me to prepare food and take it to those who were bedbound. They helped clean bedpans and figure out medicine schedules. But it was like trying to plug a dam with your finger while the water surged over the top. The generator died, and then two of the residents got pneumonia. One of the ladies with Alzheimer's just walked out the front door one freezing night. I tried to find her, but everyone else was depending on me and I couldn't travel very far. She never came back."

He took his breaths in deep gulps between chunks of information as he recalled the harrowing scene. It seemed as if he was purging, and the only way he could do it was to get the words out as quickly as possible. His buried accent rose to the surface, reshaping his words; perhaps it provided him some kind of comfort in his distress or served as a barrier for emotions that threatened to overwhelm him.

Every part of me ached for him. I imagined the kind soul before me as he helplessly fiddled with a broken generator or nursed elderly strangers who were far from their families and dependent solely upon him. It was something from a nightmare, but he hadn't been able to escape by waking up.

"I'm so sorry, Mykhail. I can't imagine what you went through, but I'm sorry," I said. "It was hard enough just worrying about my family, who could fend for themselves for the most part. What you did is amazing. You did what you could in extraordinary circumstances."

"It wasn't enough. An old woman three doors down from Baba was the first to go. Anya was fine the night before, but as soon as I stepped into her room with her breakfast I knew something was wrong. I tried to dig a grave, but the ground was frozen solid. So I put her in one of the utility sheds. It was cold, like a fridge. I don't want to think of what it's like now that summer is almost here."

I didn't want to hear any more. I didn't want to think about my sweet, caring Mykhail surrounded by death, of him struggling to care for a group of sick old people with no electricity and no help from a trained staff. I pulled him from where he kneeled, reaching my arms around him to cradle his stiff form. The words stuck to the roof of my mouth like peanut butter, but I finally forced them out. "I'm here. You can keep talking if you need to, Rabbit."

His inhale was deep and ragged, and then the words spilled out even faster. "There were all these pain pills around—so many of them were hurting. A few of them talked it out and made the decision themselves. They didn't want to slowly starve or freeze to death, and they felt guilty because I was so run-down from trying to care for them all. I found their bodies holding hands or cuddled together in their beds, with the empty bottles beside them. They left me thank-you notes." He choked back a sob, bit his lip against a painful memory. "But the religious ones said they needed my help. They couldn't commit suicide because it was a sin. If I helped them, they could still go to heaven. Baba was very religious..."

He broke down then, folding his gangly arms and legs so that he was curled in my lap. He didn't howl out his pain; if it wasn't for the warmth of his tears spreading along my chest, I might not have known he was crying at all. That broke me even more, the way even his release of grief was restrained. Words of comfort flowed from my mouth of their own volition, about how wonderful and brave he was, but I didn't know if they reached him. I told him the truth, that he'd helped his grandmother and the others. That he was a hero. Meanwhile, behind my sadness and confusion, anger simmered. Those people had preserved their own souls at the cost of Mykhail's.

The moist heat of his breath was a contrast to the coolness of his drying tears as he spoke. "She only hinted at first, but then after I'd helped the others...well, it wasn't like there are levels of sin. One more wouldn't hurt, would it? And I'd always done what she asked. I couldn't refuse her this last thing. After that, what was I supposed to do with myself?"

The details that had floated just outside my comprehension began to gel. Mykhail challenging me to shoot him in the garden and only stopping when he saw how much he'd upset Arden. The way he'd put himself between me and the people with guns. His ambivalence about the trip to Burnell. How he insisted nothing could happen between us, despite the undeniable connection between us, and never responded to my queries about the future. He wasn't being evasive about his plans—he didn't have any.

Understanding, and the heartrending fear that came with it, made me boneless, and I nearly released my grip on him. I quickly recovered though and cradled him closer. Even the horror of my dawning realization couldn't stop me from comforting him in that moment. The man I knew as warm, caring and funny, the man who laid himself bare to anyone who cared to look, had managed to keep his biggest secret in plain sight.

He wasn't planning on surviving this apocalypse.

15

I woke up from a dream that I'd stepped into an ant hill and was being eaten alive, but the painful tingling in my legs didn't stop. It was completely dark in the old chapel, but I figured it was the man lying across my legs and cutting off circulation that caused the pain, not carnivorous insects. He'd been either unwilling or unable to speak after his admission, so I'd talked my face off, combating his sudden silence with words of support and understanding. He'd fallen asleep in my arms, curling into me like a shelter cat that finally found a human who wouldn't hurt it.

I shifted, not wanting to wake him, but the slight reprieve as blood began to recirculate in my legs meant that he was no longer so completely knocked out that he was a deadweight.

I shuddered at the term. My mind was still fuzzy

around the edges, but everything he'd told me, and the conclusion I'd come to, was sharp and still just as horrifying.

"I'm sorry. I must be crushing you." His voice was gravelly, from the sleep and the emotional wringer he'd put himself through before it. He moved away from me, and in the darkness I felt suddenly alone, like an astronaut cut free from his tether and drifting in infinite black. Then pain stippled through my legs, the pins and needles of reawakening nerves shocking as it ever was. I must have made a noise, some minute sound that was amplified by high ceilings and the absolute darkness of the room.

"Are you okay?" Mykhail moved closer to me. I heard it in the creak of the pew as he shifted his thighs, felt it in the warmth that pressed close along my left side. I didn't need to see his face to know that his brows were drawn in concern for me.

"Yes," I said, but that was a lie. There was something definitely not okay, a question that was gnawing away at my heart and other vital organs. I scratched the side of my nose. "I have to ask you something though. It's kind of hard to say and I don't want you to get angry with me."

There was the silence of a breath held for far too long, then the whoosh of its release.

"Do you want me to go?" he asked. In the darkness, his voice was that of a little boy used to being shoved aside when he became inconvenient. "I don't know why I told you all that horrible stuff. I just needed to get it out. But I understand if you don't want to be around me anymore. I don't want to be around myself, really."

And there it was again.

I wanted to touch him, perhaps having grown accustomed to it as we cuddled during the night or to show him that he wasn't a pariah, so I did. I reached out to my side, slowly so I wouldn't scare him. His biceps twitched under my fingers, but when I closed them around his arm, using it as a guidepost down to his hand, he relaxed. I slid my fingertips past the impossibly soft skin at the crook of his elbow, smoothing over the hairs of his forearm and the pulse that beat at his wrist before threading my fingers with his.

"No, I don't want you to go. That's the thing, Rabbit. I've noticed that perhaps you aren't as careful with yourself as you should be." Talking about this was easier to do in the dark. I made sure my voice sounded sly and playful. He couldn't see the moisture building in my eyes or the way my lower lip quivered in anticipation of the question and of his response. "I thought you were just clumsy at first, or naive, but I'm starting to think maybe you've been purposely uncareful. I'm not judging you. I would never judge you, especially after what you just shared, but I need to know—have you been *trying* to get yourself killed?"

His hand jumped in mine, as if he considered pulling it away but decided against it. "I guess that's one way of looking at it," he eventually said, providing me with the understatement of the postapocalyptic era.

"Do you want to talk about it?" I prodded, giving his hand a squeeze. "I think it can be helpful to talk if you're thinking about…like, ending your life." The words said aloud felt like cement shoes, pulling me under with the weight of Mykhail's intentions.

His body swayed, and I guessed that he shook his head. "I don't want to talk anymore, or think, or remember."

And just like that, my open book slammed shut, right when I'd gotten to the most awful kind of cliff-hanger. What did you say to a man so full of joy and goodness, even in the aftermath of the terrible things he'd experienced, when he made the decision that life wasn't worth living? I wanted to grab him and shake him, to tell him that he wasn't allowed to do something so rash. I wanted to remind him of all the good left in the world, and how he was an integral part of it. Selfishly, I wanted to tell him that I didn't care how he felt, I wanted him to stay. But I couldn't chastise him; no matter how much the thought of losing him made me sick, he was a grown man and the choice was his. He didn't owe me anything; in fact, I owed him. For pulling me back to the surface when I'd felt ready to sink. For giving me a purpose when I'd felt hopelessly adrift.

I couldn't ask anything of him, not right then at least, but I could give. If he intended to carry through whatever plan had been hatched in a moment of despair, I could provide him with something he'd denied himself for far too long. I possessed skills beyond map-reading, and while I didn't know if they could convince him that life was worth living, they would certainly help him to enjoy the precious time he had left.

I flipped his hand in mine so that his palm faced upward, and then dragged my fingertips over it, wondering how long his lifeline was as I traced the creases in his skin. I didn't believe in fortune-telling, but I was willing to make an exception if it meant there was a strike against Mykhail going through with his plan. I circled over his sensitive skin and heard his breath go shallow beside me. "Well, then. We won't talk about it anymore. In fact, I can help you forget for a while, if you want," I said. I bent my fingers so the blunt edges of my nails scraped his palms as I kept up the motion. His hand began to tremble, just a bit. I might not have noticed if it wasn't for the complete stillness around us and the fact that I was operating by touch alone.

"You still like me?" His voice was strained, his words low. "After what I just told you?"

I leaned close to him, using my hand to find the column of his neck and then his ear before I spoke. I ran my thumb over the crenulations there and relished the shiver that went through him at my touch. "I do. You're a good person, Mykhail. I've liked you from the start, and I could more than like you if you'd let me." The darkness and my desire to draw him out made my tongue loose, but I couldn't regret the admission now, knowing there could be an even more finite limit on our time together than I'd ever imagined. "But this is not me liking you. It's me desiring you."

I caught his earlobe lightly between my teeth and he gasped. The sound activated the nodule of heat that was building in my chest, making it pulse and expand like a supernova. All of the emotions that had been stirred by his confession—compassion, pity, sympathy—were folded into the avalanche of desire that rumbled within me. It wasn't my job to heal him, nor was it within my purview, but if I could ease his suffering at all, I would. I couldn't explain how or why, but his well-being had quickly become important to me, and I wanted to show him that.

I released him and kissed from his ear to his jaw, up over those beautiful cheekbones that tasted of his tears. "You asked me about liking another person. Should I teach you about desire?"

He went stiff beside me, and then exhaled a ragged breath. He moved the hand that was still in mine, flipped the positions as he guided my hand toward the bulge in his pants. My hand was sandwiched between his palm and his thick cock, which was somehow larger than I'd guessed. "I know all about desire, in theory. I want you to show me."

"What hypothesis are we testing here?" I asked playfully, but his hand squeezed mine harder.

"No," he said. His voice was urgent in the dark, thrilling me. "What I'm feeling with you right now, this isn't an experiment. It would have to be replicable to fit that criterion, and I know I wouldn't feel the same way with someone else touching me. There's nothing to prove."

Sweet relief warmed my chest and spread through my body. It seemed I wasn't the only one freed by the darkness. He wanted me, and only me it seemed, and the feeling was mutual. I flung a leg over him so I straddled him on the pew, our faces inches apart. His lips sought mine and when they touched, he lifted his hips, resulting in a breath-stealing slide of his cock against mine. I couldn't tell if that had been his intention, but he liked the sensation enough to repeat it again, and again. My hands clamped on his shoulders as I matched his erratic thrusts, trying to guess at his timing so I could move to the left or the right for a delicious contrast against his up-and-down motions. His big hands moved over my back, first caressing then guiding me as we moved.

"Mmm, that feels good. What you're doing right now." For all his inexperience and hardwiring to obey, he didn't seem to have a problem letting me know what he liked. That wasn't common, even in my longest relationships. It heated something in me, knowing that he trusted me enough to voice his needs without trepidation. He groaned into our kiss and then dropped his head back as I rode him harder, grinding against him with the single-minded focus of giving him pleasure, chased by the spiraling thrill that throbbed through my groin.

I changed the tempo of my movements, slowing down before I brought him—or myself—too close to the edge. I gripped my legs around his thighs and swept my hands down his chest, up and under his shirt to pull it over his head. He was surprisingly hairy, given his boyish looks and lack of facial hair, and I plunged my fingers into the crinkly denseness, running my hand over the plateau of his pectorals, furred save for the smooth areolas. I pinched at them, receiving a hiss and a hip thrust that nearly knocked me onto my ass for my troubles.

"Sorry," he whispered, contrite.

I laughed and continued my exploration of his torso. "There was a mechanical bull at a bar I used to go to. I can ride with the best of them, Mykhail."

"I'm not surprised by that," he said, and then groaned aloud because I'd leaned in and circled his flat nipple with my tongue.

My hands gripped his slim waist as I alternated kissing and lapping at his chest. The last times I'd hooked up before the Flare had been with strangers, impersonal joinings that got the job done but didn't nourish something that had withered within me. But it was different with Mykhail. I knew him, *knew* him in a way that was both illogical and completely right, and it heightened everything about the experience. Each gasp and cry he emitted seeped into my bones, fueling the desire that had lain dormant in the marrow, waiting for the chance to touch him as he'd touched me. I grazed him with my teeth, reveling in the response as if I was on the receiving end.

His thick member jumped involuntarily with each pass of tongue over nipple, rapping insistently against my stomach. Opportunity only knocked once, so I climbed to the floor between his legs, unzipped his jeans and had them down around his ankles in a move so speedy that I surprised even myself. I was disoriented for a moment, kneeling before him with both hands wrapped around his shaft. Anticipation was a living thing in the air around us, physically drawing my mouth to his cock.

"Wait," he grunted, and for a moment I was awash

in disappointment at the possibility that I'd crossed some invisible line. He leaned to the side, and I heard him fumbling around for something. There was a scratching noise before we were ensconced in a golden circle of light from the match clutched between his shaking thumb and forefinger. "I want to see you," he said. He lit the tea candle beside him on the bench and leaned back, a golden god in broken glasses looking down on his supplicant. I wasn't sure if it was the candlelight or me that made his eyes glow, but I had my answer as soon as I slid my hands up and down his length. His nostrils flared, his abs went tight and he gripped the back of the pew so hard that the wood nearly cracked. It was definitely me.

In that moment, I didn't care about his warning me away. I didn't care about the fallout if I gave him everything and got nothing in return. The look on his face was sustenance enough for that burgeoning emotion that held me in its grip. I bent my head forward and licked the circumference of his head as I worked him, loving the tangy taste of him on my tongue. My lips encased the tip of his cock and I took him into my warmth, mouth meeting my fingers as they pumped his shaft.

Mykhail's hand cupped my head and he uttered a stream of Ukrainian that I couldn't understand but was sure was something totally uncouth.

I sucked harder.

I removed one of my hands so I could take in more of him, and I was tempted to unbutton my pants and get myself off too—Mykhail's groaning and thrusting and generally amazing hotness had my spine tingling and my balls heavy with need—but this was just for him. I tried to suck him down even farther, cheeks hollowed as his wide head hit the back of my throat. The flat of my tongue massaged the underside of his shaft as I pleasured him, and without warning he pushed my face away, bellowing his release in a deep, guttural tone that I never would have expected from him. My hand still pumped his length while he climaxed, the hot come spurting out for so long that I started to wonder if this orgasm was going to result in a medical emergency. But he soon slumped back in the pew, limp and completely blissed-out.

"That was incredible," he murmured after we'd cleaned up, pulled our clothes back on and settled onto the pew next to each other. Our arms were interlocked and we snuggled close, like a couple, as sunlight filtered into the chapel. The storm had passed and morning had arrived.

Incredible enough to live for? I wanted to ask, but that would have been stupid. My tongue was pretty dexterous, but it would take more than a blow job to help pull him from the brink of suicide. Every little bit counted though, I reasoned. My chest tightened at the thought of his death, and my eyes stung. "See what you've been missing out on?" I asked brightly.

"I don't think I missed out on anything," he said. I gave him an incredulous look to find him smiling down at me. His eyes were serious though. "I think I was just waiting for you, Jang-wan."

He said the words playfully, but not as a joke, and I could've laughed and cried at the same time; of course the perfect man for me was one who was set on departing the earthly plane. Of course.

We stared at each other for a long time, each trying to figure out what the other was thinking. "Mykhail—"

A vibrating sensation against my thigh made me jump in the pew and dramatically grab my leg as if some wild creature had crawled into my pocket. This sensation was a bit too strong to be physiological, even for a case of blue balls like the one that had just subsided. Then I remembered the small plastic phone I'd slid into my pocket the day before.

"What the hell?" I pulled it out, and sure enough there were two bars where Searching should have been. My pulse had just gone back to baseline but now it was racing again. The last time I'd held a working cell phone had been the night of the Flare, when my message indicator had gone off because Arden had texted me a poop emoji even though she was sitting right next to me on the couch.

I gripped Mykhail's arm. "I'm getting a signal."

We were both bent over the phone, faces illuminated like two wise men in a bootleg nativity scene, when the door to the chapel burst open. We moved to our feet in unison, squinting against the bright morning light streaming into the room. Three men charged into the small space, each taking a position so that they surrounded us, guns pointed.

I was completely disoriented, my mind not making the shift from romantic interlude to technological miracle to hostage situation as quickly as my body—my hands were up in the air and I was repeating "Don't shoot," although my brain was still a minute behind, marveling over the immaculate reception. The details filtered in slowly. The way the men were dressed alike in black body armor, had the same weapons and moved in formation as they closed in on us.

The biggest one, a beefy guy around my age with eyes that screamed "I'm a crazy asshole" from a mile away, began laughing, the sound echoing around the chapel. "Hope we didn't interrupt anything, lovebirds."

For months, I'd hoped that soldiers would come rushing in to save the day, but my fantasies hadn't played out quite like this. I thought of Arden shaking her head disappointedly at me during one of our late-night conversations. "Be careful what you wish for, John. That shit always blows up in your face."

Mykhail's bristling energy was tangible beside me, and the fear that churned in my gut switched into high gear. The men who'd broken into our sanctuary were armed to the teeth, and they looked much more willing to use their firearms than the people from Belleville had been. I thought of Mykhail stepping out from behind the tree, trying to draw their gunfire away from me. "Don't do anything stupid," I managed to eke out to him through a throat constricted with fear.

"And leave you alone with these guys?" The disbelief in his voice was promise enough; Mykhail wouldn't endanger himself just yet. He didn't have to explain what he meant by *these guys*. He meant the kind of guy who'd targeted me throughout high school, going out of his way to cross my path just so he could bump into me and call me a fag in the crowded hallway. The kind of guy who'd abruptly ask you what it felt like to suck dick in the middle of mindless party banter. At least one of them looked like the kind of guy who'd follow you to the bathroom at a bar and explain how he wasn't a queer but a hole was a hole, as he unzipped his pants.

These men were dangerous.

For a moment I thought of trying to minimize signs of gayness, but I'd never been very good at that. There was something about me that gave it away, and I'd long ago made the decision that I wouldn't be cowed by the violent homophobes of the world. But that fear never really went away, and all of the horrible things men who hated gays did to them started to play on a loop in my mind. I glanced at Mykhail; he wasn't playing up his friendly goofiness as he had during our last encounter. His gaze was hard, and he managed to project a simultaneously calm and annoyed demeanor. If he was the slightest bit afraid he didn't show it, and even though I doubted he was secretly a kung fu master who could take out these men in the blink of an eye, I drew strength from him.

Eternity seemed to pass in what was likely just a few seconds after they surrounded us. I remembered the feeling of being watched when I'd filled our bottles and shuddered. Had it been them, or had that feeling simply been some kind of omen?

"What were you doing in here all night?" the crazy-eyed man asked us, answering my question. He had hair that was just a shade too blond to be considered red and a face that only a mother could love. "You can skip the details about the gay shit though. I don't need to hear that." Funny how people who were supposedly grossed out by my kind were always so focused on us fucking. I mean, it wasn't like Mykhail and I *hadn't* had sexual relations, but that wasn't all we'd done.

"We were just gossiping." The words slipped out of my mouth before I realized it, fueled by annoyance and anger. Something that had once been a vital part of my survival, but had gone soft over the past few months, woke up and started sharpening its knives. My inner bitch. I smiled at the idiot, tilted my head as if I was speaking to a brute beast. "You sure you don't wanna hear about the gay shit? Because we were comparing notes. Did you know that the thickness of a man's neck is inversely proportional to the size of his dick?" I gave a pointedly long stare to the bulging column that was situated where a neck would be on a normal human.

One of the other soldiers chuckled, but it was Mykhail's snort beside me that felt like validation. I ignored the itch at my nose and the familiar weight of panic settling in over my shoulders. Fear was a useful physiological response, but I wouldn't subjugate myself before anyone unless I had to.

"What's that supposed to mean?" The soldier's expression was a confused proto-sneer, as if he'd caught the gist of my insult but not the meat of it, which was pretty disappointing to be honest.

"Enough, Reilly," another man said. This man had

entered the chapel last, a detail that my mind had picked up while I was in a blind panic. He was muscular with broad shoulders, his build more swimmer than defensive end. "I'm Cadet Deshawn Lewis. Me and my fellow cadets have been patrolling the area in the last few weeks, working as peacekeepers since the Flare occurred."

"Peacekeeper seems an odd term for people who just kicked down the door of a church for no reason. Is moderation something they wait until after graduation to teach you?"

Mykhail elbowed me—apparently he thought I'd exceeded my snark quotient, but I knew this was a pivotal moment. A childhood memory flashed in my mind and then disappeared. A neighbor's dog had gone Cujo on me, and I'd briefly developed a fear of them. After growing tired of me whimpering every time we passed even the smallest dachshund, my father sat me down and explained that I was the one setting the tone for my interactions with dogs. If I cowered, they would sense my fear and react accordingly. I had to create the foundation for our relationship in those first pivotal moments, to convey in some way that I merited their respect. As I looked at the men surrounding us, I realized this situation was no different.

Lewis eyed me for a while, then one side of his mouth curled. I couldn't tell if this was a sign of amusement or anger, and the fact that these guys all had big guns finally made an impression on me. When he spoke, it wasn't to berate me. "People are out here armed to the teeth, shooting first and asking questions later. Saying you're with the government doesn't always stop that. Hell, sometimes it spurs these piney fucks on. But point taken." He waited a beat. "Why didn't you ask what the Flare was?"

I suddenly felt like a small furry creature who'd mistakenly placed its paw in a glue trap. I didn't know why; it wasn't as if I was privy to some top-secret knowledge. I made a jazz hands motion on either side of my face. "What true gay guy doesn't know about flair?" I joked, and was met with a hard look.

Lewis didn't find it amusing. "Tell us where you were going."

"To the university," Mykhail cut in, sounding like a professional and not the cute boy I'd been traveling with. He gave me a sidelong glance, a censuring one. "He knows about the solar flare because I told him about it. I'm an astrophysicist, and I'm going to Burnell to see if one of my professors is there, a man who's pretty well versed in the effects of a solar flare and what could be done to help in the aftermath."

There was a subtle shifting among the soldiers; the ones in my line of sight shot each other meaningful looks, and the guy behind me seemed to take a few steps.

Mykhail continued. "So we're no danger to anyone. We're not looking to take potshots at soldiers, just going about our business."

"I see," Lewis said, which was about as opaque a reply as he could have given.

Mykhail and I were still standing with our hands in

the air, but gravity was starting to take effect and my arms began to drift down.

"Get those hands up, Ching-Chong!" This from my friend Reilly, who was apparently aiming to check off every box in the stereotypical lummox column.

"What the fuck, man?" The voice came from behind me, one of the cadets who'd simply been a scary dark figure bursting through the door. "I told you to cut it with that racist shit."

"And I told you I was tired of your PC whining." Reilly glowered at a point somewhere over my shoulder.

Lewis sighed and closed his eyes in annoyance for a moment. "Are you soldiers, or are you guests on a goddamned morning talk show? Hernandez, I told you to grow a thicker skin. Reilly, I told you if you kept it up with the slurs I'd knock you back into your momma's pussy, which I'm sure is the only one you've ever seen. Now, let's roll out."

Mykhail and I released our breaths simultaneously, expecting the soldiers to file out as quickly as they'd come in. Instead, Lewis gave us an annoyed look, as if he expected something from us.

"Um, thanks for dropping by?" I ventured, unsure of what he wanted. I twisted my hand at the wrist, giving him a beauty pageant wave.

"Date's not over yet, C.C.," Reilly said, making a concession to Hernandez by shortening the slur to its first letters. His hands squeezed the barrel and pistol grip in a rhythmic motion that seemed lewd somehow. "You're coming with us—"

"He's Korean, not Chinese, so Ching-Chong isn't correct. If you insist on using slurs, get them straight," Mykhail interrupted. Beneath my confusion, my heart did a little flip, grateful for that small act of protection. "There's no reason for us to go with you. We told you what we were doing and where we were going. You can't possibly think we're a threat."

"If you were a threat we would've taken you out already," Hernandez said. He wasn't trying to be menacing, and when I turned to look at him, I was surprised at how young he was. His hazel eyes, bronze skin, clean-shaven jaw made him look like a male model who'd accidentally enlisted instead of signing up for photos at Barbizon. He was runty compared to the other two men, but runty didn't mean he was unable to do harm. He looked plenty capable of that.

Lewis was studying us, expression inscrutable. "Well, we're all heading in the same direction, it seems. It'd make sense for us to escort you there. I presume you're going to see Dr. Simmons?"

Mykhail clammed up beside me. Dr. Simmons had seemed like an abstract, our secret pot of gold at the end of the rainbow, and now these men with guns and menacing looks were privy to his existence.

"How do you know Dr. Simmons?" Mykhail asked. His composure wavered, just for a moment.

"We've become pretty well acquainted in the last few weeks. After we ventured out from the military campus, we found ourselves lost in the wild, so to speak. We have an arrangement now though. The university is our home base, and we help protect its interests." Lewis said no more, but Hernandez and Reilly moved around us, hauling up our backpacks like a military concierge service. I thought they might search them and wondered what would happen if they found the gun, but they didn't seem interested in plundering our belongings.

"I don't recall us agreeing to hitch a ride," I said as they took our bags. "It's only a day's walk from here, so we can just meet you there."

"I don't recall giving you that choice." Lewis's hand dropped lazily to the weapon that hung at his side. Any affinity I had for him for blasting Reilly dried up in that instant.

"Let's just go with them, John." That was the moment when it hit me how much danger we were in. Mykhail prided himself on calling me the Korean name that even my own family didn't usually address me by. Now I was John again, and even though it was what I'd gone by for most of my life, it seemed foreign on his lips. That meant that he, too, could sense the aura of violation that these men emitted. It made you instinctively try to keep whatever precious item you had safe. The most important thing to me in the chapel, besides my life, was about six feet too tall to be hidden in my pocket, unfortunately.

I thought back to the water bottles I'd filled—had that

alerted them to our presence? Had we stayed longer than we should have in an unknown place? Should I have led us in a different direction? My mind scrambled to find some source of blame for the situation we were in, but there was none beyond the men who were now our captors. I wouldn't have done anything differently, because everything had led up to what happened between Mykhail and me, and I wouldn't give that up.

We marched through the front door, surrounded by three strange men who were taking us to a destination that now seemed foreboding. I'd felt trapped at home, but now I well and truly was. There was probably some lesson to be learned from this, but I was quickly discovering you didn't give a damn about life lessons when you were facing death at the hands of a group of rogue cadets in hideous cargo pants.

Mykhail paused after we exited. Hernandez started to shove him forward but then stopped out of an ingrained sense of respect. After Mykhail made the sign of the cross over his chest, he again kissed it up to the heavens. Like I said, I wasn't religious, but I still followed suit. We needed all the help we could get just then.

Hernandez's rough voice sounded from behind me. "Amen." The word was said without irony or contempt, just a respectful closure to our motions. He tilted his head forward to indicate we should start walking.

"Ready?" I asked Mykhail. I tried to sound brave. For him.

"Yeah. Thanks for this morning, and everything. I just

wanted to say that in case anything happens once we get to Burnell."

His words were oddly abrupt, but they made sense in the context of being surrounded by large men with guns. He took my hand, heedless of said men, and my apprehension disappeared. There was strength in his grip, caring and possession, and I reveled in it, ignoring the specter of death that hovered just behind me listing all the terrible things these men could do to us.

"Where's our ride?" I directed my question to the soldiers leading the way. "I hope it's big enough for all of us because I'm not sitting on Reilly's lap. Sorry to disappoint."

Mykhail laughed again, and that was the best thing I could ask for in the moment.

17

I'd only ever been to Burnell once, when I'd been the captain of my eighth-grade scholastic champion team and we'd made it to the finals. We'd been destroyed by a team from New York City, but I hadn't felt too bad since I'd been fairly certain there were at least two full-grown men on their team serving as ringers.

The university had seemed overwhelming then, bustling with cool college students who laughed and hurried to class between the huge white columns of the main hall. And now, although the brick pathways and worn marble steps were co-ed–free, the place still seemed imposing. The old buildings, fully restored to their original beauty thanks to donations by the successful and generous alumni, had a certain gravitas that my alma mater lacked.

When we stepped out of the military-style truck that

had carried us to the campus, all was silent except for the call of birds. Deer grazed in the middle of the overgrown campus green, and the rows upon rows of dark windows seemed like blank eyes watching us make our way toward the unknown. I felt like I'd stepped into one of those creepy "world without humans" artist renderings that had become popular before the blackout—computer-generated images that showed what common settings would look like as nature reclaimed them in the years after human extinction. We really are a morbid species.

The sound of the soldiers' boots on the path bounced back and forth between the old buildings lining the common, making it sound as if there were thirty of them instead of three. As we walked, movement in my peripheral vision made me realize that perhaps that estimate wasn't too far off. Other men in military-style dress were coming out of buildings, watching us as we were shepherded along like reluctant freshmen, with Hernandez and Reilly behind and Lewis in front. None of them said anything, just watched, which was infinitely more worrisome. It meant they already knew where we were going.

We reached the most majestic building, the one that capped the head of the rectangular area like an ivy-covered crown.

"We're taking them to see the Doc," Lewis said to the two young men who guarded the door with the same seriousness as the soldiers standing at the DMZ.

For a moment, I was distracted from my plight by

thinking of what chaos must have ensued at the line bordering North and South Korea when the blackout occurred. Had people banded together? Or had both sides seen it as an attack by the other and acted accordingly? So many powder kegs may have been set off that night.

"Why is he here?" Mykhail asked, drawing my attention back where it needed to be. "His office was in Bixby Hall."

"The president's office has cooler shit in it, I guess," Reilly said. "The president didn't have his own squad of troops, either."

"Someone's moved up in the world," I said and raised my eyebrow at Mykhail. I was uneasy—all kinds of warning signs were going off in my head, the kind that screamed "Why didn't you two just stay at home!" in a voice that sounded suspiciously like my mom's. But we were here now, and no matter what we encountered, maybe there was still a way to help. There had to be some logical explanation for the soldiers. Later, we would all look back and laugh at the misunderstanding that had occurred before we went on to change history. I clung to that idea, because any alternative sent this whole mission crashing into the ground.

We walked up the huge winged marble steps that dominated the foyer before being led to an office at the end of the hall. "Feels like going to the principal's office," I whispered, and Mykhail glanced my way and then to the guns carried by the men around us.

"Your high school was slightly more militarized than mine," he said.

He wasn't snappy, but he was more tightly wound than I was used to seeing him. Mykhail had run the gamut of emotions over the few days I'd known him, but this one was new. It wasn't unfamiliar to me though—he was nervous. How I'd felt every time I was in his presence before we left for the trip. I immediately thought back to the way he'd spoken about this Simmons guy, how he thought the man was so great just because he was some supersmart astrophysicist. Pffft, whatever. I bet he didn't know how to give good head.

I tried to ignore my ill-timed jealousy, but when the office door opened my jaw dropped. The man standing in the doorway backlit by the light pouring in through a huge window was totally bangable. He was of average height and average build, but his face had a kind of square-jawed ruggedness, complete with a dimpled chin, that just didn't fit with my image of an astronomer. His eyes were a cool green, and his thick brown hair was streaked with silver, making him look like some god of knowledge who had descended from the heavens to talk about star stuff with us. His expression was shuttered for a moment, but then his eyes lit on Mykhail and happiness suffused his face, making him even more handsome.

"Shevchenko!" He rushed forward and pulled Mykhail into a hug, away from me. It was completely irrational, but his use of Mykhail's last name was like a slap in the face. I'd never asked. I'd given him the surname GardenGnome, and he'd never supplied his real one. The sticky feeling of jealousy spread in my chest, but I ignored it. I couldn't keep him all to myself, and I shouldn't want to. Memories of the agonies

I'd gone through with my ex—checking his phone, hacking his email and still having the wool pulled over my eyes—brought me away from the ledge. I wouldn't go through that humiliation again, and since the large part of it was of my own creation, I could only rely on myself to stop it.

Dr. Simmons pulled away from Mykhail but held on to his forearms, staring up into his face for a moment. I chalked it up to fatherly pride, even when he finally looked in my direction and asked, "Who's your little friend?"

I was only a couple of inches shorter than him, so the size descriptor was completely unnecessary, except to put me in my place. I expected Mykhail to take my hand or put a hand on my shoulder, but he couldn't seem to pull his eyes away from the professor. "That's John."

One of the worst things about the human brain was the memory editing software that allowed it to search and find evidence to support even the most extreme suppositions. As I watched Mykhail blush and stare at this man whom he'd traveled so far to see, his words from during our walk popped into my head. *I've had crushes on guys before, obviously* and *I'm finally free from my family's restrictions* and *I said I was "pretty much asexual."* What had seemed like a cute play on words before now seemed like damning evidence. Mykhail had warned me not to fall for him, and I'd chosen to assume every possibility save one: he was already smitten with someone else.

"Nice to meet you, John," Simmons said with a smile as he crushed my hand in a handshake. I knew this was some kind of test, that I was supposed to take it like a man, given the dictates of society, but polite society had given up the ghost months ago.

"Yes, meeting new people is fun, but unless you're trying to show me how great you'd be at power-fisting, there's no reason to be squeezing my hand this hard, so..." I smiled brightly and tugged my hand from his.

He looked at me for a moment and then laughed. I gave a monotone chuckle to push the awkward moment along but stopped when his gaze dropped to my neck, eyes following the same path Mykhail had licked a couple of days before as he gave me pleasure in the grass. I wanted to reach up and cover myself in the face of his scrutiny, but resisted the urge.

"Interesting," Simmons said, and the glint in his eyes as he glanced at Mykhail made me want to cut a bitch. It was curious and insinuating, as if he was suddenly scripting a naughty grad student porn. But he quickly turned back my way and gave me a sheepish smile, one that almost made me think I was in full-blown jealous paranoia. He rested a hand on my shoulder. "I apologize. I spend so much time with my head in the clouds that I don't quite know what to do when I'm here on the ground. Shevchenko was always good at reining me in though. We worked closely during his time together here, and his loss was keenly felt last semester."

Nope, definitely not paranoid. There was something off about this guy, and I seemed to be the only one who was bothered by it. Mykhail's cheeks were flushed pink, but he didn't find anything strange about the interaction. His eyes were lit with that same fire I'd seen during our night under the stars, or when he gushed over string theory and music.

"I missed being here too," Mykhail said. "After the Flare...I hoped I would get a chance to apologize for leaving the way I did."

His words sparked the beginnings of realization, like a hair-fine fracture in a sheet of ice before it all crashed to the ground. He'd mentioned that Simmons had been upset about his leaving, but not that he was trekking to the university to apologize for that. I considered turning and fleeing from the building as it all came together—not only had I stolen Mykhail's first kiss, I'd inserted myself into what had been a journey to make amends with another man. A man who was smart, handsome and looking at Mykhail as if he was imagining a platter beneath him.

Simmons shook his head, eyes bright. "No need for that. You're here now, and that's all that matters. So you saw the CME? I thought of you when it occurred, wondering where you were and if you were taking note of it. How did you know to search it out? Was it just chance?"

"I saw that NOAA had issued a flare watch, so I added a passband filter, about one ångström wide, to my little optical telescope. I centered it at the Hα wavelength," Mykhail said, blushing madly and scruffing his fingers through his shaggy hair. Someone watching from afar would have thought he was talking about his first blow job, but that would have required him to remember that I existed.

"You pulled a Carrington, then. Brilliant." The astrophysicist seemed genuinely impressed, and for a moment I felt a surge of pride. Then the man threw an arm around Mykhail's shoulder, a motion that seemed like it was common, and guided him into the office. "What do you think the peak flux was? What designation would you give it? It was infinitely stronger than an X40."

Mykhail excitedly launched into astrospeak in reply to his mentor. I remembered what the point of my accompanying him had been, officially—to help him get to the university in one piece and then return to my family. I'd talked myself into the idea I could stay and help. I thought I could be useful, and after the past two days I thought maybe Mykhail would want me to. It seemed that fantasy wasn't meant to be. His mission was accomplished, and I was left standing behind in the hallway.

My brain wasn't registering what had happened. Despite everything, I'd convinced myself that there was something there between Mykhail and me. His handjob had been sweet but experimental, something I could have thought of as a one-time thing no matter how much that hurt. But our time in the chapel had been something beyond simple exploration. It had been, for lack of a better word, divine.

Humiliation crushed me under its wheels like a monster truck.

I had been wrong in assuming Mykhail cared for me. I'd been foolish to think I'd be able to deal with it if he didn't.

"Oof, that's rough, man." Reilly wasn't even being sarcastic. He clapped me on the back, hard, as I walked by and shook his head. "Got to hurt being someone's postapocalyptic side piece."

I couldn't even respond to that surprisingly astute observation. The inner bitch had dulled her blades and turned them into gardening implements; she was now tilling the seeds of sadness and resentment that had been planted in just the past few minutes. This wouldn't be the first time I'd dated a guy and been dropped after teaching him the ropes, but it was certainly going to be the most painful.

I recalled the weird aphorism Mykhail's grandma had passed on to him. *The devil always takes back his gifts.*

Preach it, Baba, I thought as I sighed and walked into Simmons's office, feeling like the third dick at a double penetration party. *Preach.*

18

"If you're bored, I can get one of the soldiers to find you accommodations," Simmons called across the room, waking me from my nap. I didn't remember falling asleep, but after Mykhail had mentioned how I'd come along to help and Simmons had replied with a condescending "That's nice of you. Which PhD program did you say you were enrolled in?" I'd lost interest in the conversation. Apparently so much so that I'd fallen into a deep, drooly sleep on the chaise longue in the fancy office while Simmons and Mykhail caught up. The president, wherever he was, had obviously been a fan of *Mad Men*. The office was designed like someone had created a time machine for the express purpose of acquiring mod furniture and aged single malt whiskey.

The sunlight was more golden than bright morning yellow outside the window, which meant I'd been asleep for some time. Still, I didn't appreciate the undertone of "you bother me, kid" in his words.

"I'll wait for Mykhail to see about accommodations, thanks," I said.

"So you two will be sharing a room?" he asked. There was a hint of laughter in his voice, as if he found the situation amusing.

I was ready to answer in the affirmative, but Mykhail turned beet red and looked down at his hands. Mr. Gregarious was suddenly silent, and Simmons's gaze darted between us speculatively.

Humiliation dropped down on my head like an anvil in one of those old cartoons. I'd assumed we would bunk together because I was thinking in terms of "we" now, but reality slapped me in the face, and hard. He'd barely said two words to me since we'd arrived and he'd gone all doe-eyed once his professor started paying attention to him. I hadn't been accepted into Burnell, but even I could take a hint.

The seconds ticked by, interminably, and when Mykhail didn't pipe up I stood and grabbed my pack. "Actually, I'll leave you two to talk. Sorry for interrupting your doctorate-level conversation with my lowly bachelor's-degree presence." The words sounded bratty and pathetic even to my own ears, but I wasn't the one who was good at hiding my feelings away.

I stormed out of the room and shut the door quietly behind me, not giving Simmons the satisfaction of the drama queen slam I'm sure he expected. My sinuses burned from swallowing against crying, and angry tears heated my eyes. I had been such an idiot, thinking that Mykhail's touching and kissing, that his confiding his darkest secret to me, meant anything. All it proved was that when a guy was lonely, he'd settle for anyone.

I sniffled as I hopped down the steps, not knowing where I was going but needing to get far, far away from the scene of my humiliation.

"Jang-wan!"

My heart leaped at my name on his lips, but I didn't stop moving. After leaving me hanging like that, the very least he could do was a little power walking before he groveled. Hurried footsteps echoed on the tile floor and then his hand was on my shoulder.

I whirled on him. "Oh, now you acknowledge my presence? Now that your precious professor can't see?"

His face twisted in confusion, but I was lonely and scared and so angry I could burst. I glared at him instead of taking a moment to gather myself.

"What's wrong with you?" he asked. "You've been acting weird ever since we got here."

"What's wrong with *me*?" I was incredulous. "You're the one acting like everything is normal when it clearly isn't. Why is Dr. Simmons in the president's office, huh? Why does he have armed cadets running around at his beck and call, like he's Carl Sagan meets Dr. Moreau? Have you asked him any of those things, or have you been too busy mooning over him to notice that something seriously strange is going on here?"

Something charged the air between us, a volatile energy that was ready to combust at the slightest spark.

Mykhail's eyes were stormy behind his glasses. "Okay, I don't know why you're acting like this. If you hadn't fallen asleep, you would have your explanation right now." He made a sound of annoyance in the back of his throat. "I thought you wanted to come here to find out more about the Flare and to see if Simmons is in contact with anyone about the electrical grid problem."

"Well, you could have fooled me, since I was boxed out of every conversation," I said. "All you had to do was reach out a hand or direct the conversation my way, but you chose not to. You acted like I was nothing to you."

My words echoed in the cold stone corridor of the building, repeating the sad truth to me. I had just met Mykhail a few days ago, while whatever there was between him and Simmons had years of foundation. Comparatively, I was a blip on the radar.

He sighed deeply, reminding me of my dad when my mom was on his case and he was ruing the day he met her. "I don't know what you expect from me. Was I supposed to start making out with you in front of the man who taught me everything I know? Should I have grabbed your crotch while he was telling me about the engineering students working to keep the grid operational? I told you this is all new for me.

Sorry if I'm not comfortable with that yet."

"With what? Showing that you're a human being who's attracted to and involved with another human being?" I didn't understand his sudden reticence, and the betrayal of it all skewered me. "You had no problem holding my hand in front of those soldiers, so don't give me that 'you're not comfortable' bullshit, okay? Just be honest with me. Or do you only reserve that for when it'll get you a blow job?"

I could pinpoint the moment when everything we'd built over the past few days shattered under the heel of my boot. He physically recoiled from my words, and I desperately wished I could lasso them and haul them back in. I'd let them fly in the heat of the moment, and their implication was horrific—that I thought he'd used the story of the horror he'd been through to gain a pity fuck. His face went pallid and he took a step back from me, stuck his hands in his pockets.

"Mykhail—"

His voice was tight, his expression distant, when he cut me off. "I was going to ask you to let me know where we were staying tonight once you got settled, but maybe it's better if we spend some time apart."

Pain thumped my chest as he walked away from me. "I'm sorry. I didn't mean what it sounded like I meant," I said weakly. "But don't act like you didn't just toss me aside when we got here." I stood rooted in place, hoping he would turn, even if only to glare at me.

He didn't.

Eventually, I made my way out of the building. I walked as if there'd been a gravitational shift in the aftermath of our argument and my body was now too heavy to maneuver correctly. Never, never had I felt more alone. I'd wanted adventure, love and a happy ending. Instead, all I'd gotten were a sore jaw and a broken heart, and a long, lonely trip home awaiting me. Regret poured over me like scalding oil dropped from a battlement. When I made it home, *if* I made it home, my family would be waiting to hear what I'd done to help with getting the grid back online and what had happened with Mykhail. The answer to both questions would be the same: nothing.

I didn't know where I was going when I stumbled out of the building, but I was moving fast. My angry words and Mykhail's cold reaction nipped at my heels, making me cringe each time I replayed the scene in my head. Each event, from that first night in the garden to his back as he walked away—back to Simmons's office—played at warp speed in my head, and I analyzed each one as if I was in the Kennedy assassination forum at my favorite nerdboy website. Had Mykhail looked over or to the left as he'd left me standing alone? Had he blinked two times or three, and what did it mean either way?

I needed a distraction, and badly. This was worse than the crushing sense of nothingness I'd experienced back home; at least there I'd had the comfort of my family and Arden. I'd felt useless, but only because I hadn't looked at my home as someplace where my work was valued. Now, I wondered who was monitoring the radio signals and repairing the small devices that had been burned out when the pulse of the Flare hit us. I wondered who made Arden laugh as she rocked Stump to sleep. Was my dad going out into the woods and setting rabbit traps by himself now, or had Maggie gotten over her repulsion and joined him? And Amma—who would help her with that bootleg excuse of a booty shake she tried to pass off as a twerk?

I hadn't been changing the world at home, but I had been useful. Here, I was totally alone, and more than that, I was hurt and scared. The possibility that I'd made the wrong decision inched closer to a certainty.

Evening was starting to descend as I moped my way across the campus, as I had for much of the time I'd been dating Peter the Cheater. Maybe that accounted for my going off on Mykhail. I was conditioned to think that something shady lay behind any unexplained behavior, and I'd overreacted.

That doesn't explain his batting his lashes at Dr. Simmons, a helpful part of my brain corrected. I paused on the pathway and heaved a deep sigh. It was starting to get dark and I was too out of it to leave, so any decision I made would have to wait until morning. I looked up at the row of dark buildings, seeing which one looked most comfortable to bed down in, when light flooded around me.

All at once, the lamps lining the green turned on. I stared openmouthed, not having seen electricity outside my home since the blackout. There was no way these lights were hooked up to generators. It could mean only one thing—Burnell had never gone dark.

19

I stood staring at the glowing lamp, as intrigued by it as the cloud of moths that now joined me in my gawking.

"Yo!" I looked across the green to see Lewis walking with a man and woman who were obviously civilians. He had traded the big gun for a shoulder holster holding two pistols and was dressed in a white T-shirt and camo pants. I figured this was the military equivalent of casual Friday. "I thought you two were with Simmons?" His words were friendly enough, but there was still the implication that I owed him an explanation that had rankled my nerves earlier. Now though, I would hop on any reason to get away from the ugly thoughts populating my head.

"I got bored," I said, which was mostly true. I waved up at the lights. "Since no one is surprised by this, I'm guessing Burnell hasn't had any problems with electricity since the Flare? How is that possible?"

"The university has been set up as an exemplar of how to prevent widespread power outages in the event of a CME," the man with him said. He appeared to be Middle Eastern, with olive skin and sea-green eyes. "There haven't been any problems with the electricity, with the exception of maintaining it of course."

"Thank you for explaining, Altaf," Lewis said, a hint of warning in his tone. He turned his sharp gaze toward the woman. Her mouth pressed into a line and she stared at the ground. She was striking, small-statured with smooth, dark skin and sorrowful hazel eyes. From far away, the duo had looked like extras in a generic college welcome video, minus Lewis's guns, but up close something was off.

There was a haggardness about them that seemed much more severe than even the worst midterm cramming could bring on. Dark circles under the eyes and tense expressions were the common denominators between the two. When I smiled at them, their gazes shifted down to the ground.

"I'm John," I said, giving an awkward wave.

"Altaf and Bina. They're grad students here," Lewis introduced them. The students remained quiet.

"I actually don't have anywhere to go. Is it okay if I tag along with you?" I asked. I was uneasy, but it felt wrong to just sulk around the university when I could be doing something useful.

Lewis shrugged. "Sure. These two are working a communications shift. If you think you won't get in the way, then come along."

"I think I can be useful," I said, although I had no idea of what I'd be asked to do. I tried to work up some excitement about finally getting to contribute, but the hunched shoulders of the two students undercut any thrill I might have felt. Their expressions were guarded as they glanced at me, and the woman pressed her lips together into a frown.

I'd already been worried after our armed escort to the school, but now that my anger at Mykhail had receded I was starting to get scared. What had we gotten ourselves into? I didn't know if his connection with Simmons would blind him to all the factors throwing up "hell to the no" in bright flashing lights, but I realized there was more than one way to help.

I flashed Lewis what I hoped was a convincing smile and joined the group as they commenced walking. Something strange was going on, and I was going to figure out what it was before it was too late.

I followed behind Altaf and Bina, with the heavy thud of Lewis's combat boots close behind me. I thought it was strange that he didn't walk ahead instead of trailing us like a teacher who didn't trust the students not to pass notes.

"So what exactly is communications duty?" I asked. "Are we going to be tying string to tin cans and stretching them across campus?"

Bina glanced back at me. I thought she might smile,

but her expression remained serious. "Have you not been apprised of the situation?" Her accent was African. I could tell that she came from a Francophone country, but which one of the many on the continent I couldn't begin to specify. Wherever she hailed from, the look of beleaguered annoyance on her face was universal.

"I just arrived, and I haven't exactly been given the grand tour," I said, taken aback.

"So you are not one of Simmons's men?" Her features softened when I shook my head, and she sighed.

A familiar buzz sounded behind me, and I turned to see Lewis reach into his pocket and take out a cell phone, as if that was still a normal thing to do. If he'd pulled a rabbit out of his pants I couldn't have been more surprised.

"Okay, electricity is one thing, but how is his phone working?" I asked.

Altaf gave me a nervous smile. "Mesh network, using individual cell phones as intermediary nodes instead of relying on cell towers," he said. "I can explain more when we get to my lab. That's where we're going."

I remembered how my cell phone had magically worked right before the soldiers burst into the chapel. I knew it was possible to utilize a cell phone to serve as a modem for other devices, using tethering, and wondered if this was something similar.

While I stood puzzling it out, Lewis grunted out, "Yeah, he's with me. I'll keep an eye on him," and hung up his phone. "Simmons" was the only thing he said when I looked at him.

Had Mykhail asked him to check up on me, or revealed that we'd had a fight? Would he tell him what our argument had been about? I was mortified enough without the object of my jealousy gloating behind my back. I felt a pang of terror at the thought that Simmons would be doing more than gloating, that he would try to comfort Mykhail...

We arrived at Altaf's lab, in the first floor of what appeared to be a multilab building, which was a welcome distraction from the trail my imagination was attempting to follow. It was like some sort of beautiful dream, the light of computer screens and LED displays reminding me of everything that had been lost in the wake of the Flare. Technology. Telecommunications. But not innovation, that was for sure.

"I've been working on this awhile," Altaf said. "For me, the project started during the unrest in Syria. We needed a way to communicate over the phone and internet without relying on cell towers. Mesh networking was the answer—simple and cheap, not accessible by the authorities and the algorithms are self-maintaining."

Bina looked up from her computer. "I was working on a similar project, trying to bring the internet to schools in regions that weren't wired. In this case, each phone serves as a node. We use routing protocols coded into the nodes to allow phones to join the network. Once the phone has access, it serves as another node, increasing the reach of the system."

"You know, I'd started reading up a little about this right before the Flare, but I never had time to learn more about it. This is amazing! What protocols are you using? OLSR? BATMAN?" There was a familiar stirring within me, a hunger that wouldn't be sated until I knew every aspect of how this networking was done. I thought of Mykhail and his passion for the cosmos, and how he'd compared the comprehension of new knowledge to falling in love. Despite my anger with him, I was already excited to tell him about this discovery and the possible uses. The post-Flare world didn't have to return to the dark ages. This system could be used until larger communications systems were back in place. Hell, it could replace those systems if we were starting from scratch.

I peppered them with questions, loving the fast-paced interaction and how they seemed to open up the more we talked. Altaf had a self-deprecating wit, and Bina was sharper than any professor I'd worked with.

"You're an engineer?" Bina asked.

"I studied computer science, and this stuff fascinates me. I wonder if my cell phone would work without the protocol or—"

It happened in an instant—Lewis's phone buzzed, grabbing his attention. Bina's hand passed over mine, and the warm plastic of a thumb drive was left in my palm behind it. I didn't even have time to respond.

"Alright, I have to roll out. Reilly and Penders are coming to take my shift," Lewis said.

Both Bina and Altaf went stiff at his words. The animated conversation we'd been having screeched to a halt.

"You should leave, too, John," Altaf said. His eyes had gone dull.

Bina's hands, which had just been quick and steady as she slipped me the drive, now shook as they hovered over her keyboard. She turned to me and nodded once, her eyes serious once again. "Yes," she agreed. "You've distracted us from our work enough as it is. It was nice meeting you."

I didn't take offense at her words. They were clear as day—*Get out of here while you can.*

I didn't know Penders, but the thought of Reilly being left in charge of anyone was horrifying.

"Come on, man," Lewis said. He tugged at my arm, pulling me out of the room.

As I left, Altaf moved behind Bina and placed a hand on her shoulder. She covered it with her own and took a deep breath. They didn't speak.

"You should go back to Simmons's office and find your friend," Lewis said once we got outside. "Getting late, and you need a place to stay."

"Which way is it again?" I asked, but he was already stalking off. If he'd seen me as any kind of threat back at the church, he certainly didn't now. I fingered the thumb drive in my pocket and thought of Altaf and Bina. I hoped I could prove him wrong.

I walked in the direction I thought we'd come from, not having any idea about what I should do or where I should go. Getting back to Mykhail wasn't exactly appealing, but we needed to figure out what the hell was going on. What was going to happen to the two brilliant people I'd left behind? Why did they need the soldiers watching over them at all?

My inner alarm bells were going off at deafening levels right as the wind was knocked out of me by a solid mass running into me at full speed.

20

As I fell backward, a fist connected with my stomach and my body twisted with the impact of it so I landed on my side.

"What are you doing out here?" the soldier standing over me demanded as I curled into a ball around my fanny pack. He'd hit me right in the diaphragm and I couldn't even breathe properly, let alone answer his question. Pain radiated through my torso, and then in the already abused muscles of my thighs when he kicked me with a steel-toed boot and repeated himself.

I tried to force the words out, but couldn't, and he kicked me again, his boot glancing off my tailbone. A mangled cry escaped my throat as the man grabbed me by the collar of my shirt and pulled me to my knees. "You know you're supposed to be in lockdown right now. You speakey the English, asshole? I asked why you're outside!"

Nothing he was saying made sense to me. I knew there were soldiers around, but I hadn't been told about any curfews or that the punishment for breaking one was an ass-kicking.

"Hey! Klein! Get off of him!" The voice approaching us sounded vaguely familiar through the haze of fear and pain. In a moment, the cadet named Hernandez was by my side, placing a staying hand on Klein's chest. "He's a guest of Simmons."

Klein's dark eyes went wide and he released me. I nearly toppled over, but Hernandez righted me at the last moment. My shirt hung loosely around my neck, having ripped and stretched when Klein had grabbed me. It flapped in the chill evening breeze.

"What the hell?" I managed at last. Klein wasn't as big as a Mack truck but I felt pretty flattened after being smashed by him. "Are you fucking insane?"

I thought about the gun, and for a brief, blinding moment of fury I was tempted to whip it out and use it.

"Aw fuck. I thought he was one of the Inties trying to bust a move out of here," he said to Hernandez. "They're the only Asians around here, and I just figured—"

"You just figured you'd go beast on him before asking who he was?" Hernandez finished. "You'd better hope Lewis doesn't flay your ass when he hears about this."

"Lewis is too busy making his own moves. He doesn't give two fucks what happens to some Intie," Klein said. The hatred in his voice was visceral. If I hadn't been mistaken for one, I would have thought an Intie was some kind of disgusting vermin.

"Too bad your stupid ass went and wailed on a VIP, then," Hernandez said.

I was pretty sure Simmons wouldn't be too aggrieved by the knowledge that I'd been attacked by one of his minions, but I wasn't going to volunteer that information.

"Come on." Hernandez tugged me away from Klein, and I followed because I had no other options. The man who'd volunteered to be my knight in shining armor had turned his back on me, so Hernandez was as close as I'd get to a savior. I'd take him.

"Thanks for helping me," I said. I limped beside him; a painful knot of muscle had formed in my leg where Klein had kicked me. He'd obviously been the punter for his football team. "I was just standing there when that asshole attacked me out of nowhere. What does Intie mean?"

Hernandez walked silently beside me for a while, then huffed. "Intie is short for international student. The campus was mostly empty when the Flare happened, except for the students who lived too far away to make it home. When I got here with the rest of the cadets, Simmons said they were volunteering to help maintain things, but some of them were reluctant. He told us we could stay if we helped him convince them to keep working."

Everything was happening too fast for me, and I

sincerely hoped I was still asleep on Simmons's deceptively comfy chaise. The pain radiating all over my body led me to believe otherwise, unfortunately. It was too much to process: fighting with Mykhail, being attacked, learning that Simmons had turned himself into some sort of dictator. It was outlandish, unbelievable almost.

I thought of Bina's and Altaf's frightened faces when I'd left and felt the world shift around me. The students were being forced to work against their will, and the line wasn't being drawn there.

"You realize that sounds like something from a video game or something, right? Mad professor takes over university!" I waved my hands in the air to emphasize the craziness, and to dispatch some of my nervous energy.

"If you think some know-it-all professor using students to do menial work is over the top, you have no idea what's really going on out there," he said grimly.

"You know what? Maybe I don't, although having had my ass beaten twice and almost being shot twice is more than enough. That doesn't change that what's going on here is fucked up. What's in it for you guys?"

He jerked his thumb up to the light we were walking under. "See that? Sweet, sweet electricity. Simmons has been using his pull with the board to have this campus flare-proofed for years. When we got here, all we knew was that we stumbled on a cool-ass oasis in the middle of the woods, and the only thing we had to do to stay was enforce a few rules."

"You guys have weapons though. Why didn't you just take over?"

"Because we're the brawn," Hernandez said. "I'm pretty fucking smart, but not egghead smart. Simmons is the one making the magic happen. He controls the electricity, keeps everything running and makes contact with the outside world. We don't have to do anything besides what we were trained to do." His jaw tightened. "Some of the cadets take other perks, but I'm not down with that."

"Wait. Contact...with the outside world?" I was worried about what he meant by "perks," but that was drowned out by the fact that he'd dropped a life-changing gift at my feet. When we'd discussed the mesh networks, we'd only talked about them on the structural level. I hadn't thought beyond intra-group communication because the idea of it seemed so unbelievable. My throat grew thick and I fought off crying for a second time that night.

For so long I had been in the dark, my life restricted to one house in the middle of the middle of nowhere. Leaving with Mykhail had been huge for me, but it hadn't opened up any grand vistas. But this...this was something I'd hoped for in my most sacred of fantasies, the ones I didn't voice aloud for fear that they wouldn't come true. When I spoke again, my voice was high and trembly, as if I was speaking into a fan. "There's still an outside world?"

That had been my greatest fear, the one that tormented me as I stared at the ceiling, unable to sleep, or watched my growing sister mope around the house sullenly when she should have been out learning to navigate the world. As time had passed in my family's house, it had started to feel like perhaps there wasn't anyone else besides us and the neighbors. That the whole world had shrunk down to that one point on the map and would never stretch back to its original size. Relief filled me up and pushed at my eyes and my nose, threatening to leak out.

"Yeah. Burnell is not the only place that had flare-proofed itself or with a mesh network set up. Apparently, Simmons was big on warning people about this kind of thing, so he has friends from all over who were prepped for this type of disaster. There are also some crazy survivalist dudes who think this was a government inside job. A few military bases. Some D.C. bigwigs with the Department of Energy working on rebuilding the infrastructure. But Simmons is the man with the plan right now, and they're all looking to him for help."

I thought about how casually he'd exerted his power when we'd met. He'd barely acknowledged the cadets, like a rich person who ignored the maid and pretended the dishes got washed by themselves. But if he was really the most important person to rebuilding right now, then it was hard to imagine how it hadn't gone to his head.

"If he's talking to government people, then there has to be some sort of plan, right?" I asked. "For rebuilding overall?"

"Hell if I know. I just go out on patrol, try to keep my head down." We were walking farther and farther away from the building where Mykhail was, and I hoped he was okay. Having my ass kicked, literally, and learning that the world might have a fighting chance made our argument seem less important. I had overreacted, but I hadn't been wrong. Until he figured himself out, I'd just have to operate under the assumption that he'd meant it all those times when he said there was no future for us. Tormenting myself with the why of it didn't matter, not when we had bigger problems to deal with.

I imagined Arden pretending to catch the Holy Ghost, flailing and acting a fool, like she sometimes did when I revealed I could actually reflect on myself instead of just managing her life. Maybe Simmons had contacts in California, where her parents were, and it would be possible to contact them. A whole exciting range of possibilities had just been made possible by this new information.

I reined in my frazzled emotions before speaking again. "Thanks. You didn't have to tell me all that."

"I'd want to know what was going down if I ended up someplace like this," he said, and then gave me a surprisingly cherubic smile. "You remind me of my bro. I hope someone is looking out for him." His smile disappeared. "When I saw Klein going after you, I thought… Look, it's not safe for you to be walking around here alone, man."

My stomach dropped at the implication. I thought of Arden again, of how she shook the night she finally told me what had happened to her—or almost happened to her—when I'd been knocked out. "Is that one of the perks you mentioned?"

He closed his eyes for a moment, then nodded.

I'd been friends with a circle of international students in college, and even though many of them were rich expatriates in the U.S. for a good time, a lot of them had escaped from fucked-up situations in destabilized countries. The thought of people coming here only to be faced with abuse from people who were supposed to protect them was even more horrifying. Bina's and Altaf's joined hands flashed in my mind.

"Like I said, if you think these Inties having to do some brain work is the worst of it, then you have no idea."

21

Hernandez dropped me off at what looked like a Berkshires vacation cottage just outside the campus green. "This place used to house visiting faculty or something. But it's pretty nice. There's a little library with books and stuff to keep you busy."

I didn't think I'd be settling down with a cozy mystery for the night, not having learned what I had. I wasn't going to tell Hernandez that though. I had a good feeling about him, but he was still one of the people allowing this travesty to go on.

He showed me around, and I settled in the nicest bedroom in the house. It was tastefully appointed with a large mahogany bed and wallpaper covered with a delicate, almost indiscernible herringbone pattern. If I was going to be miserable and lonely, I could at least do it in style.

Hernandez and I stood in the kitchen after he was done showing me around. I was exhausted and my thigh still burned with pain every time I walked, but it seemed rude asking him to leave after he'd saved me. "So, do you want to stay for coffee?" His eyes widened, and I waved a hand in his direction. "Real coffee, not the euphemistic kind. I have enough drama in my life, so much so that boning a soldier on the kitchen table just sounds too exhausting to even consider."

He laughed. "Man, my brother would love you. If things don't work out with you and glasses dude, I'm gonna have to hook you guys up when things are back to normal."

I thought of Mykhail, but not to wallow in sadness. There was that hypothesis of his that people would help each other through this crisis and how it had been disproven time and time again. Hernandez seemed to be an outlier though, and thank goodness for that. I smiled at him. "If your brother is anything like you, send him my way. I come with very illustrious recommendations."

He got all aw shucks for a second before declining the coffee. Before leaving me, his tone turned serious. "Be careful if you go outside alone again. A few of the other cadets are cool, but others won't give a second thought to punching your face in. Or worse." A familiar buzz sounded, and he reached into his pocket and pulled out a cell phone.

I thought of Bina and Altaf and hoped they were okay. Hope wasn't enough.

Hernandez left, having been called for guard duty at

one of the dorms where students were being held.

When I was alone, I inspected the house once again, checking the phones for dial tones and the computer for internet connections. The cadet was nice, but I wasn't naive enough to take everything he said at face value. I even went down into the basement and hit the jackpot when I found a handheld radio. For months, what I now knew to be the effects of the Flare had been messing with radio signals. But the auroras had faded, and perhaps other effects had too. I turned the dial slowly and when I finally heard the sound of a human voice instead of buzzing static, I nearly jumped out of my skin.

"—ing. This is WBUM, home of Burnell U's greatest hits. If you hear this message, you're close to the university. *Do not* come here. This place is not safe. This is a recording. This is WAFN—" I switched the radio off and left it on the shelf where I found it.

I couldn't think about who'd recorded that message or what had happened to the person who'd recorded it. I was stuck on the campus for one night at the very least, and it seemed I couldn't attempt an escape without risking another beating. All it took was one well-placed kick to make you fear another one. Worry settled on my shoulders as fatigue set in. I didn't think Simmons would let any harm come to Mykhail, but what if I was wrong? And then there was the problem of the Inties. I couldn't just make a run for it after seeing the looks on Bina's and Altaf's faces; it wasn't so much the fear, but the acceptance of their fate.

I did my best thinking in the shower, so I made my way into the bathroom attached to my room and hoped against hope as I turned the knob on the shower to hot and pulled. After a stuttering start, water cascaded from the showerhead. I peeled off my clothing and stepped under the spray, which was already lukewarm and getting hotter by the moment. It felt weird wasting water, but I reminded myself that I wasn't at home, where Gabriel monitored water usage like a hawk. Besides, if there was a chance Simmons would be taking a cold shower as a result, it was the least I could do.

For a moment, I was immobilized by regret. The big house, fancy room and amazing shower were nice, but there was no one to be excited about it with. I regretted leaving my family behind. I regretted that I'd lashed out at Mykhail instead of calmly asking him what was going on. I exhaled my grievances in a long sigh. Now wasn't the time for regrets; I needed to come up with something big and, unlike in an RPG, there was no save point to return to if my plan didn't work out. Whatever I came up with, I'd have to make sure it worked because it wasn't just my life at stake now.

I soaped myself up as my thoughts churned, gently because I was still tender where Klein had landed his blows. The cramped muscle in my thigh wasn't going to go away on its own, so beneath the steaming water I pressed both thumbs into the hard ball of muscle and tried to work it out as best I could. I let out a loud, therapeutic "Fuck!" and tears sprang to my eyes, but I kept at it. If I had to run, which I couldn't rule out given what I knew about this place, I wouldn't be able to do it without getting rid of the knot first. As a bonus, with all my energy focused on the brutal cramp, I had no room for thoughts of Mykhail or Simmons and his army of cadets. I let the pain clear my mind and tried to focus on how to free the Inties, stop Simmons and save the day in general.

When the knot was broken up and I could move my leg somewhat normally, I stepped out of the shower. I groped for a towel in the steamy bathroom, then tied it around my waist and wandered into the bedroom, hoping my insomnia would give me a reprieve. I'd come up with nothing while in the shower, and being cracked out from lack of sleep wouldn't help matters. Besides, my brain deserved a break from reality in the safety of a dark, dreamless sleep.

Or a really vivid daydream. I entertained the possibility that the ibuprofen I'd found in the medicine cabinet had gone bad because I seemed to be having some kind of hallucination.

Mykhail sat on the bed, cross-legged with his elbows at his knees and his chin resting on his fists. A rectangular box sat near his toes. I should have been frightened or annoyed, exhibited some sense of self-preservation, but he was the only thing connecting me to the real world in this strange place and I was flooded with happiness at the sight of him.

"Hey," he said. "One of the soldiers, Hernandez I think his name is, told me you were here. I heard some strange noises coming from the shower, so I ran in here ready to fight off an attacker. Then I realized maybe you were, uh, doing something else. With someone else." His eyes darted toward the towel hanging on my waist, then down to the duvet spread over the bed as if he was searching the swirling patterns that covered it for signs of life.

"Well, you missed your chance to stop an attacker for me earlier this evening. I got a post-beatdown muscle cramp and was massaging it out in the shower, *alone*, which is much less enjoyable than what you're imagining." I kept my words light; how else could you talk about someone punching and kicking at you as if you were something less than human? I wanted to tell him about the Inties, and my conversation with Hernandez, and how much it hurt when he'd left me standing in the hallway of an administrative building, but more than that I wanted be near him. I walked over and sat on the other end of the bed, daintily adjusting my towel over my knees. A bit of thigh was left exposed, but I wasn't above using my male wiles against him.

When I looked over at him, his eyes were wide behind his glasses. I'd only been apart from him for a few hours, but it seemed I'd forgotten what a shocking shade of blue they were, light refraction be damned.

He leaned forward and touched his fingertips to my solar plexus. "That bruise wasn't there yesterday." His voice was low as he circled the blossoming patch of purple with a fingertip. He pressed it just the slightest bit, and I winced. He pulled his hand away, blinking rapidly as if that would change what he saw.

"If you're intent on feeling up my bruises, I much prefer you go for the one on my butt."

He didn't smile, and for once I was glad of it. I had to joke in order to survive; that he cared enough not to laugh along with me made the pain a little more tolerable.

"Who did this to you?" he asked. "This happened after... I should have..." His jaw snapped shut, and I could tell he was gritting his teeth against an outburst. I thought of what I would instruct Arden to do if she came to me with the same dilemma, and then I applied that advice to myself.

"Remember what you said to Darlene that last night? About the manual?" I placed a hand on his knee, insatiably drawn to touch him as much as he generally seemed to be with me. "You couldn't have predicted what would happen. There's no one telling you how to navigate all this stuff. Me neither. I might have a bit of a jealousy problem, in case you didn't notice." I took a deep breath, then released the next words. "But you did shut me out as soon as you saw Simmons, and it made me feel like an idiot after what we had shared. I deserve an explanation."

I felt an odd surge of shame in the aftermath. Sometimes asking for what was due to you was harder than accepting whatever bullshit people sent your way. But this was important. Mykhail was important. If things were going to work out between us, nothing more than honesty would do. It was my turn to be the open book.

"You're right." He sighed, shifted uncomfortably. "I really do look up to Simmons as my mentor, and I was uncomfortable showing affection to you because of that."

The forgiveness I so desperately wanted to dispense

well up within me—until he kept talking.

"Mostly because of that." He looked at me, then looked away, embarrassed. "I did have a crush on Dr. Simmons when I worked under him. Today, even though I didn't feel that way toward him anymore, I fell back into the old pattern we'd established before I left."

Under him? When I'd confessed my jealousy, part of me had wanted to hear that I'd been totally off base. I'd thought Mykhail would reassure me that I'd just been paranoid and there had been nothing between him and Simmons, but that didn't seem to be the case. I mean, wasn't that always what happened when you told a boy you liked that you were jealous of someone else?

I withdrew my hand from his knee with a surprised "Oh," and he grabbed it loosely in his, exerting just enough pressure so I couldn't pull away. "Everyone had a crush on him," he explained. "He has this way of making you feel like you're so important when you talk to him. Plus, there aren't that many people in our field who are that smart and that attractive."

"Just you two, then," I said. "Okay, continue."

He pressed on. "I was his favorite from the first day of Cosmology 101. When I started working with him, he always asked for my opinion or for my assistance with his projects. It made me feel good that this guy who was so respected in our field would show any interest in me. *Me!* After a lifetime of being told everything I did was wrong, here was a man who was constantly giving me positive reinforcement.

And he had a nice ass too."

"I can't argue with that," I said morosely.

He flashed me an apologetic grimace and ran a hand through his hair. "Sorry. It's just, when I left the facility after Baba died, I was completely untethered. I thought maybe I should come back here because I knew he wouldn't turn me away. And maybe something more would happen. Not necessarily because I wanted him in that way, but because I had my exit plan. I figured if I wanted to try…well, anything, before I went through with the plan, it should be with a man I admired."

"And then I jumped you in a dark garden and ruined things for you." The familiar weight of humiliation clamped around my neck.

"Don't, Jang-wan," Mykhail said. "I told you I was glad about everything that happened between us. When I decided to come here, and it was a vague notion at best, I didn't imagine some grand love story between me and my mentor. I thought I'd see if I could help, and in our downtime maybe I'd discover what I'd been missing out on all these years. I hadn't even planned on making it here, to be honest. But then I met you, and I didn't care anymore. I thought I had feelings for Dr. Simmons, but I only admire him. With you—well, everything is different with you."

"You don't admire me?" I asked. I couldn't ask what I really wanted to. Not yet.

"I do," he said, and his voice was fervent.

He squeezed my fingertips. "But there's something more there. Something I never accounted for even in my wildest fantasies of what a relationship could be. I didn't know one person could connect with another like this. You have to understand, you've really thrown a wrench in my gears."

His words feathered over me, dusting away the distrust and apprehension that had settled over me since our argument in the administrative building. "That's all well and good, but are you still planning on..." I couldn't say it. The pad of his thumb swept under my eye, wiping away the tears that had spilled out before I could stop them. "Just thinking about it makes me want to vomit, and I have an excellent gag reflex." I squeezed his fingertips back—three quick pulses, three slow ones, three quick again. I wondered if he knew Morse code or thought my S.O.S. was simply jumpy nerves.

He shook his head. "I thought I'd figured everything out, and it made my life much simpler. It wasn't so much a suicide pact as throwing myself out into the world and hoping someone would do me a favor. I thought I was finally making some definitive choice, but in reality I was still following rules and still putting my life in the hands of others." He grimaced, as if that realization had just dawned upon him as he spoke. "I don't think that's what I want anymore, but this is still fundamentally unfair to you. I don't know if I can live a normal life after what I've done, and you can't heal me with great sex alone. There's no magic off switch inside me."

"We won't know until we check." I got the joke out, even though my vocal cords were strained by emotion. "Not to brag, but I'm positive I could find some spots that would make you reevaluate your life choices."

His head snapped back on a laugh that caught him unawares, and his knee jostled the box beside him. The sound of small objects sliding over cardboard caught my attention. He'd made a stop in the library, it seemed.

"Risk." I dragged my fingers over the faded edges of the box and raised my eyes to meet his. "So you still want to learn?"

"No," he said, holding my gaze as he lifted the lid and placed the game board down on the bed between us. "I want to win."

There was mischief in his gaze, and something else beneath it that allowed me a cautious optimism.

"I'm not going to go easy on you," I warned.

"Are you saying that I'm in for a pounding?" he asked, then laughed again at my shocked expression. "Come on, don't think I could be around you for this long without picking up some dirty wordplay."

"Stay in your lane, Rabbit." I reached over the game board and poked him in the rib.

He cracked his knuckles. "We still have a lot to talk about. About Dr. Simmons, and this place. But for right now, it's you, me and the board."

22

"Ah, nai tebe kachka kopne!" Mykhail muttered as he flopped back onto the bed and pulled a pillow over his face, yet another victim of my masterful game-playing skills.

"Another Baba-ism?" I asked, collecting the pieces and putting them back into the box. After I'd put on clothes—I may or may not have "accidentally" flashed a cheek as I'd slid on my pants—we'd played a brisk two-person game. Although he'd learned to be more aggressive, I'd still beaten him soundly.

"Yeah," came the muffled response. "It roughly translates to 'may you be kicked by a duck.'"

Maybe it was the lack of sleep or my giddiness over our oasis of normality, but the ridiculousness of the proverb sent me into hysterics. I laughed, even though it compounded the ache in my torso. I collapsed next to him, and when I wiped the tears of mirth away he was looking at me with a faux serious expression on his face.

"Are you done gloating yet?"

"Look, I had to win at something tonight. Since I can't exactly take on a soldier in training, I'll have to stick to board games." I hoped my switch back to the serious shit wasn't too abrupt. I'd allowed us an hour or so of respite and reconnection, because whatever happened next needed us both on the same page. I still hadn't figured out exactly what needed to be done, but when I did, if things didn't go according to plan at least I'd have had an excellent final night.

Mykhail sighed and then rolled onto his side to face me. After trying to get comfortable unsuccessfully, he lifted his head, pulled off his glasses and settled down again. "Back to business, huh? I was hoping we could keep living out this little fantasy. Our own house, where we play board games before bed and do unsanitary things on every available surface."

"Wait, I remember the game. When did the other part happen?" I patted at my crotch as if he'd availed himself of it without my knowledge.

"In my imagination, when you stepped out of the bathroom with only that little towel around your waist and your hair slicked back." He ran a hand through my strands, cradling the back of my head in a way that was unbearably tender. "But that will stay a fantasy for now, because we need to talk about some things."

He was so close to me now, and his words coaxed back to life something that had begun to wither in our short time apart. I thought of the flowers in my mother's garden, the ones that only unfolded their petals and opened to the world when in full sunlight. I wondered if at each sunset they felt the same sharp ache I'd experienced when Mykhail had walked away from me. He was here now, and I wanted to bask in his presence, drink in the heat and light of him. I considered pulling him close and showing him how much better a joining could be when we had a soft bed beneath us, but there was no time for the leisurely exploration I had in mind. The tightening at my groin would have to be ignored.

"I'm taking a rain check on that fantasy," I said, snuggling closer to him.

He nodded, his forehead resting almost against mine. "So, there's full power here because of Simmons's work with the Electrical Grid Initiative. He's been in contact with other survivors and government agencies too." His eyes were locked on mine, warm with some emotion that didn't match his words. "You don't seem surprised," he added.

"Because I know that stuff," I said. I couldn't help it; I kissed the tip of his nose just because I could. "You weren't the only one gathering information."

He tilted his head up and kissed me on the lips. It was a soft kiss, not something designed to seduce, but I felt the thrill of it all through my body. He sighed and closed his eyes for a moment before speaking again. "You wondered if the Flare was a worldwide event. According to current knowledge, it was."

His words were shocking, but his closeness and the way we held each other softened the blow. I'd suspected that was the case, but having that suspicion confirmed left me with a hollow feeling inside. All those stats on world overpopulation popped into my head. The human race had been billions strong and growing. "The government people he's spoken with? Do they have any numbers on casualties? Has the government been enacting any kind of plan, or has it been every man for himself, like what we've experienced?"

He was in science-nerd mode now, but lacking the buoyant, effusive energy he'd displayed before. "Obviously, the more dependent on electricity a place was, the harder it was hit. But they're thinking millions worldwide. In high-density areas, people have died off from food scarcity, accidents, loss of access to medical care. It's pretty grim, but they're starting to have some scale of the work ahead."

I suppressed the nausea that swiftly followed his words and pushed the info to the back of my mind. It was easier than I thought. The number was so huge that it was rendered unbelievable. Millions dead? Classmates, teachers, exes, all gone and likely not in a pleasant passing. A knot of anxiety twisted in my stomach; there was something more pressing. A problem I could actually do something about. Of course I couldn't do it alone. I would have to trust the man lying next to me, the man who'd unwittingly stomped on my heart that very same day. I took a deep breath and released it. "Mykhail, do you know about the students still here on campus?"

"Dr. Simmons told me there were students who hadn't

been able to make it home who're volunteering to keep everything running, and that the cadets were helping too." He seemed impressed by the idea instead of horrified, meaning either he was a sociopath or he had no idea of the truth about the students. Fucknuts. That meant I'd have the fun job of ruining his illusions. He continued, "I was weirded out by the cadets at first, but it seems like this place is proving my hypothesis right."

"That's what he told you? That they're volunteers?"

Something in my voice must have given it away. His hand slid from my head down to my arm, as if he sensed I was about to land a blow and was bracing himself for it.

"Rabbit, the cadet who attacked me thought I was one of those students," I said.

"I don't understand." Worry lines crinkled his smooth forehead. "Why would he attack you if he thought you were supposed to be here?"

"Because the students aren't free to go where they like. They're being forced to help Dr. Simmons, and he allows the soldiers to treat them however they want. I met two postdocs and they were so scared, Mykhail. I don't know what happened to them after I left. I don't know what would have happened to *me* if Hernandez hadn't intervened in my attack. He had some rather unpleasant ideas on the outcome, but I won't go into them."

Mykhail looked at me for a long time and then sat up in bed. His back was to me now, so I couldn't see his expression. "So Hernandez told you that the students here, at Burnell University, are essentially being held prisoner. By Dr. Simmons."

I suddenly wished I'd taken longer to thrash him at Risk. I cleared my throat, scratched the damned itch at my nose. "Yes. He said that most of them are international students who were left with no place to go. They're helping Simmons keep the electricity going and maintaining his communication network."

"And you believed all of this?" His back was rigid, like a shield, and I hoped my words weren't deflecting off it.

I sat up beside him and saw our reflections in the mirror above the dresser. Both of us were so tense that it looked as if someone had plopped a couple of lawn statues on the bed. I met his gaze and took a deep, shaky breath. "Yes. I believe him."

He rolled his shoulders back, then up into his signature shrug. "Well, then I believe him too."

I turned my head and met his gaze again, this time without the mirror as an intermediary. I'd expected a bit more resistance. He grabbed his glasses and put them back on and then reached out for me with one hand, absentmindedly, as he stared off into the distance.

"It makes sense, actually. I was with Simmons for so long today because he was catching me up, telling me which aspects of his research had worked out, and which hadn't. He wanted me to take the lead on some of the projects, like tracking Flare activity, so he could focus on microgrid stuff." His hand moved soothingly on my leg as he recalled their discussion. "That part was great. It was just like old times, conjecturing and bouncing ideas off one another. Then things got weird." He rocked from side to side and then seemed to catch himself in the nervous motion, pulling himself straight. "Simmons started talking about 'us' and 'them.' About finally having the government by the balls, and how he would get the respect he's always deserved now. It sounded kind of like..."

"Like a stock villain from an old movie? Did he twirl his moustache as he told you all this?"

Mykhail's hand stilled. "No. His hands were kind of busy. That's when he started asking about you and whether I'd gotten over my hang-ups. And then he kissed me."

"Excuse me?" The words came out long and exaggerated. A violent burst of anger combusted in my stomach.

Mykhail smiled at me, even though I didn't see the slightest thing funny about the situation. "He kissed me, Jang-wan. I didn't kiss him. There was no tongue or anything, so don't get mad." The fact that he chose this point in time to deploy his easygoing side wasn't making it easy to follow that rule.

I crossed my hands over my chest and nodded. "Why would I get mad? It's not like we're exclusive or anything. You can do whatever you want." I'd been crazy to imagine that he wouldn't want to sow his wild oats. I hadn't thought he'd go into detail about it though.

He sighed and raised his fingertips to his forehead as if he was tired. "I didn't feel anything."

"Maybe he should work on his technique," I said with earnest cattiness.

"Can you just listen? I didn't feel anything when the guy I'd put on a pedestal kissed me and asked me if I wanted to work with him on a groundbreaking project. I said no."

It took a moment for his words to make their way past the mental bristles I'd emitted to protect myself. "Why would you say no to that? Didn't we come all this way to help him?"

"I do want to help, but not to bolster someone's ego. Dr. Simmons has done some fantastic work, but I didn't like the way he talked about rebuilding the grid. He made it seem more like a barter than the free dispensing of information in a time of need. I cannot be a part of that."

It was corny, but I felt actual pride in him. I had thought I'd have to win him over to my side, but he'd already decided not to work with Simmons without the knowledge of the Inties and their plight. I couldn't help but point out the sad hypocrisy of the situation though. "So after all the years of fighting against the monopolization of electricity by the industry, he's now monopolizing electricity? How quaint."

Disappointment carved a frown onto his face. "He was the only person besides Baba who ever believed in me. And now this is what he's become." His voice was tight when he went on. "Do you know how far we could be into the rebuilding process if he'd begun coordinating earlier instead of power-tripping? Do you know how many lives could have been saved?"

I disliked Simmons, but I wished he'd been the good guy, if only to spare Mykhail the pain of losing yet another person important to him.

"I'm sorry he's not the man you thought he was," I said. I thought of Mykhail desperately trying to fix the generator at his baba's facility. Of how he must have toiled to keep those people alive, and how in the end he'd failed, and all the while Simmons had been living like the dictator of a banana republic, complete with an army and slaves. Simmons was far worse than the mountain men who'd attacked Arden and me, or Dale, who'd tried to take my family's home. Those men had been in the throes of desperation and illness. Simmons was a victim of his own ego, and everyone around him was paying the price.

Mykhail shoved both hands into his shaggy hair and pulled them away in frustration when his fingers got caught in the tangled mass. His leg bounced restlessly, like the animal I referred to him as. He obviously had something else to say. "After I told him no, I just wanted us to leave, you and me. Then I realized you might not want to leave with me. You might not want anything to do with me. I came looking for you so I could ask— Ugh, I don't know how this is supposed to work! We were supposed to part ways after we got here. You'd have had your adventure, I'd have had some fun. But things are different now." His eyes were glossy behind his lenses. "I don't want to say goodbye to you."

My breath caught at his words, and my heart and my brain fought an epic battle of wills. He was inexperienced and volatile, but also kind and smart as hell. He'd kissed another man but now here he was, declaring…something to me. That he didn't want to be without me. I wasn't sure if that was the same thing as wanting to be *with* me, and the difference was crucial.

I was overwhelmed with emotion as I processed his confessions. Happiness, fear and desire struggled to rise to the top, but self-preservation won out in the end. "Mykhail, you know how I feel. But I can't settle. Not even for you." The way his eyes grew wide at my words made me want to take them back, but this needed to be said. "I don't want your affection because Simmons isn't the man you thought he was. I don't want you to hold on to me because you're afraid to be alone. If we're going to be together, I can't live in fear that I'm an experiment that's about to lose its funding."

He nodded, not exactly in agreement, but in a way that said he was processing data. "After I walked away from you, I felt almost as bad as I did when I left the facility. Worse, even," he said. "My grandmother is dead. There's nothing I can do to change that. But you…if I lost you now…. it would be like what I talked about before. Like when the stars eventually push away from each other and space is just a dark, empty void. No more brilliant, blinking light that fills you with wonder and makes you hope."

A painful throb in my chest underscored his words and I bit my lip against my rising emotion. Mykhail's eyes were bright, his words fervent. He was speaking with that same passion that possessed him when he discussed something that truly moved him, and right now he was talking about me.

"What exactly are you saying?" I asked. My voice was subdued compared to the raw emotion behind his declaration, but only because the gravity in the room had apparently shifted and was compressing me from all sides.

Mykhail wasn't suffering from the same problem. His hands cupped and lifted my face quickly. His nose butted against mine and then his mouth found its destination and I was suddenly weightless. The kiss was eager, his tongue persistent, and the whimper of relief he made when I allowed him entry nearly brought me to tears. I opened my eyes to find him watching me as we kissed, as if he was scared I would slip away if he so much as blinked. I wrapped my arms around him to reassure him that I wasn't going anywhere.

"I want to be with you," he said when he finally pulled away from me. "I know I messed up, and I might mess up again because I have no idea what the hell I'm doing. But you aren't some kind of runner-up medal for me. I guess what I want to know is, where do we go from here?"

Mykhail's face was a rictus of earnest agony. Even for someone who routinely surprised me with his openness, this was putting it all out there at an advanced level. His words vibrated in the silence of the room, the immenseness of them crowding out the conflict that had seemed insurmountable earlier in the day.

But this was about more than my happiness and whether we could make it as a couple now. I shifted to avoid something pressing into my still-sore thigh, something small and plastic. The thumb drive Bina had given me. As I stared into his eyes, the plan that had eluded me all night popped into my head fully formed. I knew what we had to do.

"Rabbit." I reached a hand out to him and he took it between his. "Before we can go forward, I have to ask one favor of you."

"Is this going to be my knight's quest in order to win your hand?" he asked. He sounded almost eager.

I laughed indulgently. "Something like that."

He slipped off the bed and kneeled before me. "What do you desire, fair Jang-wan?"

I took a deep breath and then spit out the words I hoped I wouldn't regret. "I need you to go back to Simmons, Sir Rabbit."

23

I was nervous as I followed a campus map toward the building I'd heard Hernandez mention during his phone call. It was strange seeing lights along the path and in the windows of empty buildings. Nighttime now meant darkness to me, or candlelight, or the fluorescent oblong that spread before a flashlight. All of these lights on seemed excessive and made me feel like the twitchy uncle who followed you around the house turning lights off to keep the electric bill down. They also made it much harder for me to move about without being seen, which was kind of necessary.

Go stealth, I mouthed to myself, thinking of the military games I'd played for years. I'd become a master of creeping, dodging, ducking and rolling, but only with my thumbs. The rest of me was better conditioned for a dance floor or, more honestly, for sitting in front of a computer. But all those hours of mental exertion had to translate into some real-world experience, right?

I wished I wasn't alone, that I hadn't sent Mykhail away, but there was no going back on the decision now. Besides, if I'd learned one thing from our little imbroglio, it was that sometimes you couldn't depend on others. I couldn't expect Mykhail to magically know if I was getting attacked and come track me down just because we'd swapped spit. I needed to channel my inner Clint Eastwood or, even better, my inner RuPaul, and simply depend on myself to make this shit work.

A noise startled me, and I dodged into the shadows, pressing myself against a building and behind some decorative shrubbery. I kept my breathing slow and controlled as I peered through the leaves.

The sound of a sob followed by a heart-wrenching whimper reached me first, and then Reilly's familiar voice drowned it out. "Cut it out it, would you? I told you it was going to hurt. But once you get stretched out a bit, things'll be easier."

Another man chuckled in the background. "Really, you need to take this up with your admissions office. If they had admitted more women into their programs, you wouldn't be in this situation right now."

They passed in front of me then, Reilly and another cadet. The man stumbling ahead of them turned back, and bile rose in my throat.

Altaf.

His clothes were disheveled and his hands covered his backside protectively. The two cadets pushed him forward, keeping him off balance and tripping over his own feet with their jabs at his back. His expression was devastating, as if instead of the campus before his eyes he was reliving whatever horror they'd just visited upon him. That was what had been happening as I lounged on a comfy bed and played board games.

The gun in the waistband of my jeans was warmed by my body heat and seemed to be burning into my back, reminding me it was there and could be of use. Again, I felt that horrific desire to hurt, to kill, to make these men pay for what they'd done with their lives. But not yet. Not ever hopefully, if things worked out as I planned. I hadn't signed up to be judge, jury or executioner—I was simply a facilitator.

But that didn't make it less devastating seeing Altaf, who had been smiling good-naturedly and treating me like an equal mere hours ago, debased this way. I wondered where Bina was and hoped she was safe but I couldn't believe that after what I'd just witnessed. When I'd led campaigns in online gaming, I'd often have to say things to my cohorts that validated my decisions, things that sounded good and eased minds when we were in intense situations. But no matter how realistic those games were in the moment, they were fictional. And so when I sent a silent message to Altaf, asking him to forgive me for not taking Reilly out then and there, the words rang hollow.

I waited until the sounds of their footsteps had faded into the other ambient night sounds of the campus—birds of prey and foraging creatures that overturned trash cans in search of a good meal. A doe grazing on weeds growing up between the stones in the pathway glared at me as I passed her two fawns. I was trotting past her when I heard yet another set of footsteps. Apparently, like any campus, the fact that it was the middle of the night didn't mean there wouldn't be people all over the place. Unfortunately, these cadets were much more dangerous than your average drunk frat bro. I froze, hoping the deer blocked me from view but not willing to get close enough to ensure it. A hoof to the face would put a major kink in my plans.

I heard a voice, just one word, but it was enough to pierce me with recognition. Mykhail. I peeked over the mass of the deer, breathing through my mouth to avoid her animal muskiness, to see Simmons walking with his hand on Mykhail's lower back. I had no idea where they were headed, but Mykhail was all smiles for his mentor. I shoved the ugly feelings welling up—anxiety, possessiveness, doubt—into a fear-proof jar inside me and sealed the lid. I trusted Mykhail and I trusted my plan. Everything else would fall into place because it had to.

The deer snorted and flicked her tail back and forth, showing she indulged my presence long enough, so I backed away from her, hoping neither Simmons nor Mykhail would turn around.

I passed a somewhat deranged-looking statue of a half-naked dude that I knew was supposed to be Galileo only because I'd seen it on a campus map. It meant I was close to the Heidelberg dormitory. I crept toward the building and hoped I was right, that I'd heard correctly and, most important, that my intuition wasn't way off. If it was, we were screwed.

There were two men stationed outside, playing a game of cards sitting on the stone steps that led into the building. They could have been any college guys shooting the breeze, save for the semiautomatic weapons that hung over their shoulders.

"Ha! Go fish, bitch," one of the guys said. There was a silence and then the same voice said, "Were you hiding that card up your ass? No fair."

Hernandez laughed then and stood. "I gotta piss. I'll give you a minute to get over losing a game made for five-year-olds." He walked down the steps and into the brush, and I followed. I wasn't sure how to sneak up on a trained soldier without him reflexively eviscerating me, so I just imitated the last guy who'd tried to cruise me as I hiked through the park.

"Come here often, sugar?" I said in a low voice.

Hernandez almost whirled, dick in hand, but I was spared from an unplanned golden shower when he saw me in his peripheral vision. "Jesus Christ, man," he whispered, eyes searching the surrounding area for signs of his comrades. "What are you doing here?"

"Funny you should ask. I'm here to save your soul."

24

"I told you to stay at the faculty house," he whispered. "I even sent your man over to you."

"Yes, and you also told me that you don't like what's going on. I don't want to stay here, but I can't leave in good conscience, knowing there's a group of people being held against their will. And that there are men like you being forced to take part."

His expression grew hard, and for a moment he was the strange man who'd burst into the chapel and forced Mykhail and me to come with him. "You think I'm going to betray my fellow cadets? That's not how things work. There's an order of command, and I follow whatever order is given, no matter what."

I stared at him, anxiety setting in as I searched for which tack to take. I couldn't believe that my read of a person could be so wrong, but Hernandez looked ready to blow me off, if not turn me in.

"I just saw a man being dragged in this direction after being raped by two of your cadets, so you can miss me with the 'code of honor' military bull," I said. He looked away from me, and there was the smallest softening of his furrowed brow. "I've been here for one evening. You must see shit like that night after night. It's not okay. Nothing is worth crushing another person's spirit, not electricity or hot water or a damned hot meal. Is this what you joined the armed forces for? To have atrocities committed under your nose and do nothing to stop them when given the opportunity?"

He glared at me. I could see sweat breaking out on his hairline and one of his eyes twitched from the agitation.

"What am I supposed to do?" he whispered harshly. "A few of us guys have tried to change things, but we're outnumbered. And even if it didn't mean turning against my friends, who I've spent the last year training with, there's Simmons to deal with. He isn't some idiot with a gun. He has *real* power, and he needs these students to keep this place going."

I'd thought of that too. It seemed hubristic at best to think I could just come in and save the day when someone like Hernandez hadn't been able to do it. But I'd been thinking since the moment he'd explained what an Intie was to me. I hadn't known exactly what to do until the solution had snuck into my room and presented itself to me.

"Give me your phone."

He hesitated only a moment before pulling it from his pocket and handing it over. He spoke as I swiped the screen and sent out the text that could make or break my entire game plan. "I think Altaf thought he was safe, that we respected him because of his work on the phone network. Reilly started messing with him last week though. I don't know what they did to him before, but tonight he could barely walk and there was blood on his pants."

The horror in Hernandez's voice bought back the terrible images of Altaf's face. It also fortified me. "I met him. And a woman named Bina. They're kind and intelligent, but even if they weren't they wouldn't deserve this. No one does. I haven't done shit but sit around and eat Twinkies since the Flare, but I'll be damned if I leave here without knowing I did everything I could to protect these students. And I'm not the one who took a vow to protect citizens."

I knew I could count on him to help when I saw his fists clench and his eyes narrow. He was ashamed, and that feeling went a long way in motivating most people.

"Yo, are you taking a shit out there?" I'd been so focused on Hernandez that I'd pretty much forgotten about his card partner. "You know there are toilets for that, you dirty fuck."

Hernandez's gaze flicked to me.

"We need more time," I said to answer the unasked question. I still hadn't gotten a reply, and although it had been only a few moments, I was already worried. "Come on, already," I growled at the phone right as Hernandez plucked it out of my hand.

"Alright," he said. "Get ready to put your drama club skills to use."

"How did you know I took drama?" I asked. Then he tackled me.

"Dammit, stay still!" he yelled, even though I'd gone stiff with shock. "MacKenzie, I've got another one who tried to escape out here. I'm bringing him in." He hauled me up off the ground, giving me the universal wide eyes and raised eyebrows that said "Get with the program" before pinning my arms behind my back.

"Ah! Sorry! I'm sorry!" I called out. "More accent," he whispered, and I mustered up my best Asian-kid-in-an-80s-film voice. "I sorry! No hit, no hit!"

"Maybe just don't talk, actually. That accent is terrible." I didn't have time to reply with indignation. He gave me a rough shove as he pushed me into view of his patrol partner, and then said, "I found this guy trying to come out of a back window. I'll take him inside."

The cadet he'd been playing cards with was a tall, lanky bean pole with an Adam's apple that nearly matched his nose in prominence. There was an awkwardness to him that might have marked him as sweet, until he opened his mouth. "Oh. Did you stick it to him back there or something? Seems like I'm the only one not getting any action tonight.

I might have to change that." His gaze ran over my body. "You want me to take him in?"

In that moment, I learned that the taste of dread was bile at the back of your throat while someone talked about using your body as if it was no big deal.

"Nah, Mackenzie. I got it."

The man winked at me as I walked by, and it nearly reduced me to tears. Not from fear, but from anger and the desire to pull out my handgun and end him right there. But if I did that, the list of people I had to murder would be endless, because in any lawless space, rape seemed to be a clear course of action for way too many people.

I thought of the woman who'd nearly shot Mykhail in the woods near Belleville. "Men who called themselves soldiers," she'd said. They were the ones who'd turned her from a Good Samaritan into a vengeful harbinger of death. The fact that I wasn't positive it was these cadets she had encountered, that it could have been other men, spoke volumes. For a moment, I nearly slipped into despair, but then Hernandez's phone vibrated and I remembered that there were good guys, too, and that I was with one of them.

He directed me up a flight of stairs and past another cadet who stood guard at the entrance to a long corridor of dorm rooms, much like the one I'd lived in freshman year at Rochester, except the doors had all been removed. In each room I passed there were two students, each on a twin bed. Most of them were sleeping, but in one room a woman sat on the floor, staring out into the hallway. I almost didn't recognize Bina. She had a ballpoint pen clutched in her hand, as if that would offer protection against cadets who wanted to hurt her. I gave her a nod, hoping she knew what it meant. *I used the thumb drive. I uploaded the application to my phone.* She didn't speak or nod back, but her gaze didn't leave mine until I'd passed. Even then, it felt as if a piece of the darkness that enshrouded her had been embedded in me.

I didn't know if my plan would work, but seeing such blatant pain made me positive that I'd just have to try another option if it didn't—and if I survived the failure. It also made me glad for the cadet named Klein's attack; without it, I likely never would have known what was going on. Arden had taken to saying the universe worked in mysterious ways, and I was starting to believe her.

Hernandez pulled me into a bathroom where all the mirrors had been removed. "Suicide prevention," he said when he saw my confusion. He whipped out the phone and read the text message, eyes widening as understanding took hold. "I knew I liked you," he said as he handed the phone to me.

I read Mykhail's message, sent from the track phone I'd passed to him before we'd parted ways and hoped he hadn't paid too dearly to get me the information. With shaking hands I dialed the number he'd provided me with, one of the few working numbers in the world right now.

It rang and rang, and my heart stopped beating at the thought that I would fail. But then a groggy voice picked up. "Lena Thorne, Department of Energy and National Reconstruction."

I was so shocked that someone had actually picked up that I lost my voice for a moment.

"Hello? Seriously, millions of people have died and phone resources are limited, but I manage to get a prank caller."

"Lena. Miss Thorne. Hi," I said, finding my voice. "I understand you've been trying to work with Dr. James Simmons out of Burnell University and coming up against a brick wall."

"Yes. That's right. Who is this?" There was caution in her voice, but I heard a rustling as if she was sitting up in bed. I didn't know whether the fact that she was tasked with taking incoming phone calls in the middle of the night meant she was low on the totem pole or high, but I was fairly confident she'd be interested in what I had to say.

"My name is Jang-wan Seong, and I'm about to make your night."

25

Apparently the people at the newly coined Department of Energy and National Reconstruction, and by extension the acting U.S. government, hadn't been too keen on Simmons's ultimatums. Lena Thorne had apprised me of the situation—they'd been planning to show up and commence a "negotiation" anyway, but once I explained the whole keeping foreign students hostage and allowing unsanctioned soldiers to use them as they saw fit situation, they stepped up their timetable.

Hernandez stashed me under one of the twin beds, out of sight of his fellow cadets. It wasn't the most uncomfortable place I'd ever slept—that dubious honor went to the brothel in Budapest I'd accidentally booked a room in during my study abroad trip—but I thought longingly of the pillow-top mattress at the faculty house I'd abandoned. Not that I'd get much sleep anyway. The tension of an impending rescue operation and the haunted looks of the Inties had made sleep even more impossible than usual. Mykhail's unknown status didn't help either.

I kept second-guessing myself and the plan we'd enacted; rather, the plan I'd enacted and Mykhail had gone along with. I didn't think Simmons would hurt him, but I didn't know how he'd react if he found out we were trying to end his run as big man on campus. I also didn't know what tactic had been used to get the crucial information out of him. How had Mykhail gotten that phone number? Worse, how had he distracted Simmons enough to take time to text me? Every femme fatale trading her body for information scene I'd ever watched marched through my brain, and on top of being jealous I felt like a pimp.

Mykhail had told me again and again that he was used to doing what he was told, and I had still sent him off into danger. Sure, I had a good excuse—freeing the students and trying to ensure that whatever crucial information Simmons had would be open source. But the people who'd asked him to kill them out of mercy, and who'd thus driven him to seek his own end, had excuses too. He'd agreed easily, too easily in retrospect, and I hoped he wasn't using his feelings for me to propel himself into danger, heedless of the outcome. When I thought of Mykhail possibly being handed over to the more sadistic of the cadets, of him being hurt or abused or killed, the small space under the bed seemed to press down on me. If anything happened to him... My throat grew rough and swallowing became painful at just the thought of it. I closed my eyes and called on whatever benevolent forces in the universe would take pity on a heathen like me. *Please let him be okay. Please let us get through this.* That everything could end now, before we'd had a chance to even do a simple thing like learn each other's birthdays, just wasn't fair.

I threw in an extra request—for Mykhail's safety and for him *not* to be a Scorpio.

I lay in the impersonal dorm room and listened to the sounds of boots parading down the hall. I felt like a body in a drawer at the morgue, not daring to check if Hernandez had been able to maintain his position as floor guard, lest I make eye contact with a cadet and give away my hiding spot. Even if Mykhail messaged, Hernandez was the one with the phone, and there was no way to get news of it without an interaction that could draw further attention.

Lying still was easy when it wasn't a necessity, and I'd even become somewhat of an expert at it during my reign as hide-and-seek champion, but every minute spent in that dorm was an agony of itching body parts, biological urges and self-recrimination. Dust went up my nose and I was fairly certain spiders had crawled into the waistband of my pants and begun building their webs in unmentionable crevices.

After a certain point, time lost all meaning. I convinced myself that everything that'd happened with Mykhail had been a dream, and that when I climbed out from under the twin bed I would still be in my room, with Maggie snoring quietly across the way. That I'd never tussled with a neurotic astronomer among the vegetables and kissed him beneath the Milky Way. That the thrumming in my chest was caused by a fantasy man who no one in reality would ever be able to live up to.

And that was when the tanks rolled in. The growl of military personnel carriers echoing off the distinguished buildings encircling the campus green was terrifying. The floor beneath me shook as the envoy passed by, and the uprisings I'd seen on the evening news flashed into my head. Smoke wafting through bombed-out buildings. People wailing. Dead bodies. I wanted to scramble from beneath the bed and run to the windows, but machine-gunfire froze me in place.

What have I done?

I hadn't thought the cadets would fight against their superiors, actual soldiers sent by the U.S. government. It wasn't as if this was the stronghold of some dictator. I'd been wrong. And if I'd been wrong about that, perhaps I'd been wrong about everything. Gunfire started again, in quick bursts, followed by orders to stand down. My throat began to itch and my eyes began to water, and I realized tear gas was wafting in through the window.

You've turned the campus into a war zone, and Mykhail and Hernandez could be dead because of you! The thought circled brightly around my mind like one of those news tickers at Times Square. I pushed it aside. The campus had already been a war zone. Now Lewis and his cadets were simply battling opponents who could fight back.

There was movement in the halls; students were coming out of their rooms, calling to each other in confused voices. Footsteps rushed into my room and for a minute I hoped I would see a pair of ratty Converse beside the bed. Instead, there were black combat boots. "Seong! Let's go!"

I let a brief relief wash over me. Hernandez, at least, was okay.

He'd heard my name when I'd spoken to Lena Thorne and now called me by my surname as if I was one of his comrades. The small gesture fished me out of the pond of doubt I'd been swimming in. This was the right thing to do. This wasn't the moment to get existential about good and evil. The bottom line was that Simmons was using students as chattel and allowing rape to be used as a method of keeping said chattel in line. I hoped there were no casualties, but I couldn't doubt that what I'd done was necessary.

I pulled myself out from under the bed and looked up at Hernandez and Bina, whom he carried piggyback-style. She gripped him tightly, without fear.

"He said that he was bringing me to you, so I allowed him to pick me up," she said, implicating that she could have stopped him if she wanted to. I thought of her holding the pen and my throat went tight.

"Are you okay, Bina?" I asked. Altaf's terrified face as Reilly taunted him flashed into my mind.

"My ankle is injured," she replied, which wasn't the same thing as saying "I'm okay."

Hernandez interrupted us. "Whichever jackass is in

charge of the day watch launched an attack instead of engaging when they saw the AMPVs driving up. I don't understand why they'd attack military vehicles, though. They could just be confused. Rumors have been spreading about a group of Doomsday Preppers who have access to some high-powered stuff and were pillaging like it was the fall of the Roman Empire." He glanced at me as I jogged beside him to keep up with his pace. "What's with the look? I went to college."

"And I'm proud of you," I said. "But where are we going? And have you seen Mykhail?"

"No, but I talked with a few of the other guys who hadn't been down with the behavior of the other cadets. We're circling up and meeting to initiate a group surrendering of arms. White flag and the whole deal. I think it's best if you're there, since you're the one who made this happen."

Bina stared at me as she clung to his back, but still she didn't speak. Her gaze was full of questions and something that made me want to hold her hand. Hernandez turned carefully, even though the frail woman seemed to weigh no more than a hill of beans. Now I could see the welts that encircled her arms and her calves that hadn't been there earlier. Her ankle was swollen and puffy. I briefly considered punching the wall or flipping the beds as anger, the useless corrosive kind, flooded me.

I'm sorry was what I wanted to tell her, but I didn't know if that would make things better or worse. I opted for saying, "Let's get the hell out of here."

As we made our way through the corridor, our pace slowed by the need to stop and clear every open door and every corner we turned, a sick panic weighed me down and urged me forward at the same time. If he still had the track phone, Mykhail should still have been able to call. Yet the phone Hernandez had relinquished to me was silent. Something was wrong, and if anything happened to him, it was my fault. I squeezed the phone in my clammy palm, willing it to vibrate so the tightness in chest could loosen. So I could breathe again.

The phone remained still.

The world outside the dorm had gone mad. The peacefulness of the campus was a memory, and now there was the smell of smoke and itch of tear gas. Drifts of fog from smoke grenades filtered over the green. We turned away from that chaos and headed toward the space behind the dorm, where calmness still reigned. A group of seven men were standing with guns in hand, ready to move, when one of them pointed off into the distance, to the place called Thinker's Point on the campus map I'd studied.

I knew before I turned that I wouldn't like what I saw, but that didn't dull the sensation of having my heart smashed beneath a sledgehammer. I could make out two men, one a bulbous-faced almost-redhead and the other a golden geek with sunlight reflecting off his glasses. That wasn't the only reflective object. Reilly was dragging Mykhail up the hill, a gun to his back.

I watched as Mykhail wriggled out of Reilly's grip, surprising the man.

"Yes!" I cried out like a spectator at a sporting event as Mykhail whirled and swung out his long arms and legs in Reilly's direction. He obviously wasn't a fighter, but he was putting all that gangliness to good use. He raised one arm up and bought it slashing down. Reilly gripped his arm, holding it as if to stanch blood. *A knife?* Then I remembered the sharp scrap of metal he'd broken off the satellite and tucked into his pocket. I didn't know what he'd intended to use it for, given all that I'd learned after, but now he was using it to fight back. Of course, he'd managed to convert a piece of space junk into a weapon. Sagan would be proud of him.

My brief surge of pride was short-lived. Mykhail was an astrophysicist, and Reilly was military. He overreached on one swing, and Reilly took advantage, using the butt of the gun to knock Mykhail to the floor.

I dropped to my knees as if I was the one who'd been hit. My fingers sank into the grass and earth, needing to clutch on to something to keep from toppling over. "No. No! One of you stop him, please!"

I looked back at the group of men, but none of them raised their weapons. Not even Hernandez.

"Why aren't you doing anything?" I shouted, heedless of the attention it would attract.

Reilly was pulling Mykhail up by his hair now, forcing him to his knees. It was too far to run, but they had guns. They could stop this madness. My handgun was useless. I was a fair shot with a rifle, and I could hunt like a motherfucker. But sharpshooting from this distance was something else entirely.

"He's our brother-in-arms," Hernandez said. "Mutiny is one thing. Actually hurting him is something we can't do. I'm sorry, Seong." His expression was tortured, as if the invisible bonds of fraternity made no sense to him either.

"Please," I begged to the blurry figures who swam in my tear-filled vision, but all of them were bound by the duty that had also prevented them from stopping this madness themselves. All save one.

"Put me down," Bina said.

"Bina—" Hernandez began, but she slipped out of his hold and limped toward me. The gun that had been pressed against her as he carried her had slipped off his back with her.

"That is your man on the hill? With that fucker Reilly?" she asked. Her accent rendered the words lyrical, although it was a song of rage and defiance they sung.

"Yes," I said, confused.

She nodded and then kneeled beside me in the grass. Her back was straight and her form was damn near perfect as she took aim at Reilly. "These boys are cadets," she said. "*I* was a soldier."

I couldn't help the tears that ran down my face then. A miracle. I was watching a fucking miracle.

The group of men murmured in both shock and annoyance at their emasculation, but it was mostly posturing. Their awe was evident.

Bina squinted and shook her head angrily. "Ah, fuck. There's no sight on this gun, and I can't see clearly at this distance," she said. "I don't want to risk hitting the blond. But I will still try if you want me to. The risk at this distance, with this wind and that upward trajectory, will make things much more difficult though."

The relief that had just started to well up in me dried like a puddle in the desert. There was no way we could move closer. There was no time. Reilly raised his gun…and a memory of Mykhail, ever fucking nerdy and resourceful Mykhail, flashed into my mind.

"Wait," I said and reached over her shoulder. I wiggled my fingers in front of her face and curled them into a loose fist, making the space between my fingers smaller and smaller until she said, "Yes! That is perfect. Okay. Okaaaay. *Un. Deux. Trois.*" And with an exhale on the last word, she pulled the trigger.

I closed my eyes, not opening them even after the sharp report left my ears ringing and the scent of gunpowder burned my nose.

"Holy shit," Hernandez breathed.

When I looked over at Thinker's Point, Reilly was no longer in sight. Neither was Mykhail. I leaped to my feet, heart lodged too far in my throat for any words to make their way through. Had she fired too late? Had Reilly's finger been on the trigger when the bullet hit him? I felt dizzy, the bad kind of dizzy that made you want to barf and then curl up into a ball. I took a step forward and stumbled because my knees were like jelly. A support shored me up from one side. Bina. I hugged her tightly to me, the woman who'd been through so much and still managed to give a little of her strength to me.

A moment passed, and then another, and then a golden halo almost brighter than the sun rose in the tall grass and kept rising. Mykhail stood, one arm raised in the air in victory.

I don't remember screaming in relief—Hernandez told me about that later. Everything else was blotted out when Mykhail held up one half of his broken glasses to his eye, looked my way and smiled. Then I was running and he was running and somewhere in the middle we met mouth-first.

"I found my glasses!" he shouted, as if that was the most important event that had just occurred.

The first kiss he'd initiated, the kiss of a man resigned to death, had been devastatingly good. The one he gave me now was a million times better. There had always been the sense that Mykhail was light-years away, even when we were together, but now I was out there with him. We were on an undiscovered planet teeming with life and possibility.

"You fought him," I said when we took a breath. "You didn't let him kill you."

Mykhail stroked his fingers through my hair, pushing it out of my face. His fingertips gently traced over my brow bone, down to my jaw. His eyes were wide, and in the sunshine I could see how the blue was more than that, a mélange of blue and green and brown that resembled the photos of faraway galaxies in my astronomy book. "Funny, but a death march can really make you reevaluate the whole death wish thing." He hadn't stopped touching me, his fingers curving behind my ears as they tucked my hair away and then stroking my jaw, my neck, my shoulders. I reveled in the calming caresses. "I still have a few things to live for. I mean, I don't even know if I'm a top or a bottom yet. How can I die without testing some hypotheses first?"

"Do you need a lab partner?" I asked, locking my arms behind his back to pull him closer to me. A percussion grenade went off somewhere in the distance. He looked over his shoulder before grabbing my hand and running toward Hernandez, Bina and the other defectors.

"I already have one," he said. "He's also designing our lab coats. Leopard-print trim."

I knew there was a ton of work ahead. According to Lena, reconstruction had begun in earnest and they needed all the help they could get. There would be more death to deal with, more people who wanted to hurt us and many bumps on the road to recovery. But despite all that, I smiled.

Mykhail had given me the biggest gift of all—not the handjob, or the kiss, or the wonderful floating sensation as we ran down the hill together.

Because of him, I was ready to go home.

EPILOGUE

Four months later...

My parents would never admit to anything so romantic, but I was certain they'd bought the cabin just for its spectacular views of the foliage. It was the only reason I could think of for choosing such an isolated location, although that had worked in our favor in the long run. Now that the windows were no longer boarded up, you could see the surrounding woods for miles around.

Outside my bedroom, the sun was rising and the trees were at peak autumn fabulosity, an orange, red and gold explosion that spread across the forest as far as the eye could see. Stands of deciduous trees provided complementary splashes of green, little islands of subdued color in the fiery sea.

A long arm reached up and pulled me back down

on the bed, and I turned to find Mykhail watching me. His hair was mussed, his eyes were squinted, creases from his pillow crisscrossed his face and I was sure he hadn't brushed his teeth before bed last night. Despite all that, my waning morning wood still tried to make a comeback at the sight of him. His smile, halitosis and all, still made my stomach do a little shimmy of delight.

"Couldn't sleep?" His morning voice was rough and husky, a contrast to the concern in his eyes. He tugged me closer, tucking me against him and pulling the comforter over us. This was our usual morning position, but it still gave me pause every time.

Is this real? Is it possible to be this comfortable with someone? But those sounded like the questions Mykhail used to ask me when we'd first started out, so I never voiced them. I had to maintain my air of authority, even if my relationship with him was like nothing I'd experienced before.

"I could, surprisingly. I just woke up a bit early because I was dreaming about the next phase of the initiative. I figured if I was going to worry, I might as well have something nice to look at." I ran a hand over his chest, the familiar terrain soothing my jangled nerves. His rueful laugh vibrated through my palm.

"After all the planning you've done, there's nothing to be worried about. I know Lena is a ball buster, but even she can't find fault with the rollout plan for the mesh network. Plus, since you're starting with a relatively small area, it's not like it will be a huge deal if something goes wrong."

I pushed away from him, hand still on his chest, and glared. "That's easy for you to say. All you do is look through telescopes and monitor feedback all day. No one's going to come for you if you make a mistake."

He knocked my arm from under me, pulled me to his chest and rolled so he was on top. There was a devilish glint in his eyes. "If I make a miscalculation, everyone who could come after me will likely be dead. It's one of the benefits of the job." The heat of his body warmed me through, and when he began moving against me, his hips rocking into mine, I moaned. He kissed my cheek, my ear. "Besides, we're supposed to be visiting your family to relax. If you're going to think about work, we could have stayed at Burnell. At least there I can bend you over the kitchen table without worrying about your parents walking in."

After extensive research—Mykhail, perhaps making up for lost time, really lived up to the nickname I'd bestowed upon him—we were now operating under the Theory of Mykhail Topivity, much to my delight. My body reacted to the imagery he provided and to the thickness pressing into my thigh. My cock throbbed in response, and I reached down and grabbed him in my fist.

"If you're volunteering to help me relax, I have some ideas that don't even require leaving the bed." His mouth met mine, and I began to stroke, just as a knock sounded at the door.

"Jang-wan, breakfast time! I know you have an important job now, but you still have to help set the table."

My mom's sharp voice sent Mykhail and me flying apart, as effective a mood killer as an empty lube bottle.

"Okay, Amma! Geez!"

She knocked once more, probably a warning about getting too mouthy with her, and then I heard her stomping down the stairs.

***

After being forced to be my mom's pancake-flipping minion, I sat down at the table and looked over the family I missed so much every day now that I was living at Burnell. Not Arden and Gabriel, of course; they stayed at the university four days a week. The school's student healthcare center had been refitted as a regional medical center, and Gabriel was one of several doctors who'd been hired to work there. Arden had joined my project, helping to spread the reach of the mesh network to those homes that had generators in advance of repairs to the electrical grid. She was a whiz with numbers, and she loved serving as an enforcer when I had to prod one government agency or another. She was also able to work on a side project, reaching out to networked people in California. It wasn't safe enough to travel yet, but we hoped to have news of her parents soon.

A clatter at the other end of the table drew my attention. Morris had made a grab for Darlene's oatmeal and sent her spoon clattering to the ground. "That's not for you, little man," she said lovingly. Each time I returned home she looked more vibrant. I'd always wondered why my parents had risked their lives for her; now that the real Darlene had resurfaced, I was able to see why. Maybe moving to the one-room bungalow built by Hernandez and a couple of other contractors who now worked at Burnell had given her the privacy she needed to fully recover.

"Where's Maggie?" Mykhail asked. He added a scoop of sugar and some raisins to my oatmeal, plus a pat of fresh-churned butter we'd picked up at a little market along the way.

"Sulking in her room, I guess. That's where she usually is now," Dad said, shooting an annoyed look at my sister through the ceiling. "I thought we had lucked out with her, but her teenage angst was just in hibernation."

As if on cue, loud, thrashing rock music started blasting from upstairs.

My mom banged her hand on the table in annoyance. "Every day! Every day we have to deal with this devil music." She reached out and grabbed the broom and banged the ceiling, having kept it close to hand for that reason. While I was glad that Maggie was making use of the battery-operated boom box I'd given her for her seventeenth birthday, I couldn't help but feel a little bad for my parents. And for my sister. We tried to give her a true teenage experience, but nothing could make up for the things she was missing out on. While other kids would have been agonizing over the homecoming dance, or stealing drags off their friends' cigarettes behind the school if they were too cool for school dances, she hadn't even seen another person her age in months.

Mykhail cupped his hands around his mouth and shouted, "Maggie, come hang out with us! We miss you!"

She turned the music up louder in response. Now that he was considered family, too, he could be ignored like the rest of us.

Mykhail threw his head back and laughed. The sight of his happiness made me want to kiss his throat, but Amma didn't play that. I saved the PDA for later and took his hand instead.

"Thank you," I said. My voice was thickened by an unexpected surge of emotion. If Mykhail had never come into my life, I would have survived but I didn't think I would have lived. His presence had changed not only my life, but my entire family's.

"For what?" he asked, pushing his glasses up on his nose.

"For being a no-good, thieving tomato poacher," I said aloud, but what I meant was *I love you*. I leaned up and kissed him, Amma's rules be damned. It was worth the bruise from the apple she threw at my head. It was worth everything.

Want more? Turn the page for a

BONUS SHORT STORY

featuring RADIO SILENCE'S Arden and Gabriel!

It was the smell of baking cinnamon and apple that finally lured me from our bed, the mixture of crisp autumn freshness and smoky caramelized sugar physically pulling me out of my dream like a vaudeville stage hook.

I didn't mind. I'd overslept and it'd been one of those dreams, the fucked-up ones fueled by anxiety and fear that had started after the Flare and would seemingly never leave me. The world was starting to rebuild—I was even contributing in my small way with my administrative work for the Communications Department at Burnell. The dark cloak that had draped itself over the world three years ago was slipping behind us, but the memories of it were still sharp, pressing into you if you made one wrong move. Intermittent electricity couldn't burn away images of death or the scent memory of your attacker. The ever-growing phone connectivity only reminded you of those who'd never be on the other end of the line.

I inhaled sharply and then released a long, slow breath between my lips.

You're safe now. Everything is okay.

I knew that was true, mostly, but I still glanced warily around the bedroom of the little faculty house Gabriel and I shared with John and Mykhail at Burnell. The house was an oasis of safety and warmth on a campus bustling with governmental activity. It was the one demand John had made when offered a job by the Department of Infrastructure Repair; he was always thinking a step ahead.

Which reminded me…

I grabbed my cell phone from the bedside table and

flipped it open. It still felt strange, even though pre-Flare I'd be scrolling through social media before I wiped the sleep from my eyes. Internet service hadn't been restored enough to support social media. I was searching for a something much simpler: a text from my sister-in-law, Maggie.

It was her first day of school since the Flare, and we weren't there to harass and bully her until she was glad to be leaving the house. Unlike John, Maggie was dead set on pretending things didn't have to change. I couldn't blame her. She'd just turned eighteen, but she'd missed out on all the social milestones that were supposed to lead up to that. I'd been scared to leave for Burnell; I couldn't imagine what it would be like to go to high school.

My phone screen lit up. There was no message.

I jumped out of bed and grabbed my nightgown, annoyed in a way that had been completely foreign to me as an only child. Freaking Maggie. I could just imagine her stomping around her filthy room, digging through piles of clothes for the perfect back-to-school outfit. She'd roll her eyes and pretend she was too cool to care about something like the GED program for people who'd gotten an apocalypse instead of a prom. Mama Seong would be chasing her around the house trying to get her to put her guitar down and eat breakfast. I could just see Maggie glaring from behind her bangs and muttering as Mom—

I froze with the nightgown halfway over my head.

Mom?

Even after living in close quarters like we had, it was still a shock when I slipped up and thought of Gabe's mother that way, especially since I had no idea how my own parents had fared or if they were even still alive. The Seongs had taken me in—they were my family now, too, and I already knew how far I'd go to protect them—but the betrayal of how easily I fit in with them never left me. It was a physical ache that it had been Mama Seong who'd helped with my wedding updo months earlier—or tried to, although she couldn't understand the physics of my kinks and curls at all—and not my mom, who'd never pushed but always reminded me that I'd look beautiful in the wedding dress stored in her closet. That it was Seong Senior who'd danced with me at our small reception, and not my burly dad who used to spin me round and round as a little girl, as if we'd been practicing for that special moment, had made each awkward two-step seem as if I was dancing on their grave. Not that I even knew if they'd been buried…

Fuck.

I closed my eyes, pressed my fists into them to stop the flow of tears that really should have dried up already but somehow never did. Some people had lost so much—every goddamn thing they'd ever cherished. Me? I was up one hot husband and several annoying but lovable family members. How could I be sad about that? But still…

"I hear you scurrying around up there. Get a move on, lazybones." Gabriel's deep voice echoed up the stairwell, triggering that familiar bittersweet clench in my chest. The joy that he was there with me, tinged with apprehension.

For how long? What if?

"Do you have your stethoscope against the ceiling or what?" I asked. I stomped toward the door, making a racket that hopefully drowned out the roughness of my voice. I needed to get rid of the pesky feelings and slap a smile on before I faced him, even though he was almost as good as his brother at telling when I was putting up a front.

When I got to the top of the stairs and saw him standing at the bottom, arms crossed behind his back, wavy hair trying and failing to hide his dimpled smile, I realized I didn't have to pretend. He was wearing the sweatpants he knew I liked, the ones that hung from his hips just right and outlined everything, and I mean *everything*, just enough to tease me. His gaze was completely focused on me, as though I was some kind of angel descending from the heavens instead of a scrub who still hadn't showered and had forgotten to twist her hair out before bed.

The bittersweetness I'd been feeling was refined into pure sugary joy at the sight of him; the anxiety from my dream drifted away, and my pulse kicked up a notch as I approached him, taking the steps one at a time just so I could stare at him a little longer.

"My stethoscope is still in the bedroom," he said with a grin that reminded me of exactly we'd been using it for.

"Oh. That's right, Dr. Seong."

When I reached the landing, I didn't stop walking until the curves of my body were molded against the muscular planes of his. I lifted my head and wiggled my nose in an exaggerated sniff.

"Using my above-average deductive reasoning skills,

I'm guessing that you made me a delicious breakfast?" I raised myself up and down on my toes as if hopping with excitement, creating some friction that could lead to a pre-breakfast diversion if I played my cards right. I wanted Gabriel to touch me, to remind me of everything good there was in this world. The thoughts of my parents had put me on edge, but I didn't want to hide my pain. I needed to feel Gabriel pulsing into me, to hear him whisper that he wasn't going anywhere, the way he did when I woke up screaming in the darkness of our bedroom.

"What do I get if I guess right?" I asked, running my hand up over his pectorals.

He gave me another mischievous grin, but then stepped away, shoving his hands into his pockets instead of embracing me. "You win a hot breakfast, Sherlock. I didn't get up early to cook just for it to get cold. Come on."

I stood in hurt confusion for a moment as he walked away. Gabriel could be brusque, but he was always physically attentive. I thought I'd get a hug at the very least, but instead I was watching his ass in those sweatpants as he walked off into the kitchen. I mean, it was an extremely fine ass, but even his walk was a little stiff. Something about his behavior, pleasant as it was, was just off. When you'd spent the first portion of your relationship trapped in a cabin with your man, it was hard not to get really good at reading his body language.

I trailed him into the kitchen, skittering in front of him to look into eyes.

"What?" he asked. He grinned again, but this time it

wasn't mischievous. It was nervous, the same one he'd had plastered on his face when I'd walked down the makeshift aisle in the cabin's yard.

"Nothing," I said, looking at him askance as I felt the anxiety start to seep back in. He'd been joking with the Sherlock crack, but he knew very well that I hated secrets and would stop at nothing to sniff them out. The game was afoot.

He opened the oven and pulled out a tray of bubbling deliciousness. Baked apples.

"Any reason for this special breakfast?" I asked, sitting at the table and grabbing the mug of coffee he'd already poured. There were even place settings. Gabriel wasn't one for formality, but he was the kind of guy who'd do anything to keep his hands busy when he was nervous. That often worked out well for me, although that morning seemed to be an exception.

"Nope," he said, way too quickly

A sudden thought hit me. "Is everything okay? Did John and Mykhail check in? And Maggie was supposed to text but she didn't. Just tell me. Did something happen—?"

"Everyone is fine," he said gruffly. "Mom texted me that Maggie was throwing a tantrum about a missing guitar string, and I spoke to Mykhail this morning. They should be here later in the afternoon. Do you think I'd be playing Suzy Homemaker if my family needed me?"

"Oh. Right." Perhaps I'd put too much stock in my detective skills. "Well, if this is your way of softening the blow because you're having a secret baby with Mary, you both have my blessing." Mary was the receptionist at the clinic where Gabriel worked. She maintained order in the chaotic environment of a place often packed with patients—when she wasn't letting Gabriel know how she would have laid it on him if he weren't married and she wasn't old enough to be his grandmother.

He laughed, the ringing deepness of it a reassurance. "No secret babies to report. Not mine, at least. I'm pretty sure Nurse Johnson's boyfriend has been working on a repair crew in Florida for five months, and she just got good news from the Ob-Gyn."

"Look at you, Doctor Busybody," I tutted as he dropped into the seat beside me, holding two plates of apple-y goodness just out of reach.

"I think you mean Doctor Wonderful Husband, right?"

I looked at him skeptically. "Doctor…Moderately Acceptable Husband?"

His brows lifted.

"Doctor Freak in the Sheets Husband?"

He rolled his eyes, but handed me the plate. "That'll do. For now."

I dug my spoon through a dollop of fresh cream and into the soft, still bubbling apple before giving it a quick puff of air and shoving it into my mouth. The mixture of cool cream and sweet cinnamon goodness combined on my tongue in a flavorgasm that would have been perfect if not for Gabriel fidgeting beside me. His hand was in his pocket again instead of ferrying food toward his face, and his leg was jumping nervously. I willed myself not to whirl on him and demand answers.

He'll crack eventually.

I scooped up another mouthful and almost bit my tongue when he jumped out of his seat. His hand left his pocket clasping his phone.

"Hey! Hi. Yeah. Hold on…" He paced over to a notepad and wrote something down. "Okay. Okay…no, I can't wait until you guys get back…I never said I wasn't a selfish jerk, Jang-wan. Yeah, yeah." He hit the End button and then looked down at the pad.

At this point, I'd stopped chewing and sat staring at him, trying to make sense of the snippets of conversation.

"You're really not going to clue me in here?"

"Just wait, Arden," he snapped. Gabriel's gruffness factor went through the roof when he was nervous, but I couldn't imagine what was causing it. The bite of apple grated down my throat.

He took a deep breath and began punching numbers into the phone, messing up once because his hands were shaking. Gruffness was one thing, but hand shaking was quite another.

"Gabe?"

He turned and leaned back against the counter, his gaze locked on mine. I couldn't read his strained expression and was starting to really worry when he leaned away from the counter and ran a hand through his hair. He cleared his throat. His Adam's apple bobbed.

"Hello. Yes, this is Gabriel." He was using his doctor tone, the one that was grave and often used to tell people things they didn't want to hear. "Yes. Of course."

He handed me the phone, but I didn't reach for it. My stomach dropped, as if I was back in high school and my crush's number had just shown up on the caller ID. Except my crush was with me.

Who could it be?

Gabriel leaned forward and pressed the phone to my ear, and I clutched it, listening into the void.

"Hello?" The word echoed back at me courtesy of the still-shoddy phone network. Did I always sound like a stressed-out chipmunk?

"Arden?"

That voice. I'd know that voice anywhere. It had taught me the ABCs, reamed me out when I dug up his garden looking for treasure and told me I was the most special girl in the world.

"Dad?" I turned my head toward Gabriel but he was nothing more than a wavering mass of curls and hotness behind the torrent of tears spilling from my eyes. I didn't realize I was heaving sobs until his hand pressed flat on my chest, exerting a strong but comforting pressure.

"Breathe, Arden," he said gently. "It's okay. Everything is okay now."

I clutched his hand against my chest, squeezing it as though it was the only thing keeping me from shattering into pieces. Given the way my heart was pounding and my body was trembling, that might not have been an exaggeration.

"Dad? How the hell? I thought—" Words left me for a moment. There was so much I wanted to say, but I could only manage a strange hiccupping keen. I heard an answering sob and learned that I'd inherited my ugly cry from my dad. I'd never known my father to cry before and it made me smile, not just because I was a jerk, but because...

"You're alive," I croaked.

"I am," he said with an incredulous chuckle. "Somehow, I am. And I'm so glad you are, too. I knew you were too stubborn to be gone."

I didn't know anything about radio waves and the inner workings of telephones—that was John's bag. I didn't know how they could carry my father's relief over three thousand miles and wrap it around me like a quilt. But there was a gap in that comfort, letting in a stream of cold air.

"And Mom?" My voice echoed back again, wobbling like a plate balanced on the edge of a counter. Mom, who had been so sick that I couldn't stand to face her. Mom, who had loved me regardless.

"She—" The rest of his words dissolved, a garbled mess. The connection was cutting out.

No. NO.

I jumped out of my seat and Gabe jumped with me,

pacing beside me. He didn't know what the problem was, but I knew he was already figuring out how to fix it.

"Dad? Hello?"

The frayed magic that held our call together mended itself, and suddenly a prim, restrained voice was murmuring threats through the speaker.

"—I told you I would hit you upside the head with that shovel, Lucien. Now if this call doesn't get picked back up—"

I'd dreaded that tone as a child, but now it was the most beautiful thing I'd ever heard.

"Holy fucking shit." My knees went out from under me then, and I sank to the floor cross-legged, unable to make it back to the kitchen table.

"Arden Dayanara Highmore! Is that how you greet your mother?" She sounded older, weaker, despite still being vivacious. Then she laughed, the deep belly laugh that she always told me was improper when it was coming from me. "Who am I fooling? Of course that's how you'd greet me."

Years of guilt and self-flagellation rushed at me, and I was suddenly tempted to throw the phone across the kitchen. What could I say to her? How did I ask who had taken care of her in my stead because I'd been too selfish to do the job?

"Arden? Are you there?"

"I'm sorry, Mom. I'm sorry I didn't come visit when you asked me to. I'm sorry I wasn't there with you," I managed. Then the tears took my words again and I cried helplessly, in the way only your mother's voice can trigger, whether you like it or not.

"Arden." Her voice was calm and pitched just right to put me at ease. I felt her forgiveness before she spoke the words. Still, her next question scared me. "You know what upset me the most about you not being here when the world went dark?"

"What?"

"Knowing that if we never got to speak again, you'd always blame yourself. And that's it. And now that's settled and I never want to hear an apology again, okay?"

"Okay," I said, chastened. I didn't feel a weight miraculously lifted from my shoulders at her words; I was so busy being completely fucking happy that there was no room for a cliché.

"You know you would have driven me crazy if you'd been here, anyway," she added.

"Wow. Too soon, Mom."

"What? It's the truth." But even if she didn't bawl like my dad, I could tell she was crying, too. "Why don't you tell us about this husband of yours? Lucien, come close so you can hear. I'm scared I'll hang up if I try to find the speaker phone."

My dad's voice was a bit muffled by the distance from the mouthpiece, but I could still make out the humor underlying his words. "They told us there was some kind of space Flare, but when I heard Arden was married I knew what'd really caused the apocalypse," he said. "Someone finally able to tie that girl down? Pigs. Flying."

"I'm going to crush your rutabagas if you don't let

Arden talk."

"Okay, okay. Go ahead, Arden." My dad sighed his familiar beleaguered sigh. It was *then* that the weight lifted from my shoulders. Hey, clichés exist for a reason.

I reached out to Gabriel, who was still beside me, and cupped his face in my palm. I knew my hand was sticky from the apple, and who knew what bodily fluids I'd emitted during my crying jag, but he didn't even blink.

"Gabriel is probably the most annoying man I've ever met. He's grumpy and bossy and always thinks he's right. But he's also the most kind and giving person I know, and I wouldn't trade him for anything."

Gabriel ducked his head closer to the phone, maybe to hear my parents' response but probably to hide the fact that he was tearing up a little.

"That's so wonderful, Arden," my mom said. "Is he handsome, though?"

"I think our moms would get along great," Gabriel said as he shook his head and stood to give me privacy.

"He's pleasing to the eye," I said as I watched his ass walk away from me again. "Maybe you'll get to meet him one day and see for yourself."

I thought of the map Gabriel had made for me, sketching out several routes to California. Before, it had seemed like a fantasy, but now…

"Okay, the call might drop again so let's not waste any more time," I said. "Tell me everything."

About the Author

Alyssa Cole is a science editor, pop culture nerd, and romance junkie who lives in the Caribbean and occasionally returns to her fast-paced NYC life. When she's not busy writing, traveling, and learning French, she can be found watching anime with her real-life romance hero or tending to her herd of animals.

Find Alyssa at her website, http://alyssacole.com/, on Twitter @AlyssaColeLit and on Facebook at Facebook.com/AlyssaColeLit.

Printed in the USA
CPSIA information can be obtained
at www.ICGtesting.com
LVHW081207060823
754466LV00026B/507

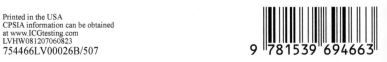

9 781539 694663